The Evolving Truth of Ever-Stronger Will

cGREGOR

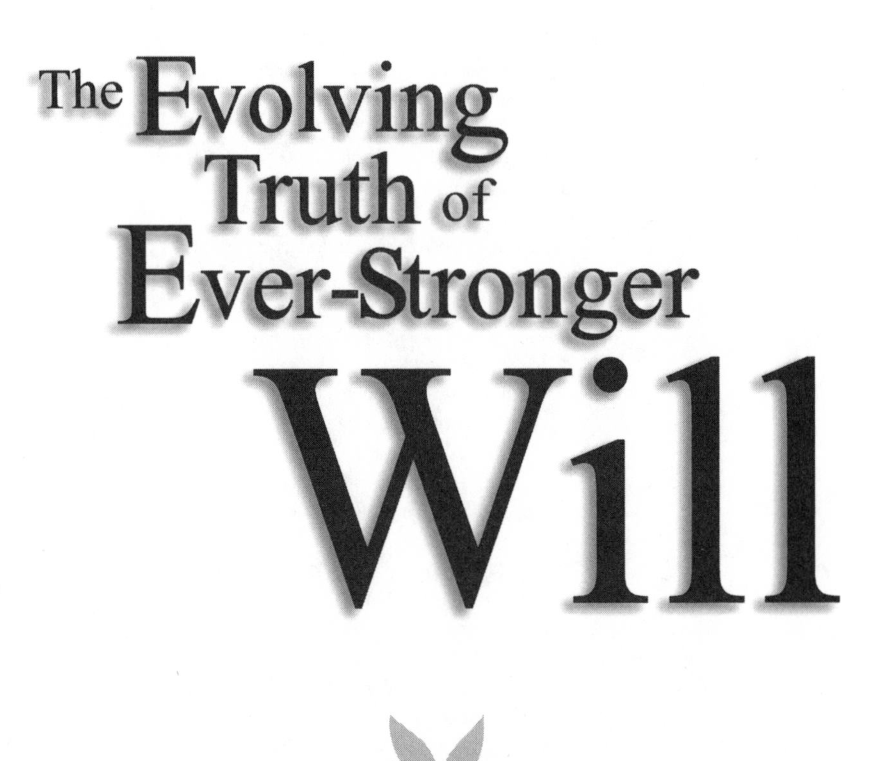

ASTRA YOUNG READERS
AN IMPRINT OF ASTRA BOOKS FOR YOUNG READERS
New York

Heartfelt gratitude to Noemí Martínez Turull for their helpful feedback on Will's story.

Astra Young Readers
An imprint of Astra Books for Young Readers, a division of Astra Publishing House
astrapublishinghouse.com
Printed in Canada

Library of Congress Cataloging-in-Publication Data

Names: MacGregor, Maya, author.
Title: The evolving truth of ever-stronger Will / Maya MacGregor.
Description: First edition. | New York : Astra Young Readers, 2023. | Audience: Ages 12 and up. | Audience: Grades 7-9. | Summary: Follows 17-year-old Will as they struggle with the aftermath of parental abuse and learn to a forge a new life for themself.
Identifiers: LCCN 2023013942 (print) | LCCN 2023013943 (ebook) | ISBN 9781662620171 (hardcover) | ISBN 9781662620188 (epub)
Subjects: CYAC: Parent and child--Fiction. | Death--Fiction. | Child abuse--Fiction. | Drug dealers--Fiction. | Gender identity--Fiction. | Self-acceptance--Fiction. | Foster parents--Fiction. | Adoption--Fiction. | LCGFT: Queer fiction. | Novels.
Classification: LCC PZ7.1.M24525 Ev 2023 (print) | LCC PZ7.1.M24525 (ebook) | DDC [Fic]--dc23
LC record available at https://lccn.loc.gov/2023013942
LC ebook record available at https://lccn.loc.gov/2023013943

First edition
10 9 8 7 6 5 4 3 2 1

Design by Anahid Hamparian
The text is set in Minion Pro Regular.
The titles are set in Futura Std Condensed Light.

For every trans, intersex, and nonbinary kid out there.
You deserve to exist in safety, joy, and acceptance.
It's not your fault the world can't always see that,
and you're not alone.
You are beautiful and wonderfully made just as you are.

Just as you are.
—MM

Chapter One

You are a monster.

You know this already. It's one of the first things you learned, one of the first lessons you felt down to the cells and atoms that make you up. Your electrons buzz with it.

Since then, anyone who has tried to tell you otherwise, you have quietly counted among the world's many liars.

You were born that way; that much you know. They called you—well, never mind what they called you. Your name is Will, and that's what matters now. That you found your name.

People think it's supposed to be short for William or even Wilhelmina or, in one annoying case, Willard.

They're wrong about that, though, just like they're wrong about you not being a monster.

Your name is Will because that's what it takes to live among people who hate you for no other reason than that you exist.

So. Will. Will the Monster, here we are, and here you are.

Your life is about to change.

Ready?

Chapter Two

You stand there, frozen, as your mother stares at you with cobra-venom hate from where she has collapsed on the floor and says, "This is your fault."

Then she dies.

You stand there, in your brown slacks and white button down and olive-green vest (you've just come from work, you seventeen-year-old curmudgeon), and you feel it as your little patch of earth shifts beneath your feet.

What are you going to do, Will?

You sure as hell don't know. You're *four months* from turning eighteen. You might escape getting put back in the system.

Right now you really wish Raz was here. It's been years since you saw her and you've never been able to find her, but whenever you're scared or freaked out or lost, you wish she was there. Like now. When you're standing over your mother's corpse.

You didn't even attempt CPR. You remember Raz once telling you that freezing is a trauma response and doesn't make you bad, but it's hard to remember that. You don't need to check for a pulse. Whatever makes a human alive is gone. All that is left is a fleshy husk. Frances is dead, her body swiftly cooling, and you are a little more monstrous.

Maybe a normal kid would feel some kind of grief right now, but all you feel is relief. A long time ago, "Momma" became "Frances." Is it so monstrous to be relieved that she's finally gone?

You're pretty certain it was a heart attack. She didn't clutch her arm or anything—you read in health class that it's different for double-X-chromosomed people—but you've always had decent instincts. And now? Time is slipping away into the bottom half of an hourglass, and while you have no idea how much of it you started with, you're also pretty certain there's almost none left. There's a window where you can plausibly tell the EMTs that you came home, and she was already dead. Problem is, you're not sure what that window is.

You don't know. What you do know is that you're not going to risk someone bringing her back.

The room stinks of the usual cigarettes and PBR and now some urine and some other smell you've never smelled before but instinctually identify as Death. Frances's last words ring through your head again anyway. *This is your fault.*

That solidifies a thought in your mind.

You've spent the past five years living in this latrine of a house with someone who literally, with her dying breath, blamed her heart attack on her only kid.

Actually, you don't really know if you're her only kid. You might not be. Frances had a lot of secrets.

Had.

Past tense already. You're definitely a monster.

Admitting it, even in your head, shores up your resolve.

You sit on the floor a safe distance away, insofar as there is such a thing—the surface of the *moon* wasn't far enough to constitute a safe distance from Frances.

You observe what is happening right in front of you. That ineffable sense of death grows more inherently "effable" as the hours slip by. In the initial seconds, there was only a vague sense of wrongness, an instinctual twitch of the lizard brain. It screamed death even as Frances lay silent. But now? Now there's more. The color has drained from her skin, making her fake tan sit in a layer of orangey-brown upon her flesh.

You remember watching crime shows that talk about lividity, blood pooling where gravity pulls it. In this particular case, that'll be Frances's ass. She's slumped against the end of the half wall, eking her way downward with that irresistible force. It reveals something morbidly true: the human body without a person in it is simply a fleshy sack of so much meat.

The internet could tell you how all this works, but you can't bring yourself to Google. You don't know how long gravity will take advantage of her limp muscles before rigor mortis sets in, the two in an unconscious battle for control of her corpse.

The limpness in Frances's face gives way to a strange rigidity. Her mouth is a tightened grimace.

You didn't realize you were waiting for it until you saw it. To be fair, you don't know enough about rigor mortis to know that it begins in the face. You learn this by watching it happen in real time.

Frances is dead.

You stand up and pick your way to the landline in the house, careful to avoid Frances's feet. Hannah always marvels at the landline whenever she braves the house for your company.

"It's like keeping a damn dodo tethered in the corner," she said the first time she saw it. "Those things are practically extinct."

Frances would never let you have a cell phone, even though you could have paid for it yourself if she didn't steal all your paychecks to pay for her pack-a-day cigarettes. She used that same cash to buy herself the newest Galaxy whatever, usually glued to her hand, but you have no idea where it is now.

Moot point. It's time.

Your fingers pick up the receiver and start to punch in 911.

You get as far as the first *one* and stop. Hang up.

You call Hannah instead. She, like the rest of the twenty-first century, has a cell phone.

She always answers when you call because she knows you can't text. She answers on the first ring.

"What's wrong?"

Hannah knows your schedule better than you do. She knows Frances's too, so she can put together that if you're on the phone when Frances is supposed to be home too, something's up. Usually you're not allowed near the phone unless it's to order Frances her dinner.

The smell of urine is stronger on this side of the room.

"Is Matt working?" Matt is Hannah's older brother, and he's an EMT.

There's a beat. "Yeah, I think so. Why?"

You say the words you hope you'll only have to voice once.

"Frances is dead." And then, softly, as if doing so any more loudly would bring Frances back to life somehow, "I need help making sure no one at school finds out, because they'll have to report it to CPS. Do you think he can help?"

The hospital or coroner might not be much better if they tell the school, but maybe, just maybe—

There's another beat, and this one feels like *holy shit*. "I don't know, Will. But I'll try."

You give her a little more information, listening to her breathless questions, and then you both hang up so you can wait for Matt to show up.

Hannah doesn't say she's sorry. She knows Frances too well for that.

Again, you wish Raz was here.

When you were three years old, Frances left you in a dumpster in Hagerstown, Maryland. Yeah, you know, you know. Usually that's an ignominious honor reserved for babies, not toddlers, but Frances was always one to buck tradition. You spent the next six or seven years bouncing from (usually awful) foster home to (often worse) home until sometime around your eleventh birthday you landed with *her.* You only know her by the nickname everyone called her—Raz. She was shortish. Beautiful brown skin darker than your olive tone. Plumpish. She had a mass of waves that she kept raspberry-red from the shoulders down and were dark brown at the roots. She said the color made her feel powerful. You blurted out in awe that it looked magical, and you'll never forget how she beamed at you and how the warmth of her smile beat back your instinctual shame.

The first time you saw her, you *knew* it was going to be different. You're not sure you were ever that right before Raz or have ever been so right since.

Raz was amazing. You don't think you were her first foster, and you hope you weren't her last, because everything was just . . . *different* with Raz.

She made you blueberry pancakes on Saturday mornings and let you put as much butter and syrup on them as you wanted (spoiler: a lot). She was cool with you drinking a little coffee so you could be like her, more sugar and milk than caffeine, but you felt grown up. She let you lock the door of your room until you learned you didn't need to do that there. She bought you new clothes—actual—new—clothes. She'd find random shows to binge-watch with you on Netflix, and it's because of her that you've seen every episode of *Friends* (she hated Ross with a fiery passion, so you did too) and every time there was a joke that would have never made it past the writers' room in the twenty-twenties, she'd turn to you with a spectacular eyeroll and say, "Progress we've made: Exhibit G" or something like that. She also knew *everything* about the shows, the actors, the bloopers, all of it—and shared it gleefully.

But most of all—more important than coffee or pancakes or privacy or nineties sitcoms—Raz helped you find your name. Frances had given you one, or someone had. But Raz knew how much you hated it, and not only did she listen seriously as you rattled off ideas, but she seemed as invested in it as you, firing off trivia about every name you suggested. Among the ideas: Raven, Imogen, Eleven (you had marathoned *Stranger Things*), and Ash (and *Pokémon*). Then one day, you said "Will," and Raz's head snapped up and her feet did little excited kicks.

"Will," she said, as if trying it out. "You've got a lot of that, kid."

You hadn't even thought of it that way, but the moment she said it, you knew that was it. You read a fantasy series once, and the sorcerers in it used Will to do magic. You discovered, much later, that the series' author had been a Frances—like your mother and the worst of your foster home mothers. That only made you cling to your name with hotter ferocity.

You never got to tell Raz that. You've always wanted to show her how your name became your armor.

Raz just got things.

She caught you one day staring at your skin and knew why. It wasn't that you were really that much different-looking than the other kids at your school (you weren't) or that you wished you were something else (you didn't). It was just that you didn't seem to fit. Anywhere. With anyone. Except Raz.

"Sometimes people live in the between spaces," Raz said. "Like you and me. According to the world, we're almost one thing and not quite another. Not white enough or Black enough, not Dominican enough or female enough, not male enough or whatever enough. But we're enough. We're us, and we're real. We might feel like we live in the Upside Down sometimes, but—"

"The Upside Down is full of *monsters*," you blurted, interrupting even though you never interrupted Raz. Something about *Stranger Things* got to you, and you didn't realize what until then.

But Raz just smiled and reached out and smoothed a bit of dark hair back from your face. "That's only how it looks to people who weren't born there, Will. People make monsters out of what they fear or don't understand, because they know it could just as easily be them."

So your name is Will.

Raz worked her own magic to get the system to allow for the name change. It took almost the whole year you were with her, but she did it.

She took you all the way to Hershey Park to celebrate, and you rode roller coasters all day and she screamed alongside you. That night on the drive back, she told you that she was working on something she wanted to ask you about, and you were pretty sure she was going to ask if she could adopt you.

Three weeks later, though, Frances showed up at your—Raz's—door with a stolen four-years-sober chip from AA or NA or something and a social worker saying that you had to go with her now.

Raz told you to go to your room, and you heard raised voices coming from the living room, at least some of it about your name change. Your body remembered the sound of Frances's yelling. You felt each decibel climbing your spine like a ladder, burrowing into the base of your skull. The weight of your suitcase as you lugged it down the stairs after Raz helped you pack it with tears beaded on her eyelashes. The pure fear leaking out of your pores, all of it mingled with fresh fury when you saw the look of leashed rage on Raz's face at Frances's smugness.

Raz pressed a piece of blue paper into your hand as she hugged you goodbye, fiercely staring into your eyes and holding your hand tight around the scrap, murmuring, "It's the way back to that in-between space," and you knew she wasn't supposed to give you her information but she did it anyway and that more than anything told you she really had been planning to ask you to be her kid forever.

You cried on the way to Frances's house. Not big hulking sobs but little streams of water that wouldn't stop and just drip-drip-dripped off the side of your face.

At first, Frances seemed sympathetic.

"It'll be good, Will," she said. "You and me. Fresh start."

She said it an hour into the drive, winding through the hills of western Maryland, each curve taking you farther and farther away from Raz.

You think for that moment she actually might have meant it. It was the one time you ever remembered her saying your name without building it out of knives.

But then you woke up the next morning in a strange bed in a stinky room of a stinky house and discovered that she'd burned the scrap of paper Raz had given you. You found the edge of it, blue with a yellow-brown char, in Frances's ashtray.

Frances waited for you to react, smoking silently and watching to see if you would, and you didn't.

But you knew she'd left a scrap of it on purpose.

To show you that she may have thrown you away like trash, but she had fished you back out before you had a chance to be someone else's treasure.

To show you she hadn't forgotten that you are a monster, but that you are *her* monster, and that she would not let you go.

Matt arrives with the coroner and the ambulance together about twenty minutes after you call Hannah. No sirens, no flashing lights even. Not that anyone would see them. Your house isn't that close to anything.

He meets you at the door, his partner and the coroner hanging back, and you wonder what Matt told them. You don't really care, though the muted pity on his face bothers you. He takes one look at Frances, sighs, and then turns to give a hand signal to the others. You don't see their response beyond a ripple of movement in your peripheral vision that implies a sudden lack of urgency.

Matt's about six feet tall, with brown skin closer to the olive color of yours than to his sister Hannah's, which is so pale she's almost translucent. His hair is darker brown, and he has nice hazel eyes that sometimes lean toward green in the right light. Right now, they're watching you as if he's waiting for you to do something.

He doesn't offer any condolences either, just like Hannah. That says enough.

"Hey, Will."

"Hey." It feels stupid to say that tiny little word at a moment like this.

He follows you into the house. Matt walks over to Frances and touches her cheek, sighs, then closes the door behind you after a brief nod to the others outside.

Matt became an EMT because he found his best friend dead just after they graduated from high school. You suppose he's a good person to have on hand here. He at least knows firsthand what it's like to find someone close to you dead. Even if the circumstances couldn't be more different.

"You see what happened?"

When you hesitate, Matt holds up his hands.

"Officially, on the record, you found her dead, okay? Maryland law says we can pronounce her dead at the scene without needing a medical opinion if rigor mortis is in effect, and she's in the early stages of rigor. We won't attempt resuscitation, but we will need to inform law enforcement so they can alert the medical examiner. It's not for an investigation, just protocol. I don't want you to worry about that." Matt pauses, blowing out a breath. "Not a person in Bright Springs who knew Frances who wouldn't feel sorry for you even if they don't know you from Lizzo. Frances didn't make friends, Will."

"I know."

"I'm telling you that you can tell me. You ain't got to worry that anybody will come after you for this. Hell, when I told dispatch who was reported deceased, Renee crossed herself and said that maybe god really is merciful."

That startles you a little. You have no idea who Renee is, but you hadn't realized so many people knew Frances. Then again, you didn't have to spend much time with her to know her. A Frances drive-by was usually enough to make people steer clear next time they saw her coming.

"I don't want CPS sticking their useless heads in," you say finally, the words singeing your insides. "They didn't give a shit yesterday, and they sure as hell better not try and pretend they give a shit today. I've got one year of high school left. One, Matt. Four months until I'm eighteen."

He nods. Runs his fingers through short hair. "I can't promise anything, but you've got people in your corner. Technically I'm supposed to run it up the chain if I suspect abuse or neglect—"

You can't help the sharp sound that erupts from your throat.

"—but frankly, Hannah told me enough for me to suspect that yesterday would have been a more appropriate time for that than today." He sucks his teeth. "Shit, Will. I could maybe get in trouble for this, but I'll tell whoever that you're staying with family or something if they ask. Maryland doesn't have an official emancipation process, really, so if we can just hold out till you hit eighteen, you'll be good to go. This town can be shit, but it's also a small town where my mom's name carries some weight. Cops might not love her, but they know she's not someone to mess with. We won't let anyone try to rip you out of here. I don't want to see you up to your nose in strangers who think they know best any more than you do."

It's weird to think Matt's on your side. Nobody under the age of twenty in this town besides Hannah falls in the category of Team Will, but from what Matt's been saying, the adults (some of them, anyway) might be willing to look the other way while you bust your ass to survive this mess until eighteen.

Matt might say he won't let anyone try to rip you out of here, but he can't be certain they won't succeed anyway. You know too well what happens to kids like you. Your trust in adult authorities to do the right thing—or to listen to you at all—is at such low elevation, it's practically the Dead Sea.

Matt goes over to her again, presses his fingers against the skin of her neck. She was a skinny thing, in spite of all the beer she drank, but taller than you and—

"I think it was a heart attack," you say finally, because you have to say *something*. "She was getting up to get a beer because I hadn't come home yet, and when I walked in the door, she had kind of keeled over at the half wall there. She saw me, and I kind of froze. She slid down and"—*This is your fault*—"Then she was just . . . gone."

"There's likely nothing you could have done," Matt says. "Even if you'd started chest compressions immediately, by the time we got here, it would have been too late. We would have tried to resuscitate her for at least fifteen minutes, but she would still be dead."

You think he's saying this for your benefit, so you don't feel guilty for letting her die without trying to help. Or for letting hours go by before you called anyone.

"Thanks," you say, because you think that's what you're supposed to say.

"You want to stay at our place tonight? Hannah was going to make up the air bed in her room just in case."

You take a deep breath, your body's reflexes forgetting about the stench in the air. You want to say yes, but something stops you.

"Maybe tomorrow," you tell him instead. "I'm going to need to . . . clean up."

That you're having this conversation two feet from France's dead body isn't lost on you. That Matt's treating you differently—like an adult instead of his kid sister's friend—isn't lost on you either.

He nods. "Okay if I let them in now?"

"Yeah," you say, stepping backward.

You look at Frances for the last time, then you open the door before Matt can and go outside.

Perching on the end of the tiny porch, you scuff your foot in the gravel as Matt and his partner go in. Hearing them go through the motions is surreal. Words like "no brain activity" muttered loudly enough to reach you, the beep of machines. The zip of a bag, the plastic gasp of an air pump, the creak of a gurney.

You hear someone ask about "the kid," and for a moment, you hang suspended over your body, which has tensed like it's the one in rigor mortis.

"Hell of a start to adulthood, this," is all Matt says, and it seems to be enough. Only a grunt answers it. Matt adds one more line, and you think it's for you. "But I think Will had to grow up long before crossing that line. They're a hell of a fighter, and they're not alone."

The tension in your body relaxes in increments—albeit with diminishing returns.

Not long later, the sheriff's department shows up, a couple of young deputies. Thankfully, the cops only ask a few questions, mostly to Matt. He fields everything with finesse.

"Hannah's best friend" is a phrase you make out amid the cloud of dissociation, as well as Matt and Hannah's mother's name, Dana.

"They're not alone," Matt says again to the cops.

Eventually, they leave. You stay.

Time stretches out longer than the two hours you spent sitting on the floor next to Frances's body.

They're not alone.

Matt didn't tell them a single outright lie—except that one.

With the cops gone, the EMTs work quietly. Understanding seems to echo in the silence.

Maybe, just maybe, you'll get through this for real.

But you know this is only the first hurdle. And you know you cannot trust the system to leave you alone.

You don't go back in until Frances is gone.

Chapter Three

You learn more in that following week than you'll likely learn from a book all year—like how expensive dying is. Matt finds a funeral director to handle the death certificate. There's a window of nine months for dealing with Frances's assets and reporting everything to the state; that gives you time to turn eighteen.

You learn a lot that week about *assets*. You learn this after digging through Frances's papers her car is paid off.

The house, an old double-wide on two acres of land off State Route 6, is also paid off.

She didn't have life insurance or anything—you're pretty sure about that since, well, your job pays the bills, and that wasn't one of them. *You're welcome, Frances*, you think.

Part of you wants to let Matt involve his mother for real. Dana Straczynski does immigration law, but Matt says she has colleagues who might help you pro bono.

Dana's a single mom on purpose, and unlike Frances, she's actually good at it. You don't have a flaming clue in hell who your dad is, but it's for way different reasons than why Hannah and Matt don't—Dana used sperm donors to get pregnant. You've always sort of envied their family. Dana's so . . . competent. You wonder sometimes what it would have been like to stay with Hannah and Dana.

Maybe you could trust Dana. Though she only met Frances once, the way she always used to say, "Will, if you ever need to stay a couple nights a week, just say the word" pops back into your head and calms you enough to believe Dana probably wouldn't call CPS and have you dragged back into foster care for four months.

You learned young that four months is plenty long enough to fuck up absolutely everything. That's why you never told Dana; the known quantity of Frances was preferable to getting thrown back into the system.

Never mind that you would never give Frances a foothold to terrorize Hannah's perfectly imperfect family for reporting her. Frances ruined everything she touched.

Including you. And the carpet she died on.

No one in Bright Springs bats an eye when you rent a steam cleaner, which you do the day after Frances dies, and you spend the next two days using it on every carpet in the place. Vacuum, steam clean, dry, repeat.

The action has a feeling of ritual to it. Cleansing. Purification. Maybe even exorcising.

It works for the first one, but the other two are questionable. No matter how hard you scrub that carpet, something oppressive remains in the air, an undertone of death.

The house reeks of smoke that you think you'll never chase away, but without Frances adding more to it every day, you're surprised to find how quickly it fades into a sort of stale background ambiance. Mostly, anyway. Sometimes a wave of it hits you all over again as if Frances blew cigarette smoke directly into your face, making you choke.

You try to ignore it. When that doesn't work, you scrub some more.

It finally starts to sink in when you hop in your car to go get more Windex *just because you can*, that you have made a choice and acted on it for maybe the first time ever. Yeah, it's to go buy cleaning supplies, but no one is going to *stop* you. You could drive to Pennsylvania if you wanted to. And no one would scream at you or hit you for it when you got back.

Instead of simply a tool, suddenly your car means freedom.

You're really fucking glad Frances let you buy the twelve-year-old Nissan Sentra junker because she realized it was easier for you to pay her bills if you could drive to work, and she sure as hell wasn't going to let you use her vehicle.

But now you also have Frances's car, a four-year-old Chevy Malibu that no one will probably want to buy from you since it reeks of smoke and rose-scented air freshener.

Anyway, the point is, you're pretty self-sufficient, since you've had to be. You know how to cook and take care of yourself. You just need to get through a few more months before you'll be on your own. You could even apply for colleges.

I mean, yeah, don't get ahead of yourself. Senior year's a thing you still have to survive, but there's something past that finish line now. Relief, maybe.

When the first day of school arrives, you meet Hannah at the coffee shop, The Daily Grind. It's far enough from school that you pretty much never see anyone else there.

You're in jeans and a T-shirt. And a binder, which you never dared wear in front of Frances but would put on when she was passed out at night and you had a few brief minutes of quiet to just *be*.

Now you can wear it, but you get out of the house as fast as you can as if Frances will rise from the grave—or, more appropriately, the crematorium—to forcibly strip it off you.

For an article of clothing so constricting, it feels liberating.

Hannah pulls up in her Jeep. It's fire-engine red, and she definitely did not pay for it herself. You wonder what that would be like, to just have someone give you a car on purpose. Not because, like, they died.

The gravel parking lot crunches under your feet when you open your door and get out. You already have your coffee, and when Hannah gets out of her Jeep with a silver travel mug in one hand, you see she clearly didn't plan to buy one.

"Hey," she says. She sounds just like Matt did.

"Morning." To your surprise, she closes the distance between you and hugs you with her free arm, hard. It shocks your skin into goose bumps in the mountain air and because you weren't aware of how much you needed that. Human contact.

You let the hug go on long enough to become a little awkward, then pull away. Hannah likes hugs, but you're usually not one for them. She's your exception.

"You ready to face the hordes?" Hannah's pale skin glows as a beam of sun breaks through the orange-rimmed leaves of the nearest tree. Her red-brown hair (a lighter shade than Matt's) turns gold where little baby strands claim the sunlight, but as ethereal as she looks, her gray eyes are flat.

"Not really." It's a ritual, this little exchange. Whenever you meet before school, which you always do when one of you is having a shitty time at something, you have to psych yourselves up to do battle. Today though, it's especially true.

"If you change your mind about telling my mom, I found a couple of people in her directory who do probate." Hannah looks at you hopefully, as if you'll give her the green light.

Shaking your head, you instead change the subject. You reach in your back pocket and pull out Frances's Galaxy. "I have a cell phone now."

The note of distaste in your voice is unmistakable. You knew Frances's passcode because she was terrible at hiding it. She'd whoop your ass into another dimension if you tried to use it, so holding it now feels gross. Phones are personal, and you've now been far more up close and personal with Frances than you ever wanted to be. You took one look at her camera roll and almost threw it across the room. Bunch of selfies, mostly, with her making doe eyes at the camera. You should just find a way to delete everything, but you're a little afraid you're not allowed to?

Hannah looks at the phone like it's a huntsman spider. Belatedly, she says, "I guess that's a good thing to have, but—"

"Yep."

"Have you been going through her stuff?"

"Not much. It's weird as fuck." At her understanding nod, you waggle the phone at her. "This is bad enough. But I guess I'm going to have to."

"I ain't touching that phone. It's probably haunted. If you want, I'll come over today and help you get started with the other stuff." Before you have a chance to accede to that or process the *haunted*, she brightens. "You can add me on Snapchat now."

Weirdly, that makes you feel better.

It's almost time for you to get going to school, but you don't want to, and you can tell Hannah doesn't either.

She's pretty, in a quiet sort of way. You think under other circumstances she would have been kind of popular herself (your friendship notwithstanding), but as it is, she's got Tourette's syndrome and started out school with a massive stutter, and Matt being all things small-town celebrity wasn't enough to shield her from the absolute dickishness of kids once he was out of sight and out of mind. When you met her, it was a few months after Frances stole you back from Raz and you were just starting to get boobs and hating it, and she'd spent the summer in speech therapy, and when she saw you at school she zeroed in on you like a heat-seeking missile and gave absolutely zero fucks that you were fully intending to be a sulky loner freak.

She picked you, and since that mere fact reminded your still-broken heart of Raz, you just . . . went with it.

You smile at her suddenly.

"What." She doesn't make her inflection rise at the end.

"No one I'd rather face the hordes with than you," you say.

She outright beams at you.

Bright Springs High School *suuuuucks.*

You pull into the student parking lot behind Hannah, and already you see a veritable *fog* of football players at the entrance, chest bumping and slapping each other on the back as if they are piss-marking everything in the vicinity as theirs.

Hannah parks at the back of the lot, with you next to her. Your tattered backpack is light on supplies—you were so busy with the whole Frances-is-dead thing that you forgot to go school shopping. Right now you think you have one pencil with half a lead left and last year's binder that is half full with last year's notes.

The sound of Hannah's slamming car door makes you jump.

"Side entrance?" Her eyes are on the blocked entry from the lot.

You nod vigorously.

But you only make it as far as the grass.

"H-h-hey, if it isn't H-H-Hannah!" You know that goddamn voice. Levi Strand, resident sphincter crust. He's a little under six feet and you're pretty sure he fake-and-bakes his white-ass skin because he's starting to look like Donald Trump, but people at this school fawn over him. Well. They fawned over Trump, too, but unlike Trump, Levi's got straight As, rumors of a full-ride football scholarship to University of Maryland, and oh yeah, his dad's the superintendent.

In case you were wondering how he gets away with his bullshit. If you weren't already, you're about to.

He zooms between you, and you can smell the leather of his letterman's jacket.

"Piss off, Levi," you say.

"You can talk!" Levi feigns shock and holds his hands up as if to say *ooooohhhh, I'm soooo scared* and then goes back to ignoring you. He loops an arm over Hannah's shoulder, and she shrugs him off. Her pale face is already flaming red.

"How 'bout that date this week, H-H-Hannah?"

"Oh my god, Levi, *piss off.*" You round on him, which he isn't expecting, and he actually runs right into you. For a moment, you freeze with the shock of it. What are you *doing?*

"Will." You don't think he's ever looked at you directly before. Now he gives you a long once-over that you feel ripple across your skin. Another surprise—you don't think he's ever even said your name. He looks at people like they're rabbits and he's some kind of lion, when he's just a hyena. "Why don't you let me and H-H-Hannah decide this?"

"It's decided, Levi," says Hannah, shocking you all over again. "Go. Away."

To your additional surprise, he does. He backs off a step, looking over both of you once more. Then he smirks.

"Later." He throws a look over his shoulder as he walks back to the gaggle of football players, managing to look as if leaving was his idea.

"Did we figure out some sort of over-under on how long it would take for one of those shitheads to do something shitty?" You mutter it, kicking at a clump of patchy grass among the otherwise pristine green swathes of turf.

"Nope, but this might be some kind of record," Hannah says. "Table!"

She says the word loudly, but not loudly enough for anyone to hear. She must be really stressed. Usually she doesn't have outbursts anymore, and contrary to what a lot of people think about Tourette's, she doesn't shout obscenities unless the Capitals are playing, and that has nothing to do with Tourette's and everything to do with Carlson being a defensive BAMF.

"You okay?"

"Other than feeling like I got dipped headfirst in a septic tank, fine."

You make it inside the school, feeling like the day's already been a week long.

It's right before your fourth-period calculus class that the second weird thing happens.

Ashton Gray is talking to Hannah when you walk into class.

Last year Ashton kept to herself almost as much as you and Hannah did. None of this would be particularly notable, except the fact that Hannah has had a crush on Ashton since your first year of high school.

She's a pretty girl. Brown skin, black hair, dark eyes. Her face is heart-shaped, and she has definitely bloomed over the summer. Blah to bombshell in three months, though you'd never let Hannah hear you say the blah part. And holy shit, Ashton is *sparkling* at Hannah.

Like, if you were to picture Cass from *Dragon Age* with stars for eyes right now, you wouldn't be too far off the mark with Hannah's expression.

You feel a pang of something that isn't shock and isn't jealousy, you think. You're ace (demi, but who's counting?), and even if you weren't, Hannah and you are just friends, with the word *just* the same sort of application you'd use to say that a meteor is just a rock.

As a demi person, you resent people assuming romantic love is the be-all, end-all goal.

Ashton tears her eyes away from Hannah when you sit down in the seat next to Hannah, which she's saved for you, of course.

"Hey, Will!"

"Uh, hey."

"Good summer?"

"Eh." You don't really want to be rude, but what are you supposed to say to that?

"I was supposed to give this to you." She holds out an office slip to you, which you take, bemused. Ashton looks a little uncomfortable, but then brushes it off. "I'll see you in seventh," she says to Hannah, then gives you a little smile and leaves the classroom.

Third weird thing is the way Ashton's smile at you almost looks shy, as if she's worried about what you think of her.

You stare after her. "What just happened?"

Hannah looks around. There's only fifteen or so people in the class, and if Levi's in it, he's not here yet, but she still turns pink.

"I don't know, dude," Hannah says. "She just kind of came up and started asking me about my summer and about, like, this book we're reading for AP English"—one of the two classes you don't have with Hannah—"and I don't know. She was probably just making small talk while she waited for you."

She looks so bewildered that you can't help but smile, in spite of the little surge of sharp feeling that this time you think is jealousy. You know you're terrible for feeling it, but you do anyway. Hannah is your only friend. If she and Ashton hook up, you'll be spending your senior year alone. Really alone. You and Hannah have an established dynamic. One easily upset by things like Hannah thinking you're mad at her if you're too quiet for too long. Ashton would be like a bomb.

(Come on, Will. You're being ridiculous. You really think Hannah would just ditch you like that? Then again, of course you do.)

The office slip is pretty innocuous. It's a summons with a note scribbled at the bottom that just says, *Check in with Suzie*, which means the counselor wants to see you. That itself isn't weird. You met with her once a week last year because your teachers said you were overtired, which was true. She wanted to know why, you told her half-truths for twenty minutes once a week, you went on with your day—it was a whole thing. Looks like she wants to start up again.

Or could she have found out about Frances?

Nah. You're pretty sure that would have merited more than a simple check-in request.

You think.

Seventy-eight percent sure.

You put the note out of your head. You'll deal with Suzie the Counselor tomorrow.

Just then, Levi strides into the room, somehow with an extra two-foot radius of invisible-but-palpable force field beyond his actual body. People spill away from him before he gets within bumping range. Mrs. Cantor, the teacher, gets up from her desk the instant the bell rings.

Levi sits in the chair on the other side of Hannah, a smirk on his stupid face even though he's not looking at her.

Apparently, people here find him attractive. Sure, he's symmetrical enough, but his faux-tanned skin and repulsive personality makes it seem like his skin is just a thin layer of orange-y butterscotch over a rotten onion.

As if he heard your thoughts, the butterscotch-coated onion turns to you. Smiles. Holds your eye contact a few seconds too long without blinking. The sensation of looking directly at him burns like lasers, but you stubbornly stare back. A glint in his eye, he raises his thumb and index finger to his lips like he's taking a hit from a joint and blows an invisible smoke ring at you. What? Then he turns to Mrs. Cantor, who's going through first-day stuff already.

It's going to be a long rest of the day.

Chapter Four

Hannah, to her credit, always pretends not to hate your house. She never pretended to feel anything but contempt for Frances on the few times they were face-to-face, and in the slightly more-frequent event where Frances left for a few nights unannounced, Hannah came over and never acted like your house was the shithole that she probably thinks it is. Not really, anyway. You'd see her nose wrinkle at the smell, but she'd always say it was allergies. Hannah is a very diplomatic person.

Hannah stops just inside the doorway.

"It's safe to take your shoes off now, I think," you say (this is an important distinction, considering the state of the floors before now). "I cleaned the carpets to within an inch of their life."

In great trust of this statement, Hannah takes off her royal blue slip-ons. "I had no idea the carpet had a color."

"Right?" It's sort of bluish now. It definitely wasn't before.

She's staring at the spot on the floor. "Is that where—"

"Yep."

"Jesus. Doesn't it freak you out?"

If I hadn't seen her die with my own eyes, I never would have been able to sleep at night, you think. But you don't say that. Not even to Hannah. She doesn't know you're a monster, or at least she doesn't let on if she does. Someone who wasn't a monster would have tried to save Frances.

"Not really," you say instead. Even though Hannah is literally here to help you rifle through Frances's things, you change the subject for now. "Want a Coke?"

In the week since it happened, not much has changed around the house other than the state of the floors and the once-stained walls, but you have stocked the fridge with Coca-Cola and the freezer with a shit ton of microwave dinners Frances never let you buy. If you can avoid it, you won't cook again until you turn twenty.

"Sure," Hannah says.

You get one for each of you and throw a pan of Tater Tots into the oven to heat up, setting the old-school timer before you remember you've entered the twenty-first century and can probably do that on the phone now.

The timer makes a nervous little buzz, but you're used to it. Right now it's almost as if it knows its end is nigh. It's been a good timer. It can rest soon.

Hannah cracks open her Coke and glances down the hall to where the master suite is.

"You been in there yet?"

"Only for the carpets," you tell her. You haven't been able to bring yourself to go through anything yet. For one thing, it stinks worse in there. Frances smoked in bed, and it's a goddamn miracle she didn't die because she went up in flames.

For another, you really would rather not go through her stuff at all. You thought about filling your car with it and hauling every bit of it to the dump, but you like the environment more than you hate Frances, so you decided the better thing to do is sort it out and donate what you can.

Hannah's got her eyes trained on the door, and you know that little frown that bunches up her lips on one side. She's Preparing Herself.

"Let's get this shit over with, Will. When it's done, I'll help you paint all the walls and tear up the carpets if you want. Make it your house."

You're not sure if it'll ever be your house, literally or figuratively, but it's a nice thought.

"Okay," you say. You fill your lungs with lemon-tobacco air and follow Hannah down the hall.

Frances's room is just how you left it, of course. Her bed remains unmade and a glass half-filled with cloudy water sits on the nightstand.

You don't have a clue where to start.

"Shall we see what kind of skeletons she's got in the closet?" Hannah sets her Coke down on the dresser, which has ring marks all over it, and flakes of ash that missed the ashtray now cover the surface like nuclear fallout.

"Steel yourself for actual skeletons," you mutter.

Even though you've had to come in here a lot to get Frances's laundry and clean, you're always a bit taken aback by the size of her room. Or maybe it's less the actual size and more that your need to "get in, get stuff done, get out of range" made it feel bigger. Like it could trap you there where Francis could zero in on your presence as her most convenient target.

"Right," you say. The closet's a wreck. Naturally. "Any clothes that look like they can be donated, chuck on the bed. Anything that needs to be doused with gas and set on fire, toss it on the floor."

"All the underwear, then."

Horrified, you nod fervently. "Yeah. Definite yeah. In fact, I'll get a trash bag now and save us a step."

The kitchen's starting to smell like Tater Tots when you grab a big drawstring bag from under the sink. You pause for a moment, then snatch two extra and head back to the room.

"How did she afford all this?" Hannah has two sequined dresses in her hand when you get back. One of them is blues and greens, Hannah's favorite colors. She's never bold enough to actually wear jewel tones, though. She sticks to earth-toned neutrals, but she grips the peacock-colored dress like it's a treasure.

You give Hannah a long look. There's been a decent amount of your reality that you haven't shared with her. You find you're tired of hiding it.

"All my checks got deposited into a joint account," you say quietly, then add a sardonic, "I'm too young and irresponsible to have my *own* checking account, according to the law."

"A joint account." Hannah's tone is dead level.

"A joint account."

You didn't make much money, but you did work full-time at the library all summer for ten bucks an hour and your checks evaporated. Getting paid to spend thirty-four hours a week away from Frances made that part almost worth it. Being around books all day was a bonus.

"Will."

"Hannah."

This time there's a small rift in her voice. A crack that's not quite anything you can pinpoint. "You could have told me."

"There was nothing you could have done." Paying for Frances's fashion is near the bottom of your list when it comes to the Sins of Frances.

She goes quiet. You know her mind is going through the options of coulda-shoulda-woulda, and she knows you and your history just well enough to know that you never would have forgiven her if she had called CPS on Frances. CPS stopped giving a shit long ago. A two-minute conversation could have kept you with Raz, and you hate them for it.

Maybe the system helps some kids. They didn't help you.

Hannah walks past you to throw the dresses on the bed as if they're Frances herself.

Her neck is red around her collar bone. She's . . . really angry.

It's probably good you didn't tell her till now.

"That's a fucking two-hundred-dollar dress." She bites off each word. "It's not couture, but it's—"

"I know."

You've done the math enough times. You worked twenty hours to buy Frances one of those dresses.

More. Taxes are a thing.

"Let's just do this," you say.

The two of you work in silence for a while. Whenever Hannah or you aren't sure about something, you hold it up and the other either nods or shakes a head, deciding the fate of each garment. Before long, you've got one entire side of the closet done.

Hannah turns to the other side of the closet and pulls out a couple more garment bags that likely contain a month or so of work you did.

"What's that?" Hannah peers around one of the crinkling bags.

"What's what?"

"It's a box or something."

"What?" You knew better than to mess with the garment bags, so this box is news to you.

Hannah tosses the garment bags onto the clean—clean*er*—side of the closet and kneels down.

The box is more like a little trunk. It's got a gold clasp with a lock on it.

"It's locked." Hannah jiggles the clasp, then yanks on it, but aside from a clicking noise, nothing happens.

Her eyes meet yours.

"There has to be a key around here," you say.

It looks like a diary lock. You can visualize the key since they're so simple. Some of your old foster sisters had them. You know there was no tiny key like that on Frances's keychain.

"You check the dresser," you tell her.

Hannah hops to it like you're a drill sergeant. You go to the nightstand, where the ashtray sits, caked with gray and odorous. There's a small cupboard and a drawer in nice condition despite the grody state of the table bit where Frances's beer cans languished and where she dribbled booze and ash everywhere. You open the cupboard first and behind you, you hear Hannah pull open a drawer.

"Jesus Christ," she says.

You turn around, and she's dangling Frances's Colt .45 between two fingers like it's a months-dead skunk instead of a gun.

You shrug. "I don't think it's loaded."

At that, Hannah takes a firmer hold on the gun and checks the magazine and the chamber. You forgot her mom used to take her shooting. If you remember correctly, it was because Dana keeps a gun in the house and was adamant her kids at least know how to handle it safely. Hannah hates guns.

"It's definitely loaded," she says, then carefully moves a small switch.

"The safety wasn't on?"

"N-ope." She puts the gun back and keeps rummaging through the drawer.

Disconcerted, you turn back to the nightstand.

The drawer is as fruitless.

Hannah just about slams a drawer on the dresser. "Nothing here. She must have really not wanted you to find it."

"Or she got drunk and ate it for fun."

Hannah rolls her eyes at you. "Maybe it's under the mattress."

You help her pick up the mattress, both of you fumbling with the awkward, floppy weight. You peek under the mattress, but you don't see—

"There!" Hannah crows at the exact moment your eyes find it. A small lump, taped to the box spring with brown masking tape.

"It might not be the key," you say.

Together you set the mattress back down so it hangs off the foot of the box spring. Hannah snatches off the little lump and looks at the back of it.

She doesn't say anything, only holds it up triumphantly to you.

A small brass key. Well, hell.

She peels it off of the tape and hands it to you. "You should do the honors here."

Honor's definitely not the right word for this.

You head back into the closet, where you kneel beside the box with Hannah beside you.

Irrationally (not irrationally at all) you hope the key doesn't fit. So you won't have to know what's inside this box.

Tough titty. The key fits.

You turn it and press the little brass tags on either side of the lock. The box pops open.

The first thing you notice is the money.

Hannah says something under her breath that's probably a curse, but you barely hear it. There's got to be at least a thousand dollars here, mostly in dingy twenties.

You don't stop to allow the irony of Frances literally locking away your own earnings from you to catch up. Instead, you pluck the bills out of the box and drop them into the lid of the box.

Underneath it is a pile of envelopes, haphazardly thrown in the box. You pick one up at random. There's no return address, just a scribbled out TO section. It's open.

You pull out a piece of blue paper.

Blue paper.

Stop here.

Breathe, Will.

Feel your heartbeat for a second and brace yourself, because the ground is about to shift beneath your feet.

You're about to find out that Frances spent more time lying to you than you previously thought, which is impressive. It's not your fault for not realizing it. Frances is—was—an exceptionally practiced liar.

The problem isn't that it's yet another lie on top of heaps of other lies (or in this case, under a heap of them). The problem is, as is so often true in these cases, the surprise of the thing. It hits you in a way you didn't think you could *be* surprised.

You know that paper. And you know that handwriting.

The smell of blueberry pancakes cuts through the lemon-smoke and dirty laundry.

You're holding a letter.

From Raz.

And it's dated last year.

Chapter Five

Some people can't pinpoint the instant their life changes. Even you've missed some doozies. You had no way of knowing that a knock on the door meant getting wrenched from another temporary family, or that when you came home from work on a normal day, Frances would be gasping her last breath. But this one?

Oh, this one, you know. You feel this change in your marrow, because it's not just a crossroads type of change, it's one of those rare retroactive-revision ones, the kind that makes you rewrite everything you think you know.

You also know instantly that this letter you're holding isn't the only one that is from Raz, because it's only the top on a stack about three inches thick at its apex.

A jangling sound starts, far away and disembodied, like you're hearing it from under water.

Hannah jumps up and takes off, socked feet making small thumps on the carpet with her running, and it takes you a minute to understand that the jangle is that old timer you've heard a thousand times before. Just as disembodied, you hear Hannah say loudly, "How the fuck do I turn this off?"

The timer continues its one-man band show for another few seconds, then goes silent.

All of this has happened in the span of a few breaths, really. Time might have frozen for you, but it didn't for Hannah—she kept ticking along while you got sucked into the flames of your life burning up like the cherry of one of Frances's cigarettes.

So when she comes back with a massive plate of Tater Tots, a shallow pink wasabi bowl full of the mayo and ketchup mixture you both love, and another one of ranch dressing, she manages to plunk back down beside you, get settled, and pop a steaming Tot in her mouth before it occurs to her that you haven't so much as twitched from where she left you.

"Will?"

You're not even sure you can answer. Your eyes have started to make words out of those familiarly crafted squiggles on the page.

Dear Will,

The leaves are starting to change, so naturally I've been making soup every day even though it's still eighty degrees outside. I'm also trying to learn how to make bread without my bread machine, but last time it came out hard as a rock, so I might end up sticking to what I know. I'm no Monica, right?

Work has been good, in the sense that it's keeping me busy. My boss has been pushing me to travel more, but I'm not sure how I feel about that. The cat doesn't like it much when I'm away, even though the neighbor feeds her and scoops her litter box. I finished getting the kitchen remodeled, which she didn't like either since it meant I had to keep her cooped up in the upstairs bedroom while the workers were here. I hope you're well.

(Something's crossed out here, but you can't make it out.)

I hope junior year's treating you okay. High school can be pretty rough.

You'll get through it, though. I know you will.

The letter's not signed.

You turn it over, looking for more on the back. There's nothing there.

"Will?" Hannah repeats your name. "What is that?"

You never really told her about Raz. She knows you were a foster, but your time with Raz was so brief and perfect that thinking about it made you doubt that it had ever happened at all.

"It's from an old foster mom," you say finally. Your hands are quivering holding the letter.

"Whoa. Why does your mom have it then?" Hannah stops. "Did, I guess."

"I don't know. I didn't know she wrote to me."

The carpet in here looks almost new, without much tread wear or dingy ash fading. Plush against the palm of your left hand. Your fingers dig into it like a grappling hook.

Full of more letters, the box in front of you taunts you.

"What's wrong?" Hannah asks. "I mean, besides the obvious fact that your mom is basically a drunk dragon. Was. That letter has to be kind of old—"

"It's from last year," you say, holding it out for her to inspect.

She reads it quickly. "Did you two write to each other a lot?"

The wave of helplessness crests in your chest so quickly that you feel like it washes you away. You're swimming in it, surrounded by stinging salt water and grit.

The Tater Tots are going to get cold. You make yourself take a couple and dip them in the fancy sauce. You don't really taste them.

"Never." You look at Hannah now, and you can almost see how wild-eyed you must look because she hands the letter back and grabs your free hand, not caring that there's a smear of sauce on it and some shiny grease from the Tots. "I don't even—I don't even know what this means, Hannah. Nothing in this letter makes any sense. Like . . . why would she even keep writing to me if she never got a response? How the fuck did Frances keep all these a secret? There have to be at least twenty or thirty of them here—would she even be allowed to write to me? Legally or whatever. I have no fucking clue."

Hannah looks closely at you, then pushes a wave of dark hair out of your face. You didn't even notice it.

"She meant something to you, didn't she?"

For a second you think she means Frances just because your brain has not yet accepted that these letters actually exist, but Hannah motions at the letter.

"I think . . . she was going to adopt me," you say. "The year with her was the best of my life. She—she helped me find my name."

You've never told anyone that before.

"Shit." Hannah takes the letter back and peers at the date. "If she wrote this just last year, she obviously still cares about you, Will. You should find her."

"There's no return address." You don't remember where she lived, not exactly. Some things about living with Raz you remember with perfect clarity, like Michelangelo himself carved them into your memory. Others feel like you tried to watch them through clouded glass.

"Then we'll look through these letters until we find a clue. Don't you want to tell her you never got the letters?"

Hannah's question stops you cold, halfway to grabbing another Tater Tot.

All this time, Raz thought you never wrote back.

You didn't even know, and you managed to probably torture someone. She kept writing all this time even though she never once got a response. One of the only people on the planet you ever loved, and you managed to let her down without even trying.

You can almost hear Frances laughing at you. *This is your fault.*

You and Hannah spend the next hour organizing the letters chronologically in the living room. You also count the money. It's about seven hundred dollars, which is nice, you guess. You're already going to have to pay a grand for Frances's cremation. Frances's ashes currently sit in their most basic urn in her car, because you didn't want her in the house.

The "to" address on each envelope is scratched out. Never a return address. But there's postmarks on each of them, all Hagerstown—where you lived with Raz—except one. The other one is marked Frederick, which also doesn't seem abnormal, since it's just a bit farther south than Hagerstown.

The stamps are kind of cool—special editions. You lay them out on the floor by year, then in order by date.

Letters begin the month Frances took you back. There are four from that year. Then they drop into a pattern. March, May, December. The year you turned fourteen, though—there's a blip in that pattern that you wouldn't have noticed if you had read them as they came. That year she sent one in August, too. But then it goes back to March, May, December . . . until last year.

There are three from this year. One arrived three weeks ago. You haven't been able to open that one.

"She wrote you like clockwork," Hannah says, sitting with her arms around knees pulled to her chest. She stares out over them. "Real letters."

"Frances never let me use the internet, so it's not like she could have emailed me, even at my school email." Frances didn't even let you get online to pay bills, making you probably one of the only seventeen-year-olds of your generation to know your way around a checkbook. The only time you've ever been on the internet at all is at Hannah's house or at school or at the library.

"Frances was fucked up," Hannah says.

You make yourself pick up a letter—no, still not the most recent one (that one's too scary)—and choose the August one from the year you turned fourteen. The envelope's stamp is a black-and-white image of a cranky-looking white man with a big, bushy white beard. The stamp says "Leo Tolstoy."

Dear Will,

Here it is, August again. Feels like it hasn't been here in a while. Silly thought, maybe, but I can't seem to shake it. There's a famous Tolstoy (he's the guy on the stamp) quote about time and happiness, but I can't remember it off the top of my head. I must be getting older.

Speaking of which, so are you. Almost fourteen, now. Starting eighth grade. I hope middle school is nicer to you than it was to me, but just know that it will get better. Maybe when August comes again. ☺

I've always wanted to drive up the coast and watch the leaves change. I'm not ambitious enough to start down south, but maybe starting in Baltimore would work well enough. Though there's a great pizza place in the Inner Harbor where you can build your own pizzas, so I might get distracted by that and never leave to see the leaves.

Look at me, going on and on. I hope you're doing well, Will.

You show it to Hannah, who reads it quietly.

"Was she always this scattered?" You think Hannah is trying to be diplomatic when what she wants to say is *nuts*.

"No," you say. "A little weird, yeah, but not like . . . this kind of weird. She sounds like a grandma with Alzheimer's or something."

The next letter is in December, and it pretty much just wishes you a happy birthday. But the closing of it catches your eye.

Time marches on, come what may.

You stare at it for a minute. You're a smart kid—and not a trusting one. Sometimes a side effect of not trusting anyone is that you have a massive tendency to overthink everything. Like the letters' timing—Raz sending you letters in the exact same months every year had to be deliberate. She either wanted you to know you could expect them, or . . . she wanted you to look at where the pattern changes.

Okay. *Okay.*

Your skin feels prickly. Good. It should.

The letter's still in Hannah's hands as she reads it a second time, muttering under her breath. She always sort of mumbles whatever she's reading when she tries to read silently.

You grab the one from August of last year.

Dear Will,

What do you know? August did come back. It seems to have taken its time, but sometimes such things are worth it if you want to really be. I bet you're starting to look forward. About to start junior year, about to turn seventeen. Only one year left before you hit the big one-eight and get to do whatever your Will self wants to do.

Next August will be a big one for you. The last August of your high school times. An entire chapter of your entire life, coming to an end. But there are new beginnings to be had, too. Don't let that last August just pass you by. I hope by then you'll know or at least have an idea of where you truly need to be next.

You read the letter a second time. Now you *know* Raz is talking to you. Really talking to you. Having a conversation she planned over the course of years, though?

This year's August letter—you feel a panicked pang as you become utterly certain of something: this is the last letter. It's over by Hannah, in the bottom rightmost corner of the little grid you've made of all the envelopes.

There's something in here she wanted you to know.

You lean across Hannah's feet and grab it.

Dear Will,

Remember what I said last year? It seems August has come again indeed. This is a special last August for you. You're a senior now—all your hard work and patience has paid off.

The leaves are starting to change here, and it always makes me think about change itself. And pizza, for whatever reason. There's not much pizza where I'm spending my autumn—I'll be off the grid with family on a much-anticipated hike through the changing leaves—but nonetheless. So many choices for you to make. Big ones. Hard ones, maybe. Life's seldom full of easy ones, as I know you know. You're a warrior, Will. Never forget that. You are powerful.

Did you ever read any Tolstoy? You should at least Google him. Fascinating man.

I'm afraid I have to wish you a happy birthday early this year. I wish I could do it in person.

That's it. That's where it ends.

Wordlessly, you hand the two letters you're holding to Hannah.

"She . . . kind of unraveled at the end there." After reading, she hands them back.

What. "No, Hannah, don't you see what she did?"

Hannah looks at you blankly, shifting to sit cross-legged and stretching her back.

"All this talk about August and leaves and pizza. She laid a trail in her letters for the past four years. She wants me to do something, but I don't know what it is."

Slowly, Hannah takes the letters back from you. She lays them out on the carpet, every August letter in a row.

"What if Frances had just burned the letters or chucked them? Why didn't she?" Her voice is quiet.

"Frances liked to have things she could . . . hold over me. If she'd told me she had letters from Raz, she probably could have gotten me to do just about anything. Or just shown them to me to burn them in front of me."

"Frances was *fucked up*," Hannah says again.

You shrug. Far as you're concerned, this is normal parental behavior. Well. You guess it's not, but it's your normal, and that's the normal you have to live with.

Hannah stares at the letters again, and you do too, reading them over and over in sequence. After a minute, Hannah grabs her phone.

"What are you doing?"

"Googling Tolstoy."

"What."

"She said to."

Touché.

"Okay, so she said to Google him. This is what comes up." Hannah holds her phone out so you can see. There's Tolstoy's face, sure enough. Birth, death, brief bibliography, and then—

"Quotes," you say. You resist the urge to snatch Hannah's phone away.

She reads out, "'If you want to be happy, be.'" She snorts. "Just like that. Okay, the next one's not that bad. 'Everyone thinks of changing the world, but no one thinks of changing himself.' I can get on board with that one, sexist pronoun norms notwithstanding. Last one here is, 'The two most powerful warriors are patience and time.' Whoa."

Your spine feels tingly now. Raz wanted you to know she was patient. That patience is powerful.

"She said she wishes she could wish you happy birthday in person," Hannah says suddenly.

"Right, but she said this was the last letter. How the hell would that even happen?" Then it hits you, because this is all coming a bit fast for you to be anything but slow. "She wants me to find her."

Suddenly excited, Hannah sucks in a breath, eyes wide. "She even told you when and where, Will. She told you *when and where.*"

Tolstoy's face vanishes from the screen of Hannah's iPhone as she types in *baltimore build your own pizza inner harbor*

She makes a chirpy sound of triumph and holds out her phone. "Flamey's Pizza. There. Your birthday. Baltimore."

Baltimore's like . . . a three- or four-hour drive from here. But you feel like you could get there on a pogo stick if you had to, because

Because

BECAUSE

It's Raz. It's *Raz.*

Something wet drips onto your lap, and Hannah drops her phone onto the letters.

"Hey," she says. "Hey, you okay?"

There's nothing you can really do but shake your head. The letters feel like they should take up the entire room. They are huge and bubbly and iridescent like the giant soap bubbles you saw someone making at a park once.

"She still wanted me," you suddenly blubber out, and then Hannah's arms are around you, squeezing you tight, holding your atoms together where they want to fly apart.

"Will, you don't have to wait until your birthday. You don't."

You can't see Hannah's face because your own face is smushed against her clavicle, but you think you feel one of her own tears soaking into your hair.

"I want to find her now" is all you say.

"Then we will."

Chapter Six

When Hannah leaves, she takes all the to-donate clothes. Three enormous bags full of your hard-earned cash, converted to textiles and so much trash. Having it gone feels liberating. Your brain buzzes from the emotional labor of the day, explaining everything to Hannah, having to talk so much your voice is almost hoarse.

Exhausted, you throw a microwave dinner in to nuke (seriously, it kind of feels like Frances died and *you* went to heaven), and when it's done, you read every single one of the letters at the table, while poking at an enchilada and drinking another Coke.

You're never going to sleep tonight, but you don't care.

So you sit there at the table, ignoring the dug-in roots of your desperate desire for a parent, a real parent. You also inspect each one of the letters for any sign that Frances could have solved the puzzle of Raz's messages. You don't think so. The paper doesn't look like it's been handled. Fold and unfold something enough times and the creases will be a dead giveaway.

It's not until you finish the mixture of green chili rice and black beans you stirred together that you remember the scratched-out addresses on all the envelopes. You put your empty enchilada tray into the makeshift recycling bin beside the table. Frances not only didn't recycle, but she wouldn't let you recycle. "No fucking point. They used to give you a nickel for every can. Damn waste of effort." That is a decent microcosm of Frances herself, actually.

You don't know it yet, but you are now grieving for Frances. Yes, grieving. As awful as she was and as much as you hated her, you are and will continue to mourn for her.

You'll never get to see her face when you tell her you found the letters. All opportunities to fight back are gone forever. These letters and why she really kept them will remain a mystery.

And if nothing else, the finality of her sudden death robs you of any chance you ever had for resolution.

You've stacked the envelopes in order of date (the postmarks help) but now you look more closely at the scribbled-out addresses.

Frances had to have done that part; the letters got to you, didn't they? Well, not you-you, but within fifty feet at least.

(You're getting warmer.)

Involuntarily, your head turns, and you gaze at the front door. Beyond it, really. You're imagining the exact location of the mailbox.

(Even warmer.)

You get the mail every day. There's a pile of random junk and bills and typical mailers from the school in the fruit bowl, where you used to put it for Frances to open, which she never did.

(Very warm.)

The mailbox is all the way at the end of the driveway, at the road.

(Getting hot now.)

Even if Raz sent the letters at predictable times throughout the year, the days they arrived within the months are pretty scattered. Sometimes earlier, sometimes later. Frances wouldn't have known when they were coming.

For all Frances's . . . Francesness, you really don't think she would have gone through the lengths of walking all the way down to the mailbox every day only to look for a letter and then leave anything else there for you to pick up later.

(Hotter. You're right on this one, you know. That's too much effort expended for someone who made you wait on her hand and foot.)

You suddenly feel the intense sensation that you're being watched.

Sometimes you'd feel that when Frances was still alive, her eyes like the burning cherries of cigarettes boring holes into you that smoldered and stank of moldering tobacco.

But she's dead.

You shake it off and turn back to the task at hand, even though you catch a whiff of stale smoke.

This is where you have a small stroke of brilliance. You carefully rip one envelope down both sides, unfolding it until it lies flat, inside out, on the table. You get up and rummage through the piles of magazines and crap on the shelf under the coffee table until you find Frances's rolling paper. Come to think of it, there's probably some weed somewhere too. Not that it appeals to you. You can't afford to let your guard down, chemically or otherwise.

You grab one, then the half-leaded mechanical pencil from your bag. You really need to go school shopping.

Placing the rolling paper against the envelope's inside, you lightly pencil over the imprint of Frances's scribbles like you're shading something.

You hope Raz wrote the address in ballpoint.

She did.

You watch as the ghost of backward letters appear. You see a P, then an O.

A PO Box. Frances had a goddamn PO Box.

(Bingo. Took you long enough.)

You can't make out the number, but that doesn't matter. You almost fling yourself away from the table, dropping the pencil in the process, where it rattles off the edge and lands on the linoleum with a sharp report. Frances's keys. They're here somewhere, because you used them to put her ashes in the front seat of her car. Where the hell did you put them?

You find them on the hook by the door and feel sheepish. Frances never used the hook. This is one of those moments where you have to get used to living alone and *not* having to account for someone else leaving their key ring in a pair of jeans they drop in a pile with one leg crawling toward the bedroom because they were so drunk that they started peeling them off before they got in the bedroom at all.

The keys for the house and car are easy to spot. There are two silver ones that look like they're to padlocks in the dilapidated shed out back and one brass key with a round top that says *Property of USPS, DO NOT DUPLICATE.*

You found it.

It was Frances's, and it's one of her secrets. You can almost hear her screaming with rage that you dared to lay a finger on it. That stale smoke smell returns like tendrils reaching out to grab you. Holding the key tighter in your hand—*she's dead, she's dead, she's dead*—you feel the jagged edges cutting into the soft pads of your fingertips, but you don't let go.

You're tempted to drive into town right now and find the box if you have to try the key in thousands of boxes until you find one that fits. Instead, you transfer the key to your own ring. You'll go after school tomorrow when it's open.

You don't know what to do now. This secret whispers through the air like the sound of ice subtly cracking beneath your feet.

On a normal night, Frances would be parked in front of the television, inhabiting the depression in the left cushion and a cloud of smoke at the same time. You'd be doing dishes after dinner. If you went into your room, she'd holler at you to get her a beer.

None of that is happening.

You're alone.

She's really gone.

So why is your skin still prickling all over?

By the time you make it to school the next day, bleary-eyed and chugging your second latte (bought with the hidden Frances money), you've totally forgotten about the note you got from Ashton, so when Suzie the Counselor accosts you and Hannah at your locker, a rock the size of the Titanic drops into your stomach.

"Got time for a quick chat?" Suzie is a short white lady with curly brown hair that grays at the roots in steadily increasing increments each month before snapping back to brown again. She reminds you a little of Samwise Gamgee.

Hannah looks at you quickly, obviously sensing your unease even if she doesn't dare intervene. "I'll tell Perez where you went."

Usually teachers add a huffy *mister* or *Ms.* or *missus* when a student last-names another faculty member, but Suzie-who-first-names-herself doesn't. It doesn't make the rock in your stomach any lighter.

You follow her through the hall, ignoring the few kids who glance at you for walking with Suzie; at least none of these students are Levi.

Suzie's office is principal-adjacent. Just as you arrive, you have to stifle a grimace because while you haven't seen Levi himself, his dad—Superintendent Strand—is just coming out of the principal's office. Probably there to get Levi out of detention, or maybe to bully the principal, depending on how far the Levi-butterscotch-onion fell from the tree. Superintendent Papa Onion barely glances at you, his forehead creased as if this is the last place he wants to be.

You hurriedly follow Suzie into her office and plunk down in the blue-upholstered chair your tailbone has come to know and despise, chucking your empty coffee cup into the trash beside her desk.

"How are you doing, Will?" Suzie asks this as she lowers herself into her chair. She adjusts a stack of papers on her desk.

"I'm okay," you say. Your brain is working overtime to try to gauge if she knows Frances is dead by analyzing the expression on her face.

No luck. Frances broke your calibration for normal people's mood reading a long time ago. You wish you'd kept the coffee cup to give yourself something to fidget with. In its stead, you find a rough tongue of plastic on the chair's arm and press it into the pad of your finger several times while you wait for Suzie to inevitably ask more questions.

She watches you poking yourself with the plastic for a beat before speaking. "Did you have a good summer? I know you were feeling anxious at the end of last year."

You press your finger harder against the plastic. It's stiff and digs into the flesh. Suzie can't know—it would be tremendously manipulative of her to lead you around like this if she knew Frances was dead, but then again, it's what Frances herself would do.

"Worked a lot." That's nice and noncommittal. "Did you have a reason for wanting me to come in? It's only the second day, and I'd rather not miss too much."

"Yes, actually." Suzie pauses, a small frown on her face. She taps the pad of her index finger against the desk, which is a habit of hers. "Can you think of anyone who might have a reason to send you mail here at the school?"

The question is so unexpected that the Titanic-rock in your stomach loses its mass and you have to latch a hand onto the arm of your chair with the sudden void of whooshing air in your core. "What?"

"Anyone at all?"

You stare at her, because obviously you can think of one person.

"Yes," you say. "An old friend. Frances doesn't like her."

The present tense comes easily, and Suzie knows you call your mother by her first name anyway, from when you would talk to her last year. You were careful not to give her more than the very basics; she never pried. Much.

The frown deepens. Suzie's frowns are always a little lopsided. The left side of her mouth crunches up more than the right, and her left eye closes just a smudge more too.

She seems to battle with herself for a moment, but then she scoots her rolly chair back and rummages in a drawer for a moment.

You recognize the handwriting on the outside of the large envelope she produces in a heartbeat. Your finger stills on the plastic. Raz. Definitely Raz. You resist the urge to snatch the envelope out of Suzie's hands. Maybe Raz was worried you wouldn't work out her puzzle? Hell, you never even wrote her *back*. The mere fact she kept writing to you is either super obsessive or super dedicated, and you're pretty sure it's the latter. You try to school your face into something resembling neutrality when Suzie presents you with the envelope. It's been opened; the outside is addressed to the school.

No return address.

Suzie sees you twitching toward it and reaches inside. She slides a regular-size mailing envelope out of the bigger one and shows it to you. That one isn't open. The outside says, *Please deliver to Will Farkas.*

"It arrived two days ago," Suzie says, watching you without blinking as if she expects you to snatch it right out of her hands. To be honest, you're not sure you won't. "Principal Lopez gave it to me after our morning meeting."

"Thanks."

"You can open it if you want," she says. At your look, she hurriedly adds, "You don't have to open it here, of course."

She's probably smoldering with curiosity. You give her a wry smile.

"Thanks," you say again.

"If there's something wrong, Will, you know you can always come and speak to me about it," she says.

Your smile widens, and it feels more like a baring of teeth.

You nod to her, take the letter, and hurry out the door with the plastic's bite mark leaving the pad of your finger pink.

Here's the thing. You could talk to Suzie. You could tell her what happened. You thought about it last year, even, because Frances went on a hell of a bender and swung a chair at you. Gave you a nasty limp for a few days, and a bruise the size of a softball.

But you didn't tell her then, and you won't now.

Unlike Matt, she's not going to risk her job to leave you alone. She gets your pronouns right and has pushed the rest of the faculty to do the same, but she always gives off the sense that she thinks you're *damaged*. She's always looked at you a bit like a mangy mutt from a shelter who she doesn't quite understand. Like you might bite.

Okay, so you are pretty damaged, but she'll never believe you that it's just your fault. Taking you away from Frances wouldn't have solved anything. Frances dying might not have either, but hey, it's a step up.

You scurry away from the office.

Your fingers are damp and sweating on the envelope. You take two steps down the echoing hall toward your first period government class, then spin on your heel and head to the bathroom instead. The school put in a couple unisex accessible bathrooms a few years back (no, not for you specifically), and when you started as a first-year, after some frustrating arguments with Principal Lopez, he relented and agreed that you could A: use those bathrooms as long as you yielded to any students who had more pressing needs for them (fine, obviously) and B: change there for PE because you sure as hell weren't going to go in any binary locker room. Nope. It's worked fine for three years. They're always empty when you need them.

Like now.

It smells like bleach in here, which'll give you a headache in approximately an hour, but you don't care. You hang your backpack on the hook on the back of the door and look at the letter in your hands.

It's definitely Raz's writing. For some reason, its existence weirds you out more than the stack of letters back at home.

You slide one finger under the flap on the back to open it and promptly give yourself a paper cut.

Ow.

Pulling out the now-expected blue paper, you pop the bleeding finger in your mouth and shake the paper to unfold it.

Will,

I don't know if you remember me or if your mom ever gave you the letters I've sent you over the years, but I couldn't not take this risk. There are so many things I want to tell you, and I wish I could do it outright. The letters I sent directly to your address I expected your mom to open.

She seems to know Frances pretty well for only having met her the once.

I hope, if you got them, that my little code worked. If you didn't get them or didn't get it (I've never tried to communicate to someone using that kind of method before, so I probably sucked at it), this is what I wanted to say:

For days after your mom took you away from my home, I felt sick. I couldn't sleep. I kept seeing your face over and over again, this defeated look in your eyes and a kind of triumph on your mother's face that has haunted me for years. I want you to know, whatever it is that you decide to do, Will, that I was trying to adopt you. I didn't want to get your hopes up at first, but then I was informed that you were being reunited with your mother and that it would be impossible. I have worried since all that happened that it was my fault, that my starting the adoption process is how Frances found you. For years, I have just wanted to make that right.

I don't know who you've become. I only know that I hope you're okay, and I haven't stopped loving you even for a moment. For whatever reason, I couldn't shake the feeling that you'd gotten thrown into a bad situation. Your mom never responded to my letters, and since you never did, I assumed (believed, strongly) that it was because she didn't give mine to you.

If you want to know me, meet me at Flamey's Pizza in Baltimore's Inner Harbor on your eighteenth birthday. I'll be there all day. I live in the area now, though I'll be out of town for a bit before then. You don't have to come if you don't want to; I'll never hold it against you.

But if you want to, then maybe we can catch up. You might think I'm crazy for saying it, Will, but I wanted to be your mom from the moment I met you. You're almost an adult now, and maybe you don't need that, but maybe you do. Maybe we could still be family.

I hope you're well.

Love,
Raz (Esmeralda Olmos-Adams)

Holy shit.

For the next eighty seconds, that's literally all that goes through your head. If you could have rubbed some kind of magic lamp and asked a genie for anything over the years, this letter is pretty close to it.

So naturally, you immediately distrust it.

She didn't give her address, but you're pretty sure you remember her having a cell phone back when you lived with her. Part of you wonders if Frances kept all those letters just to copy the handwriting and send this.

You at least have Raz's name now. Her whole name.

But this one lines up with exactly what you and Hannah deduced. Down to the pizza place's *name*, for Christ's sake.

You want the letter to be everything it says it is. *Everything.*

Are you even capable of wanting anymore, Will? You're so used to your hand getting slapped if you so much as hold it out to look at your fingernails, let alone to reach for anything.

But this aches. It aches hard. Your whole body feels like you stepped into a human-size bug zapper.

So you make a decision. You're going to go with it. But you're not going to wait until your birthday.

You stuff the letter into your backpack and leave the bathroom just as the bell rings.

Chapter Seven

Hannah drives behind you to the post office after school. You try to forget that the last moment of waving at her in the school parking lot before your mini-caravan into town was also a wave at Ashton, who was standing by Hannah's Jeep, speaking animatedly. Ashton waved at you, too, which makes it worse.

Too much is changing.

When Hannah parks beside you, her lips have a little smile dancing around them that sends more sharp pangs through you. You should be *happy* for her that Ashton's paying attention. Like . . . you remember that she danced with Ashton at your first high school dance and came back looking so smitten you half expected her heart to cartoonishly beat out of her chest or bluebirds to make little feathery poofs into existence just to swirl around her and sing.

You're just being selfish, of course. You want Hannah all to yourself. Especially now, with everything.

She sobers a bit when she reaches you though, and you hate that just looking at you is enough to drain away her giddiness.

"You don't have to do this," she says. "I could go in—"

"Small town, Hannah," you interrupt her. "Everyone knows your mom, and by extension, you and Matt. And Frances is just this side of infamous. No way you could pass for Frances's kid."

"Okay, okay," Hannah grumbles.

The post office isn't that big, and it definitely isn't crowded. It smells like the inside of a brown paper bag. Hannah follows you past the PO boxes to the counter. There's only one person in line before you, an older woman picking her nose with her thumbnail.

You wait, outwardly patient, until she leaves. The postal employee at the counter looks a little like Mario (as in Super).

"How can I help you?" His mustache wuffles when he talks.

"Hi. Uh." You fumble for your key ring. "My mom gave me her key and asked me to pick up her mail, but she didn't tell me which was her box."

You see him take a breath as if to stop you, so you barrel on.

"I know you're probably not supposed to give out PO box numbers and stuff, but here's my ID," you say, handing him your driver's license. "Her name's Frances Farkas."

"Ah."

The guy stops reminding you of Mario, and all you see is the broom dog from the old cartoon *Alice in Wonderland*. You suddenly really want his mustache to start going all brusha-brusha-brusha back and forth.

You also suddenly realize you probably could have gotten this info yourself if you hadn't stopped making your little pencil rubbing of the address as soon as it said PO box, but as discussed, your brain isn't quite at a hundred percent just now. No one'll blame you but you.

"That one. Box three-oh-nine." He draws each number out.

"Thanks," you say.

Another customer has come in, and he gives you a shrug-nod combo before his mustache *does* make a slight brusha-brusha as he seems to move his mouth in distaste.

Hannah meets you at the nook where the boxes all live. Now that you're standing here, you don't know what to do. Which is to say you know exactly what to do, but doing it seems a lot less than fun.

"Which one is it?" Hannah asks. You tell her.

She finds PO box 309. It's one of the normal-size ones, about six inches by six inches. You put the key in, having another one of those moments where you hope the damn thing doesn't fit. It does.

There's a small stack of envelopes in there, a couple of them padded yellow ones. You pull them all out, but there's nothing in Raz's handwriting.

"I don't want to open them here," you say. What you want to say is, *why the fuck was Frances getting more mail in a secret PO box?*

"You can come to my house. Matt's off work today, and Mom won't be home till seven or so."

"Okay."

You try not to keep looking over at the pile of mail on the passenger seat while you follow Hannah to her house. She lives in Bright Springs proper, not far from school or the post office. Then again, nothing in Bright Springs is far from anything else unless you live in the sticks like you.

Matt's car is in the double driveway when you pull up.

Inside, Hannah gets a couple cans of strawberry soda (she guzzles the stuff) and hands one to you along with a snack pack size of Doritos. She's got an entire box of fruit snacks under one arm when she nudges you down the hall toward her room.

She doesn't close the door all the way in her room. You sit down on the foot of her bed, putting your soda on the edge of the desk that bumps up against it. The mattress shifts as she joins you on it, moving her pillows around to lean against the wall to face you.

The mail you put in a pile between you. You take the top envelope, an innocuous white envelope addressed to Frances Farkas. There's a Hagerstown return address on this one, another PO box. You start to slide your still-paper-cut finger under the flap, but Hannah waves a hand at you.

"There's a letter opener on the desk," she says. "Mom got a bunch made for the law office but the printer screwed up the font kerning or something."

The envelope opens with a satisfying hiss of sliced paper instead of flesh. There's a letter inside—or at least you think at first. You pull out a folded piece of white printer paper (thicker, actually), and when you unfold it, five crisp hundred-dollar bills fall out. You're pretty sure your mouth does a similar move. The bills are that glossy blue, the bluer strip palpable on the surface and the green seal actually glittering.

Hannah's breath whooshes in. "What."

Gingerly, you set the money aside.

The next envelope has money too. Not as much, but you put that with the rest.

Then you come to the padded envelope. You're not stupid, Will. You both feel some vague sense of vindication and a quickly accumulating sense of dread and trepidation as you slice open the flap of the padded envelope. The vindication is because this confirms that you're not nuts—that Frances's "freelancing" was *not* answering internet surveys or focus groups or whatever other bullshit things she told you it was. The trepidation and dread? You're pretty sure you have at least an idea of what you're going to find when you dump the contents of the envelope onto the bed, but it still sends a little shockwave through you when out tumbles about ten equal baggies of weed and twice that number of pills.

Naturally, it's at exactly that moment that Matt knocks. Both you and Hannah are too gobsmacked to answer, and the lack of any strangled *I'm changing!* means he opens the door to Hannah's room, saying, "Thought I heard you come home, Hannah. Hey, Will—" Then he stops with one hand still on the doorknob and stares. "What the actual fuck are you doing?"

Your vocal cords refuse to cooperate, so you just hold out the envelope wordlessly so he can see who it was addressed to. Hannah finds her voice first.

"Frances was getting mail at a secret PO box in town, and we went to check it and all this was in there, Matt. It's not *ours*."

You don't think he'd care about the weed, but the pills—those are what he's staring at. You don't know much about drugs (the irony of this is not lost on you), but you do know that oxycontin has been all over the school and the town, and you also remember exactly *why* Matt is an EMT. Jacob. His friend he found dead, courtesy of too much oxy.

You didn't know Jacob well. Once or twice, he was over when you were, and a couple of times you played *Mario Kart* with him and Hannah and Matt. You remember him as a tall white guy with big blue eyes and eyelashes so long and thick people at school actually talked about them.

But you also remember a couple of times hearing him laugh wrong at school. Not wrong like laughing-at-someone-vulnerable wrong, but laughing wrong in general. Laughing in a way you think you've laughed before, like something is so deeply poisoned, so broken at its very foundation and there's no glue that'll hold it together. It boils out of you in laughter that might release a few endorphins but deep down is the same feeling of seeing a puppy starving to death.

Matt's feet aren't moving, but the upper half of his body is trembling so finely it could be called a vibration.

"Matt," you say, because your brain is processing something you're sure he'll say any second now: this is a lot of oxy, and your mother—

(Your mother. Your mother. Your mother.)

—Your mother was clearly dealing it.

Your mother was dealing opioids.

Your mother could have sold Jacob the drugs that killed him.

There isn't an expletive strong enough to break through the numbness that suddenly coats your brain, but if there was, it would be repeating like a skipping record over and over and over.

"Will," Hannah says. When you don't answer because you and Matt are still staring at each other and having the same thoughts at the exact same time, your horror mirroring one another's, she says it much louder. "WILL."

You and Matt both look at her so quickly it's almost creepy.

"There are no postmarks on these," she says quietly. She points at the envelope you're still holding out to Matt like a shield, and you look down at it.

She's right. You look at the others scattered about the bed.

Matt comes in and closes the door, then on a seeming second thought, depresses the lock on it.

It doesn't sink in for a moment, then you say, "Jesus Christ, that means someone at the post office—" at the same time Matt says, "Someone had to put them there," and you both look at each other again.

So you watch Matt sit down on the floor. The air in the room feels like there is a lattice of stretched, taut wire covering it floor to ceiling. Like everyone feels that moving risks cutting themselves to ribbons like a hardboiled egg in a slicer. You swallow.

"We can't tell Mom about *this*," Hannah says. "You know we can't. Not with drugs involved."

Matt nods, eyes unfocused as if he's stuck inside his own head.

"Raz," you say quietly. His head snaps up at the sound of your voice, but he seems to be present again, his gaze quizzical as he waits for you to go on. Drawing a deep breath buys you a second. You may be a monster, but Raz has always wanted you. She has always tried to take care of you. This steels you. "Raz will know what to do."

"Who's Raz?" Matt looks at you sideways.

So for the second time in your entire life and the second time in two weeks, you tell someone your story.

Matt sucks with computers, so Hannah takes point on Googling. She's pretty quick about it, too.

"Found her," she says after a few minutes typing and clicking around on her MacBook Pro, which was a year's worth of birthday and Christmas gifts last year. "Looks like she works for a nonprofit in Baltimore."

"Can you find her address?" You hate asking it, because you hate the idea of being able to just find someone's address on the internet.

"Gimme a minute."

You look back at Matt, who's now sitting with his legs outstretched, leaning back on his hands. He keeps looking over at the pills though. You can't really blame him.

"What do you think we should do with it?" you ask him. He's the closest thing to an adult in this room.

Maybe that means him treating you like an adult made you peers.

"I don't know," he says. Then he says something you absolutely should have thought of: "That much oxy's not cheap. Whoever her supplier was won't *not* notice if one of their dealers doesn't check in or whatever."

The words make you feel queasy, and Hannah's typing stops for a moment.

"We could go to the cops," Hannah says, but Matt violently shakes his head.

"No. Hard no. They'd probably find a way to charge us with possession and then keep the shit for their damn selves, not to mention pocketing the money."

"But—" Hannah tries to cut in, but Matt goes on before she gets farther.

"Hannah? I respond to a lot of calls. Trust me when I say it's a seventy-thirty chance of getting one who will make this problem worse and one who won't. Considering Will's situation? You want to risk that?" Matt pauses long enough to see Hannah dip her chin ever so slightly. "Plus, you remember the talk Mom gave you when I started driving you around, right? About what to do if I got pulled over and you were in the car? To tell them immediately about your Tourette's in case you'd have an outburst and to also tell them firmly that I am your brother?"

He stops again until she nods, his emphasis on *I am your brother* ringing out in the silence as he holds up one brown arm. Hannah's nod is a slow bob almost like she's under water. You can see the wheels in Hannah's head turning as she seems to dredge up the years-old memory. Matt's forehead tightens as if he sees it too. You'd bet money on that talk never retreating far enough into his mind to necessitate excavation. You weren't there for the talk, but if you had to guess, Hannah's takeaway was more about communicating her disability to protect herself than identifying herself as Matt's sister to maybe help protect *him* with her privilege. Matt shakes it off after a moment, a sight that gives you a pang.

He goes on. "I played football for years with one of the guys on the force—Bridgers, who always had my back—and I still wouldn't trust him. I once turned up at a call and he'd handcuffed a victim of a crime. If you want to bet Will's chances on those odds in this town, I've got a bridge to sell you for your college fund."

Silence takes up all the space in the room while you watch Hannah struggle.

Hannah has a sort of . . . pure optimism about things sometimes. Some of it's just unvarnished privilege. She has a lawyer for a mom who buys her cupboards full of fruit snacks and brand-new gadgets and all these other things Hannah takes for granted but you look at with sparkly eyes the way Abu looks at that ruby in *Aladdin*.

Matt has some of that, but he also has maybe more in common with you than he does with his sister. He's brown enough to stand out in this mostly white town, though his good looks and two state wins in football and track made his face a known quantity. Doesn't protect him in Hagerstown if he goes there. Or Pittsburgh. And on top of that daily thing you share with him, that liminal space of being Other-ish and uncategorizable, he's got trauma. Before Jacob died, he smiled a lot more. He was going to go to UMD on a football scholarship but instead did EMT training and now shows up to help when other people find loved ones dead. Or awful abusive parents, but still. There's life before seeing someone you knew dead, and there's life after it.

This is your fault.

You shake the intrusive thought away.

Anyway. Hannah may live a different reality, but at least she listens to the both of you, and adjusts her perspective accordingly. At least you think she does. So when you nod at Matt again and look up to Hannah, her lips tighten and her chin dips again to say she gets it. She goes back to typing.

After minutes of less-fraught silence, she drums her nails against the keys without pressing them, the way she does when she's feeling impatient. Then she looks up.

"Found her. I think." She turns the computer around. "I paid the ten bucks to buy the information—did you know that's a thing you can do? *Buy* people's addresses? Jesus—Anyway, there's a Baltimore address. We could go there day after tomorrow, find some excuse to make the trip."

You're nodding before you can think. "Yeah. *Yeah.* I can drive. If we leave early in the morning—"

"*I'll* drive," Matt says, sitting up and interrupting you. "I'm off work that day, and my car gets better mileage."

Hannah looks like she wants to protest or thinks you might, but you just shrug. "Okay."

"Okay," she says.

"I'll just stay here Friday night," you say. "We can leave around six and be there by nine or so."

Hannah wrinkles her nose, but after a moment, she says, "That'll work." She brightens. "We can stop at Wawa for breakfast and coffee."

You can't help the small smile that tugs the corner of your mouth. Hannah loves greasy breakfasts.

Matt reaches up and takes a pack of fruit snacks from Hannah. "You really think this person will know what to do?"

Though he's no longer got that unfocused look about him, his voice still has a distant quality, like there are layers of history he's trying to be heard through. You know that feeling too well yourself.

"I hope she will." Your stomach does a somersault.

You go home soon after that, but before you do, you stand next to Matt as he flushes every tablet of oxycontin down the toilet. His body heat mixes with yours, giving you the alien impression that his commingled anxiety and relief and yours are feeding off each other.

When they're gone, he turns to you.

"Do whatever you want to with the weed," he says.

"What am I going to do with that?" After six years in a smoke-filled house with Frances, smoking is the literal last thing on earth you want to do.

"I honestly don't give a fuck, Will. Make brownies. Snort it. I do not care." Then he hastily says, "Don't actually do that last thing. Forget I said that."

You crack a smile. "I don't know a lot about drugs, but I think even I know you don't snort weed."

Hannah shudders at the thought as she gathers the weed into the yellow envelope, the rest of the envelopes stuck inside it. She stands up and hands it to you. "If we end up at the mercy of the cops, none of this'll look good. It's still way over the decriminalized amounts even if we weren't underage, but at least we're no longer in possession of narcotics."

"Right." On an impulse, you hug her.

She hugs you back.

You kind of want to hug Matt too, because he looks like he needs it. He's standing there looking at the two of you with this lost expression. Not lost—haunted. After an awkward moment of hesitation, you do hug him. You think he's surprised, because his whole body tenses up, but then he relaxes, and his arms tighten around you.

"We'll figure it out," he says to you like he's the one comforting you, and maybe he is? You're suddenly not sure who needed the hug more. Matt just kind of seems to get it right now.

Hannah looks back and forth between you, a little perplexed, a wobbly smile trying to find purchase on her lips.

And then you leave, hoping you don't destroy these two people who are trying to help you.

Chapter Eight

You barely notice Friday at school. You go to class, scribble until you run out of lead, then borrow a pen from Hannah to get through the rest of the day. You *really* need to go school shopping.

You pass Levi on the way to your car, and he gives you another one of those weird, knowing smiles you hate so much. He's either plotting your demise or just thinks he's funny, and you're not sure which. To make it worse, there's a lone first-year just trying to get to his own ride, and Levi shoves him so hard he yelps and crashes into the beat-up maroon sedan parked next to Levi's Beemer. Blond heads within the car all crane to look at the source of the noise, followed by a burst of raucous laughter. Levi's eyes never leave yours as if to say he's demonstrating what could be you.

Unease scrabbling up the ladder of your spine, you get out of there. The unfortunate kid manages to right himself and scuttles off in the opposite direction. In your rearview mirror, you see Levi leaning against his car with an inscrutable expression as you pull out of the parking lot.

As planned, you crash Friday night at Hannah's so you're ready to go in the morning. When 6:15 rolls around, you're on Interstate 70, Matt at the wheel and Hannah in the back with her legs up on the seat, having what appears to be a religious experience with her sausage, egg, and cheese biscuit. You sip from your giant minty iced coffee that is basically chocolate milk for big kids and worry that drinking this much this early in the drive will be a problem for your bladder before you get to Baltimore. (You're right—are you psychic or something?)

Concentrating on tiny details is the only thing keeping you from having a full-on anxiety meltdown.

The hills around Bright Springs are starting to paint themselves with oranges and red-golds as the sun climbs into the sky. The car smells like sausage biscuit and Matt's cologne, which is surprisingly not awful. Matt turns on some music—Sigur Rós—which fits the mood you're in. Quiet and wistful and a little haunted.

Anything louder would be overstimulating in the extreme. But the colors of the leaves, the soft music, everyone's unspoken agreement to not have a 6 a.m. conversation—it all helps you ignore the purpose of the day.

You've never been to Baltimore. The city's skyline appears as you merge onto Interstate 95 after two hours of driving, and you feel a momentary shock at how big it is. Matt navigates through the city—though not avoiding any potholes, since that's impossible in Baltimore, he says—and points out some stuff as you go.

"Inner Harbor's up around this corner," he says. He nods toward your side of the car.

You roll down your window a little, and a thrill goes through you at the smell of the sea.

"How do you know so much about Baltimore?" You can't tear your eyes away from the small flashes of sunlight on water.

"Mom takes us here sometimes. When we go on vacation, we usually spend a night in the city and fly out of BWI the next day."

Just like that, your little illusions crumble and you're Will the Monster again. You feel a familiar hunger gnawing at your stomach. Vacations. The idea of a night in a hotel overlooking the harbor before a trip to Disney World or SeaWorld or any of the other worlds Dana has taken Hannah and Matt over the years. They're . . . you fumble for some sort of description. They're Bert and Ernie in their nice home and nice life and you're . . . Oscar the Grouch in your garbage can. It cuts keenly through some of your wonder, but a small part of you clings to the way the sun dances on the waves. You can't hear the water over the buzz of traffic and occasional honks, but you wish you could.

You can almost hear Hannah's eyes on you. She leans forward between the seats and pokes you in the shoulder.

"On the way home we can stop and walk around," she says. "Have dinner at Five Guys or something. Right, Matt?"

Matt glances over at you, casually, but you feel him sort of . . . resonate with whatever he sees. "That sounds like a good plan."

Your eyes are burning with something hot and painful and you hate yourself because underneath the gratitude and the warmth you feel for Hannah and Matt, there's a searing fury that you cannot tamp down. Anger that they've had this life and you've just been . . . adjacent to anything good for all of yours. You feel what you feel and loathe yourself for it.

Matt turns the car north, out of downtown and up a hill, and while Hannah's phone sings, you stare out the window and try to mold yourself into a person.

Fuck. You are all over the map today, and you know why. You're driving to find Raz. Of course your emotions are a hurricane.

The unidentifiable gnawing vanishes when you reach Raz's neighborhood because holy shit, it's a queer hipster paradise. Matt turns the car down 36th Avenue, and you almost keel over. If downtown was a surprise, this is like tumbling all the way down the rabbit hole into Wonderland. There are craft cocktail bars and a brightly lit sex shop with queer-friendly, sex-positive slogans on the outside. You outright gape. You're gray asexual (or demisexual, depending on your brain) and demiromantic, but when you think of sex shops, you think of the one in Bright Springs—which is the building version of a dingy FЯEE CANDY van.

"Holy shit," says Hannah. She looks almost as shell-shocked as you feel, staring at the sex shop with pinpricks of pink on her cheeks.

"Johns Hopkins is right over there," Matt says absently, gesturing behind you. You think he's blushing a little. Bless.

The road makes a T, and Matt turns right. You pass a bookstore called Atomic Books that has social justice stickers all over its front window and books front and center by Ta-Nehisi Coates and N. K. Jemisin and you want to *cry*. Giddiness bubbles up in you at the sight. Never once did you expect to want to hug a bookshop.

For the first time, you feel the tornado in your heart ease into something else. A light breeze. A zephyr. Something that could bear you skyward on an updraft rather than tearing you to shreds.

Looking around, whatever comes after high school starts to take shape. Something that's more than just surviving without anyone finding out Frances is dead.

Somewhere like here you could . . . *be*. Exist. You could live in this loud, bustling place, or one like it. You could stop being the Only Something in a room.

You could have this, Will.

Matt turns left a moment later and suddenly pulls into an open space before you realize why.

"We're here," he says.

You freeze.

You were so distracted by the glorious neighborhood that you forgot that it was *Raz*'s neighborhood and now you are on Ash Street, which is *Raz*'s street, and you follow the line of Matt's finger as he points to a house, that is *Raz*'s house.

It's a pale yellow-sided detached house, unlike most of Baltimore's famous brownstones and row houses Matt pointed out as you drove. It's got a yard and an actual goddamn picket fence, though it's natural wood and not painted white. There's a car in the driveway that makes you start, because you recognize it. She drove you to Hershey Park in that car, a forest-green Subaru.

Your breath is shallow and feels high in your chest.

"You ready?" Matt asks.

"Give 'em a minute, Matt," Hannah insists. Then, to you, "Take your time. There's no hurry."

It's that more than anything that makes your hand (your fingers are ice cold) tug the door latch and open the car door.

Will Raz even recognize you? How would she know what you look like? When you lived with her, you were short and lumpy and bunched up like an inchworm mid-inch. You got taller and you're sort of muscular now because ever since the "Frances chair" incident, you've started every day with planking and push-ups and other things you could do in your room to stay fit, mostly so you could fend off Frances next time if she got violent—

Stop, Will. Chill. Breathe. This isn't easy, and it doesn't have to be.

You hear Hannah and Matt follow as you walk to the fence and push open the gate. It's not a long walk up to the door, but it feels longer than the three-hour drive you just took to get here.

You raise your hand to the door knocker before you can stop yourself.

The sound it makes is startlingly loud in the morning air, and Hannah jumps beside you, even though she had to see you were about to use it.

You wait for any sound of stirring behind the door, those rustly movements and thumps that say someone's coming. Nothing.

"It's Saturday," Matt says. "Maybe she's sleeping in."

"Knock again," says Hannah. "Or ring the doorbell."

You ring the doorbell. It makes a big *ding-dong*, just like the onomatopoeia.

Again, nothing.

Then a yowl cuts through the air, and this time Hannah's not the only one who jumps. Around the right corner of the house trots a fluffy black-and-white cat, who sits down in the dewy grass and yowls again. The cat has a mostly white face with an absolutely *extraordinary* black mustache and goatee that are at once dignified and absurd, if that's even possible.

"Aw, kitty," says Hannah. She starts to walk toward the cat, one hand outstretched. The cat meets her halfway, sniffing at her offered finger for a moment before rubbing a cheek against Hannah's hand. "Look at you!"

In response, the cat slinks past her and heads toward you—no, to the door. Jumping up to paw at the wood, the cat meows again. Maybe that yowl is just this cat's voice.

You offer your hand like Hannah did, though you don't know cats very well. This one has a collar. When the cat lets you stroke its head, you gently work the collar around so you can see the tags. The first is just a rabies tag, followed by one that says "Home Again" and has a microchip number on it. Finally, the name tag.

"Lieutenant Sebastian," you read. You stare at the cat, wanting to laugh except you feel like you have a balloon in your chest that's about to burst because no one answered the door, but here is this *cat,* and if anything on the planet should be called Lieutenant Sebastian, it is this cat with the extraordinary mustache.

There's a phone number on the tag and you get out Frances's—your—phone to type it in.

"The cat's name is Lieutenant Sebastian?" Matt says.

"Oh my god, he's perfect," Hannah says.

"She, actually," says a voice from the driveway.

You're so startled that you drop your phone. Thankfully it's A: in a case and B: only about a foot to the doormat because you're squatting to examine the cat's collar. Your first thought is *Raz,* even though the voice isn't anything like Raz's.

You look up to see . . . well. Not Raz. At all.

You can't help staring.

It's a person about your age. Curly black hair that's shaved on the sides with a recently washed, damp mass of curls on top, white skin that probably burns in two seconds flat, *blue*-blue eyes. Pierced lip. You register other details a half-second later. Flat chest, lean build, really tall—wait. This person is wearing heels. Black ankle boots with three-inch heels, to be exact. Black skinny jeans, tight black T-shirt, blue glitter eyeliner.

You suddenly feel underdressed for a . . . Saturday morning . . . in your jeans and binder and white T-shirt and black pleather jacket.

"I mean, if you have to give a gender to a cat," the person's saying. "Are you looking for Raz?"

The name jolts you out of your staring. "Raz? You know Raz? Do you live here?" Questions tumble out of your mouth. Your face feels hot, and it's not the too-warm morning sun or the air that promises mugginess even in early September.

"Yeah, I know Raz, and no, I don't live here. I live there. I'm Julian." The person points to the duplex next door, a big brick building that may have been one large house once upon a time before being divided into apartments. Peering a little closer at you, Julian goes on in careful, measured words. "I'm gender fluid. My pronouns are they/them." Then they wait as if to see how you'll respond.

You can't feel your tongue. It's dried out like a slug on the sidewalk in July. Somehow, you string words together.

"I'm agender," you manage, realizing maybe you should have said your name first. "And uh, Will."

Not much better.

You start to introduce Hannah and Matt, but Julian cuts you off. "Wait. Will? *You're* Will?"

Out of the corner of your eye, you see Matt and Hannah exchange a glance.

"Yeah," you say. "How do you know my name?"

Julian puts one hand on the fence. Silver nail polish glints in the sun. "Raz's told me all about you," they say. They look troubled. "Did she know you were coming?"

You shake your head, and something about Julian seems to . . . tighten.

"Shit." Julian looks at you—no, at Lieutenant Sebastian—then frowns.

"What's going on?" Matt says, breaking his silence. "Why'd you come out here, anyway?"

Julian's tongue fiddles with their lip ring, like a nervous tic. "I heard Lieutenant Sebastian scratching at my door while I was getting dressed, but I thought it was the other neighbor's cat until I heard the meowing. Nobody sounds like Lieutenant Sebastian. But she's an indoor cat. I thought she'd just gotten loose or something, and I was going to get her back inside."

"That's not all," you say. You don't like the dread that suddenly pools in your middle.

"I haven't seen Raz in two days," Julian says. "Which isn't that weird, I guess, and she said she was going on a multi-day hike or something last week, but her car hasn't left the driveway, and if the lieutenant was out, well. I saw a light on over here last night and assumed it was her since the car was still there. I thought I must have misheard when she was leaving, but . . ."

No. No no no no no. You feel the cat butt her head up against your hand, which is shaking. "She didn't answer the door."

See? Nothing gets better for you. The thought sticks in your mind, and you can't dislodge it. You dared to hope, but now Raz isn't here. She's not here.

"Will?" Hannah speaks for the first time. "Maybe we should call the police."

"No!" You say it loudly, but it sounds way too loud until you realize Julian said it too. You look up at them, and their blue eyes meet yours.

"Sometimes I feed the lieutenant for Raz when she's at work late," Julian says. "I know the code for the garage door."

They beckon you to follow, and you do, picking up Lieutenant Sebastian (who weirdly doesn't protest) and waiting for Matt to open the side gate on the fence.

Julian goes to a key pad on the side of the garage door and stands obscuring the numbers so you don't see the code. You don't blame them for that. The door gives a mechanical jolt and starts to open, whirring and shuddering like it's up too early. When you're all in, Julian hits the button to close it again and flicks a light switch on the wall.

There's a bunch of shelves with camping gear on them. Raz took you camping once.

"Hey," Hannah says softly, putting one hand on your back. "You okay?"

You shake your head tightly. Not a negative—you just don't know yet. Lieutenant Sebastian is warm and solid in your arms, where you've got her positioned with her front paws on your left shoulder so she can be upright. She starts sniffing around and squirming when you reach the short set of three stairs to the house.

Julian opens the door into the house, and you set the lieutenant down before she can claw a hole in your shoulder. She bolts into the house with a trailing *prrrrrrrrrow.*

"Raz?" Julian calls her name softly. The door has opened into the kitchen, which smells so familiar and so like Raz your eyes well up. Cinnamon. She used to boil it in a pan every few days. From the pan on the stove, looks like she still does.

Julian walks through the kitchen to the right and into a living room where their breath hisses in. "Shit. Shit."

For a moment you don't see why—then you see the sliding glass door that leads to the small back yard. It's open. About six inches, but still. Definitely wide enough for the cat to slip out.

"She wouldn't leave a door open like that," you say. Maybe you shouldn't be that certain, because it's not like you've lived with her for the past half-decade, but you *know.* If Lieutenant Sebastian is an inside cat—and you remember Raz saying something after seeing someone's cat dead in a street that people should keep their kitties inside, especially in cities—then . . .

Julian almost leaps to the door and closes it, locking it.

“I don’t understand,” they mutter, nudging at a long stick on the floor with one booted toe. “Raz is religious about keeping this secure. Raz!”

This time they yell it. There are stairs right in front of the front door—and you head for them.

“Raz!” You call out her name as you climb, and you hear the others following you.

You don’t know what you’re going to find upstairs, and fear grips you harder with each step, trying to claw you backward. What if you find her dead like Frances? What if someone murdered her? What if—

There’s no one in the first room, which looks like a guest room, except (you can’t think about this now, you can’t think about this now), *except* that it’s got a *Stranger Things* poster on the wall and *ohgodohgod*, a drawing. You remember that drawing. You drew it for her at school one day and that’s—that’s the house in Hagerstown where you lived with her and the two of you standing out in front of it and oh god, that’s even the same *comforter* you had on your bed there, and the stuffed elephant you couldn’t find when Frances stole you back and—

“There’s no one here,” you hear Matt say behind you, like he’s speaking across a chasm of a thousand years.

You don’t know how long you’ve been standing in this room—in *your* room, you know it’s yours, that it’s meant to be yours—but clearly Matt and Julian have finished searching the rest of the upstairs.

“I drew that,” you say stupidly, pointing at the picture on the wall next to the poster of Eleven’s face. You turn and see them all in the doorway, watching you.

Hannah’s hanging back now as if she doesn’t know what to do. Her eyes are wide and frightened, and she leans back against Matt’s shoulder almost unconsciously. Her chin jerks with little spurts of movement to the left, a physical tic of her Tourette’s syndrome, and you know she’s trying hard to fight it because she doesn’t want you to focus on how she feels right now, and she’s such a good fucking *friend* and you don’t know what to do.

Julian comes forward, graceful in all black, looking like something out of another world, a world you want to live in but you're stuck in this one. Your eyes are burning again, this time not with self-hatred.

"Hey," Julian says. To your surprise, they take your hands and hold them tight. It seems to tether you to where you stand, anchoring you so you don't just dissolve and float away. "I know you don't know me, but I feel like I know you. Raz talks about you all the damn time, and I know she was hoping she'd get to introduce us someday. There are some things . . ." Julian tenses again suddenly and trails off. Then they go on, seeming to choose their words carefully. "If Raz isn't here, that's probably a good sign."

"What?"

Julian glances at Hannah and Matt as if trying to decide whether the pair of siblings are trustable or not. "Raz was afraid that your mom would . . . do something if she found out Raz tried to get around her to contact you." They pause, then go on all in a rush. "I only know because I saw a big envelope addressed to Bright Springs High School when I was saying hi to her one morning as she left. Raz was so nervous that she just blurted out that she was trying to contact you without—without your mom knowing. She's usually careful about what she shares, but she looked exhausted and must've felt guilty. I told her she wasn't doing anything wrong."

Your mind whirls through all of that information. They know about the letter. The one Raz sent to the school. Which means they *don't* know. About Frances.

"Afraid Frances would do something?" Hannah says at the same time Matt says, "Afraid Frances would do *what*?"

Julian looks back and forth between you and the pair of them for a moment, hesitating. "She came here once. I didn't actually see her, but I heard her yelling at Raz even over the shower. By the time I got dressed and made it outside, Frances was already gone—other neighbors had chased her off—and Raz was crying into a pulped begonia Frances had destroyed. She told me who it was but wouldn't say much more. I don't think she wanted Frances to know I existed."

Julian's voice says what I feel—Raz would try to protect them. Because she couldn't protect me. Julian knows who Frances was when she was alive. But they don't know something else.

Before Julian can go on, you say quietly, "Frances is dead."

Chapter Nine

The words hang in the air after you say them.

"Your mom is dead?" Julian says after a long beat with no one speaking.

"Yeah," you say. "*Frances* is dead. About a week ago. Heart attack."

Slowly, Julian looks at you, squeezes your hands once more, then says, "I don't know all of your story, but what I have even briefly encountered with your mo—with Frances—I guess I don't know whether to say I'm sorry or just to tell you that you're going to be okay. Or both."

You haven't said this in front of Hannah or Matt, but something drags it out of your mouth anyway. "I'm not sorry."

The vehemence of your words almost makes you stumble. You immediately scrunch your eyes shut as if that'll keep Hannah and Matt and Julian from seeing what a monster you are (no matter how much Hannah thought Frances was an asshole, being glad she's dead is something else altogether), but when you open them again, Julian's blue eyes are still looking into your own.

You break the eye contact, but you don't let go of their hands.

Julian just nods, sucking their lips against their teeth, and says, "You're going to be okay. Better, probably."

You don't know why, but you really needed to hear that.

Inexplicably, you get that—that *watched* feeling again, ember eyes searing into you out of nowhere. Julian's hands are warm and solid in your freezing cold ones, and after a moment, the sensation fades, but your nostrils burn like you've just inhaled the first puff of smoke from one of Frances's cigarettes.

Matt looks uncomfortable in the doorway—maybe because he's experiencing being the Only Something in the room as the only straight cis person? Or so you think at first, until he says, "I don't want to be Chicken Little or anything, but should we maybe be considering that if Raz would never leave her door open and no one is here and Lieutenant Sebastian was out, *and* that Raz was afraid of someone, maybe someone else was here? And they might come back?"

Hannah turns sharply to look at her brother for a split second before you notice her gaze flicks to your intertwined fingers with a glint of something unreadable in her eyes. She looks back to Matt as if forcing herself. Julian's fingers fall away from yours as if they've just realized how long they've been holding a near-stranger's hands.

"That's probably a good point," Hannah says. "Though they didn't take anything, if anyone was here."

"That we noticed," Julian murmurs, and you look back at them. "Let's go to my place. I'll feed the lieutenant on the way out and make sure her box is clean."

You nod, and Julian leaves. Matt goes with them, but Hannah hangs back with you.

"Are you okay?"

"I don't know," you say. You don't. A week ago, Raz was just a bittersweet memory. Now you're standing in her house, in a room she clearly left for you. And let's not forget that she appears to be missing. She'd said she was going out of town on a hike, but you don't leave your door hanging open and your car in the drive.

“I really think we should call the police,” Hannah says. That glint is still in her eyes, and you wish you could tell what it *is*. Usually, you have some sort of read on Hannah, but right now everything feels off, wrong.

“What are they going to do? They’ll probably just say there’s some forty-eight-hour rule like they do on TV shows, and even if they do file a report, then what?” At best, they’ll push some paper around and give you a cup of coffee while they tell you to stop worrying because Raz is an adult and she probably just got spacey despite not even knowing her. You suddenly put your finger on one feeling, at least. A shitty one. Helplessness.

Hannah looks uncertain. You want her to understand this. The police are not your friend. The one time you called them, when one of your foster parents punched a foster sibling so hard he passed out, they only made it worse. For you, for your foster brother. What if Raz broke some sort of law by writing to you all these years without Frances’s consent? Harassment or something? You can’t risk them going after her.

There’s a gulf between you and Hannah right now, even though she’s only a couple of feet away. It widens every time she pushes about the police, and this time it seems to have widened more. Because Julian understands this? You don’t know.

Normally, you’d rush to reassure Hannah. Today, though, the thought is too exhausting. So you don’t, whether it upsets The Dynamic or not.

“Let’s just go downstairs,” you say finally. “Maybe Julian will know something that’ll help.”

Once Lieutenant Sebastian is fed and has a clean litter box, Julian leads you next door to their place. Their home is clean and tidy inside. It smells like coffee and berries.

“You live here alone?” Matt asks. “What do you do for a living?”

“I’m an emancipated minor, or as close as you get in this state,” Julian says. “Have been since I was sixteen. Eighteenth birthday’s in a few months, fucking finally. I bus tables downtown Thursday through Saturday night and do online school during the day."

The look on Julian's face is none short of irony when they meet Matt's startled gaze, but instantly you relax a little. At least one person here will understand you, you think. You think.

"You can afford this place on that? Damn." Matt looks around.

"Yeah, it's a nice restaurant. I make a couple hundred bucks a night." Julian shrugs like it ain't a big deal, and maybe to them it's not. You get that, too.

Matt whistles though, scrubbing his hair with a palm. "More than I make. Damn."

"What do you do?" Julian asks.

"I'm an EMT." Matt's wry smile makes Hannah bristle, as if his answer annoys her, which you don't understand. "We're in the sticks, though. The hospital in Bright Springs can barely be called one. Rent's probably cheaper, too. And I still live with my mom."

You listen to them chatter while Julian pours coffee. You can feel Hannah's silence throbbing like a fresh bruise. The look on her face is a mixture of, well, the way you've seen her look when she's picked last for a team in PE. Like she's on the outside of a circle and everyone else is within.

That's how you've felt your whole life.

You ask Julian where the bathroom is and head there. You don't really have to pee. You just wanted to be alone for a minute.

The duplex is small, everything close together the way some people would call cramped and real estate agents would call cozy. There's an open bedroom next to the bathroom, and you can't resist glancing through the door. The sheets on the bed are rumpled black jersey, but there are silver-metallic-threaded pillows in the shape of stars on it, and framed pictures of nebulae hang on the walls. Other than that, there's no furniture you can see, but there's a closed laptop with stickers all over it on the nightstand.

The bathroom is small and tidy and smells more strongly of the berries. There's some mixed-berry body spray—the cheap kind, but it smells really good—sitting on the sink.

Without really thinking about it, you pull your phone out of your pocket and unlock it. The screen is still on the dial pad where you'd punched in the number on Lieutenant Sebastian's collar.

Before you can stop yourself, you hit the green button.

There's silence for a moment. You wait for a ring.

Nothing.

After a second or two though, there's a beep. "Hi, you've reached Esmeralda. I'm sorry I missed you, but if you leave me your number, I promise to get back to you. If I want to. Toodles!"

The sound of her voice is yet another shock. You pause too long after the beep and almost drop your phone in the toilet.

Then you say quietly, "Raz. It's Will. I came to your house, but you're not there. I'm with Julian. Please . . . please let us know you're safe."

You hang up.

For a moment you stand there with your toes hanging over a cliff you didn't realize was under your feet. Frances is gone. She was apparently dealing. Now Raz is missing, the one person you trust to help. You sit down on the closed toilet then, listening to the sound of your pounding heart until it slows enough for you to go back out to face the others.

Julian is midsentence when you get back. ". . . all I know is Raz would want to know that Frances is dead so she could take care of Will." They look up. Meet your eyes.

Julian sees the cliff you're standing on. You don't know how, but they do. When you lock eyes with them it's like the very strength in their gaze steadies you and makes your footing more stable. Something about Julian (okay, this is no mystery—they're nonbinary like you and you never meet anybody like you) makes you feel seen for the first time since, well, Raz. It makes the gulf between you and Hannah feel bigger. It makes Matt seem far away.

Maybe it's the need to break this fragile feeling in the room. Maybe it's Julian's face; you don't know why you say it, why you ask this question when you know it's going to hurt.

"Raz really talks about me that much?" It comes out of your mouth in a voice that almost doesn't even sound like yours. It's surprisingly resonant, deeper than you expect to hear in that moment.

You wish you'd been able to go on puberty blockers. They're like a grand a month, and you never had health insurance until the library, and even then without a sympathetic government, a lot of insurances won't cover them. Not to mention Frances would never have allowed it.

But now you're just distracting yourself from what you asked.

Julian watches you, cradling their coffee mug (it's dark blue with stars scattered across it) in both hands.

"All the time," they say.

Your eyes start to burn, but for once you ignore it. "She said in a letter she wanted to adopt me."

"That never changed," Julian tells you. They give a wry, self-loathing smile that you know too well. You understand it way too well, that smile. You've worn it. "I used to be really jealous of you, actually. Raz is just—"

"She's perfect," you say.

"She's perfect," Julian agrees. Their smile turns warm. "I just happened to move in here, you know? I have a cousin who owns this building and was willing to let me move in with no credit and all that, as long as I didn't fuck anything up. For a while it was really weird, just living alone. Having my own space and not having to worry about—not having to worry."

There it is again, that sense of kinship. Julian understands more than just being nonbinary. Your eyes are still burning.

"Anyway," they say. "Raz was always just really sad when I first met her. It was a couple of years ago. But she realized I was living alone and just was alone a lot, and she started inviting me over for dinners and trying to give me some kind of . . . normalcy? I don't know. And then she started talking about you."

It's almost like you can feel fingers on your insides, pulling you in different directions.

Raz was always thinking of you. But she's gone—off somewhere and maybe not safe but demonstrably Not Here—and all this time, these years, you were resigned to your life with Frances.

"I guess you wouldn't know," Julian says suddenly. "How hard she fought for you."

"What?" The burning in your eyes turns to prickling, and you blink several times.

"I don't know all of it, but she told me once that she was meeting with CPS at least every few months. She'd drive up to Hagerstown to meet with the Washington County people and try and get information about how you were doing. That didn't change, just became less frequent, and she'd always come back furious. *That* didn't change either."

You think of the letters, postmarked in Hagerstown. She sent the letters every few months. A tear crawls over the edge of your right eyelid, and you bat it away.

Hannah reaches out and takes your hand.

"Thank you," you say.

You're not sure if you're talking to Hannah or Julian, and when they both say "of course" at the same time and then stare at each other, you mostly just feel embarrassed.

Your stomach chooses that moment to growl loudly.

"Sorry," you say.

"Did you just apologize for being hungry?" Julian grins. "Totally something I would do, so I'll say to you what Raz always says to me when I apologize for my own stomach or, you know, looking at someone by accident: apologies are only for when you've caused someone harm. Not for existing."

It's your turn to be jealous of Julian, for having Raz sayings and for having had two years with her, to get to know her. You think you are going to love Julian. You think you can't do anything but love someone who just . . . understands.

Hannah's hand tightens on yours, almost too tight. "Five Guys?"

You nod. Then you look at Julian just as a wistful look passes over their face.

You understand that look, that certainty-of-being-left-out look, that knowing that when someone says, "are we going?" it's a "we" that excludes you. You heard once that there's an actual verb form in some languages for *us but not you*, and you remember Hannah being appalled by it when she heard of it in class, but she just used it in English. Her hand feels possessive, like a claim to your skin.

It's such a Frances feeling that you have to actively shake it off. This isn't Frances. It's Hannah, your best friend.

And you know she's going to feel a pang when you do the thing you wish more people had done for you in your life and say to Julian, "Wanna come?"

You also understand that when Julian just gives a quick shake of the head with what's meant to be a playful smile, they don't mean it. They want to go, but they already understand they wouldn't be entirely welcome. It hurts you somewhere you didn't think Hannah *could* hurt you. She's now got Ashton, but she's holding your hand like Julian is invading. It's the very thing you've been trying to stave off in yourself, for her.

That gulf gets a little wider.

You're not used to easily understanding someone, and the thought of walking away from it leaves you feeling bereft. People are *not easy* for you, but Julian has felt effortless from Moment One.

So you do something uncharacteristic.

"Can I—" You pause, feeling stupid. You're still blinking too much, but you don't want to leave without a way to contact Julian, so you just sort of hold out Frances's phone—your phone now—and thankfully, Julian takes it and keys in their number.

"Sent myself a text," they say. "I'll ask the neighbors if they heard from Raz and leave a note on the door for her, and let you know the moment I hear anything. And Will?"

You are halfway up from your chair, and Hannah has just dropped your hand, and Matt's still watching everything and saying nothing. You stop.

"Yeah?"

"Text me any time. Day or night. If I don't answer right away, I might be at work—boss is a Grade-A barf nugget about phones at work—but I'll hit you back as soon as humanly possible."

"Thank you," you say. "And likewise."

"It's good to meet you."

Usually you can't quite tell if people mean what they say, but you are pretty sure Julian means this. They seem . . . lonely.

You understand that too. "You too, Julian. Really."

With that, you head out the door.

You try to enjoy exploring Baltimore for the rest of the early afternoon, belly full of burger and fries. Matt and Hannah keep the subject light as you wander about that red brick harbor and smell the ocean and listen to its waves, but all you can think of is Raz.

All you can think of is Julian's words. *I guess you wouldn't know. How hard she fought for you.*

And you, monster that you are, are just that much gladder that Frances is dead.

Chapter Ten

It was only a matter of time before somebody missed Frances.

Back in Bright Springs, you've set yourself about cleaning the house more. From the moment you walked in, all you could smell was that sickly smoke clinging to everything as if you hadn't spent the past few weeks scouring the place to exorcise it. You feel like it seized the opportunity to creep back in through every crack and cranny while you were away, seeping back into the carpets, the air, the couch cushions.

By the time you're done, your eyes burn with the smell of lemon and bleach, and it feels like Frances's clammy hand has you by the scruff of the neck in retribution.

Just a headache, you tell yourself. Just a goddamn headache.

It's almost nine thirty at night, and you run three huge garbage bags of Frances's junk down to the big can for collection tomorrow. Gone is the hideous collection of small harlequin clowns she kept in a small hutch in the corner of the living room. Gone is all her underwear and socks and bras (though you did find several of your own stained T-shirts in her clothes). Gone are the stacks of tabloids. You vow never to let another one of your dollars subsidize that trash.

So when her phone goes off, you actually have the tiniest jump of excitement and hope that it's Julian.

It's not. It's a number Frances didn't bother to save, and it's a text.

Where tf r u

Your heart gives a jump. This could be one of her . . . drug people.

The phone buzzes again. What if they saw that you read it? Hannah once said how much she hates people knowing if she's read a text or not. You do a quick search online to see how to check and hurriedly go to the settings to see if read receipts are on (they're not, thank Dog).

Band's gr8 tonite. U said u'd be here n bring the snaccs x x x

The next message is a selfie of some dude in an actual cowboy hat outside a club you think is in Hagerstown. Ugh. UGH.

Nope nope nope nope nope.

What the hell does he even mean, "snaccs"? Do you even *want* to know?

You block the number and flop down on the sofa on the opposite end from where she used to sit, swallowing over and over.

Sometimes Frances would bring people home, and you'd hide in your room as much as you could until they were gone. On the times you got lucky, you never had to see them.

You haven't looked much at Frances's phone, other than that one glance at the camera roll that made you want to throw it across the room. You don't know if you should look more. You don't want to. The idea makes your gut feel like that red tide in Miami washing all its dead fish up on the shores of your stomach lining.

Having a stare-down with your dead mother's cell phone is not the way you want to be spending your Saturday night.

To distract yourself, you grab her laptop (it's a MacBook Air, and she bought it a couple of years before you got the library job—you never asked how she paid for it). The laptop isn't much better than the phone, but at least you know her Amazon account is linked to the joint bank account.

You plan to deposit the money you found in the PO box on Monday, so you know you'll have enough to get whatever you need for school.

It's weird as hell, to be able to open up Amazon and just . . . shop?

Splurging on a new backpack seems like a good idea—this is your first encounter with the concept of *retail therapy*. The one you pick is all swirls of midnight blue and cerulean galaxy pattern. It's JanSport. You've seen other kids with those your entire life.

You get yourself notebooks, pens (you've made do with leftover pens from Hannah's mom's law office for years), and the nice kind of mechanical pencils with extra lead. And just before you're done, feeling a teensy bit guilty, you throw in a watercolor sketchbook, brushes, and a set of paints. You used to paint with watercolors in art class at school where Frances couldn't stop you. Anything at home was as good as shredded if she thought you liked it.

Your heart is racing when you finish.

Everything should show up Monday, and you're so excited. It's your senior year, and you bought all your school supplies with your own money, and you live *alone*, and Frances is *gone*, and it's only when the confirmation page for your last purchase pops up that you realize you, a kid, are feeling reckless and wild and exhilarated over completing a task that someone should have been doing for you your entire life.

You are feeling reckless and exhilarated over something that, to Hannah and Matt, would be merely routine—boring.

The thought sours your good mood a little, and that's understandable, Will. It's one thing to live a terrible normalcy; it's something else altogether to take baby steps away from that terrible normalcy.

Frances shouldn't have ever been *anyone*'s normal.

Your life is pretty fucked up, and you know it just a tiny bit more today than you did yesterday.

You look at Frances's phone—*your* phone now—and realize also that for the first time when you're feeling upset, you could text someone. You could text Hannah.

There's already a text. Your heart gives an ominous thud when you see the number—it's the same one you just blocked.

Fine your loss bitch

Maybe you did it wrong. You Google how to block a number on this phone and go through it again. It's exactly what you did before, and you finally drop it next to you like it's a coiled cobra.

The cobra doesn't strike. It won't; it's just a phone.

But when you reach for it again, it's not Hannah that you put in the To box of the text message, because a rough-edged, painful part of your heart knows that this isn't something she'd understand.

So you text Julian instead, even though it's just after midnight.

Hey, it's Will, sorry to text so late

There's a moment where you regret hitting Send, but no more than thirty seconds later, you get a response.

Will! I just got off work and am about to drive home. Gimme twenty minutes and I'm all yours. Feel free to start talking and I'll answer as soon as I get home!

Just that response, a very adult response from another seventeen-year-old, eases the tightness in your rib cage just a bit.

You start typing, your thumbs still not used to the motion and the predictive text making you even slower because you have to keep deleting stuff.

I'm just sitting here ordering all my school shit for this year and I just . . . it feels like this huge deal and this exciting thing and then I realized that it's really not??? It's just this normal thing for most people, and I got excited over a backpack (you'd like it, I think—I'll send you a picture) and I guess like . . . do you ever feel jealous over . . .

You hit Send because you don't know what you are trying to say. The words don't feel right. You try again.

Okay, so Hannah and Matt, they are all excited about being an adult and I mean, Matt still lives at home and everything but he's saving up money for a house down payment *and that's like . . . some real adult shit.*

And Hannah wants to move out and go to college, like . . . really wants to. And that's the same thing I'm already doing. School, work, home. Maybe someday just work and home but like . . . fuck, I don't know what I'm saying. Sorry.

To distract yourself from waiting for Julian to reply to your word vomit, you go to the kitchen and throw some Tater Tots in the oven. You set the timer on the phone, which feels wrong, so you cancel it and set the old jangle timer. *Last time*, you think.

No reply yet.

You go into your room. It's never really felt like yours. Anything that got put on the walls was at risk of getting torn down by an angry Frances, and anything you didn't take especially careful pains to hide was at risk of disappearing (even things you did hide, which you always found out the hard way until you got better at hiding shit). Unlike the disaster that was always Frances's room, it's tidy in here. Of course, that was because Frances made you keep it this way.

In an act of rebellion, you strip, leaving your clothes on the floor.

You dig through your drawers until you find a pair of boxers and a T-shirt and put them on.

When you get back to the living room, you turn on the television (another purchase that happened with your money—a 4K HDTV that Frances made you drive to Hagerstown to get on Black Friday last year, which you jumped at because it meant you got to leave the house at midnight, stop at McDonald's on the way, and spend a blissfully anonymous night in a long line of people ready to trip all over each other to get electronics). You put on a nature show. You always liked learning about animals when you lived with Raz. Frances said nature shows were boring.

As if thinking of her triggered an olfactory memory, one of those strange waves of stale tobacco and warm beer rises into the air. You go to the window and throw it open, taking a deep breath of night air. For a moment, you think you see a glowing pair of cigarette cherries at eye level in the brush off the edge of the driveway, but when you blink, it's gone.

Getting the phone from the kitchen counter, you see Julian's replied.

No, that's legit. DON'T APOLOGIZE. It's like . . . jealousy that other people got to be kids when you didn't, maybe? Like being an adult is a thing that is supposed to be exciting and not something that just gets handed to you when you still Need An Adult, you know? Is that what you mean?

Your heart gives a little *fwub* at the message because it is exactly what you mean. Exactly.

Yeah, you type back. *It gets to be this exciting thing for them because they got to be kids and have people help them with things and love them unconditionally and idk.*

You're proud of yourself for using a texting acronym.

I feel like I'm getting to be more of a kid with my mother dead than with her alive. I was always the grown-up, and she was just the . . . dangerous toddler.

You've never really been this honest about what it was like living with Frances. Not to Hannah, not to anyone.

There's a pause, and you wait, breathing in the smell of cooking Tater Tots and barely catching a hint of that old stale smoke smell. Even more than the open window, this conversation is somehow banishing Frances's toxicity.

I'm really glad you texted, Will

The message comes from Julian a moment later, and your heart gives a little *fwub* again, this time not because your brains are in sync but because, well. You're not really sure why. You swallow. You don't know it at that moment, but that thing you're feeling? That slight tingle, the low-down belly slip, the way it's suddenly just a tiny bit harder to breathe? It might be the beginnings of a crush.

Maybe not. Maybe whatever you're feeling for Julian in this moment is tied up in aesthetic attraction and because they're a conduit to Raz.

But maybe it's something else. Maybe it's someone you connect with being glad to connect.

That's a heady thing. One you're not too familiar with.

You might not recognize all of these things in this moment, Will, but you know *something* important is happening.

The timer starts to jangle. Your Tater Tots are done.

You text back, *Me too, Julian.*

You text Julian through most of Sunday, light back-and-forth that makes you feel floaty, as if just the conversation will make your feet detach from the ground. Julian seems as hungry for your conversation as you are for theirs—you remember your snap assessment that they seemed lonely. You tell them, in veiled terms, about Frances dealing. They agree Raz will know what to do, and their agreement means everything. The drug complication doesn't scare them away; they keep chatting away with you, leaving you feeling warm. It's a good feeling. A confusing feeling. Hannah texts you too, mostly about Raz. You're not used to people texting you. It's strangely exhausting.

When you get to school Monday, Hannah's not there yet, so you go inside by yourself. The halls are too quiet; it's early, but you wanted to get breakfast in the cafeteria.

A too-familiar voice stops you in the hall just outside, though, and too-familiar Timberlands on the aqua-green tile invade your view of the floor.

"Will," says Levi.

His arm, too fake-tanned and muscled, lands in front of your face as he blocks your path, hand against the wall to stop you. You almost run into his elbow.

"Levi," you say flatly. "What do you want?"

With Frances dead, he's literally the last person you want to see on the planet.

"What do I want?" Levi leans over a little to look you in the eye. He smells lightly of cigarette smoke and some kind of expensive cologne. "I want what I paid for."

Shit.

"What the hell are you talking about, Levi?" You think you keep your voice level. You already have an idea of what this ass-crack wants since *I want what I paid for* has a distinctly new meaning after discovering Frances's PO box.

"I want. What. I. Paid. For. You know what I'm talking about, *Will*." He says your name with a sneer.

"You're going to have to spell it out for me," you say, and then, like a freight train of words barreling over the edge of a cartoon cliff, add, "if you can spell."

Your vision flashes white in front of your eyes at the absolute nincompoopery of insulting Levi Strand to his face.

To your absolute shock, he laughs. It's not a mirth-laugh, though. You have the sense that he simultaneously hates you more and maybe respects you a little for what you just said. He's got a four-point-oh GPA, for Dog's sake.

"Okay," he says. His words come out like they've been scraped level. "I paid your trailer trash mother for a delivery, and she hasn't showed in days. You're going to get her to fix that."

You're not a good liar. You've never been a good liar. But something about this human toe-jam gives you a reserve of calm you've never thought you'd find. Instead of attempting to lie, you tell the truth. At least part of it.

"Levi," you say, "Frances has never told me what she did for a living. I pay all the bills myself, and I have since I was old enough to work. If she owes you something, maybe you should talk to her and stop bothering me. Or maybe you should just get your daddy to do it, since you get him to take care of all of your other little problems."

And then you walk around him and into the cafeteria, the calm disrupted by the sudden calculating look you left on his face.

You aren't sure you actually thought it would be that easy, but either way, when you leave to go to the bathroom in the middle of your last class of the day, the halls are quiet again, and Levi finds you again.

"I told you to leave me alone," you say.

"And I told you I want my shit." He leans against someone's locker. "I'm not playing with you, Will. Tell your mother this isn't funny."

"Tell her yourself. Or didn't she give you her phone number?" It takes all the self-control you possess to keep your voice and face calm, because frankly, Levi scares the crap out of you.

"You have until the end of this week." He hits the locker with his fist with a bang, but you've lived with Frances for years.

You don't jump.

"Get it." That's all Levi says before he leaves, strolling down the hall and around the corner like he knows he's won.

How did he even find you now? Has he just been waiting outside your classroom all period?

Ugh.

But it's a problem. Another problem.

By the time school ends, a headache is pinching at your temples, and you're not sure how you're going to make it through work.

You don't see you have a text until you're inside and already reshelving returns. You're crouching to shelve something on the very bottom row when the phone—your phone—slides out of your back pocket and lands face up. The screen flashes on with the jolt and shows Hannah's name.

She must have texted you when you were driving.

I overheard one of the football players saying that Levi's been giving you shit.

And then time-stamped a few minutes later:

Are you okay?

You like the library. It feels like a multiverse at your fingertips. You can open *The Death of Jane Lawrence* or *Please Don't Hug Me* and poof, you're in another world where the characters feel more like you. You don't want to think of Levi here.

You write back after finishing the first section of the cart.

I don't know how to make him stop. It's not like I can pick up where Frances left off. Like I would anyway.

There's no response for a while.

Mary, the head librarian, smiles when she sees you checking your phone. "Your mom finally let you get a phone, eh?"

Your face gets a bit warm. You forgot you're probably not supposed to be on your phone at work, because hey, you've never had to worry about breaking a rule you couldn't. But it is—yours. It's yours now. In an unexpected surge of emotion you can't identify, breaking a rule with it almost seems to cement your ownership.

"Sorry," you say belatedly. "I'll put it away."

"Will," Mary says with a soft chuckle. "I'm glad to see you have one. As long as you're not sitting and texting or watching TikToks when you've got something to do, I'm not going to bust your chops about it."

Oh.

Mary is a nice woman. A little shorter than you and with blonde hair she blows out every morning, she's got a kind face and looks like she would be just as suited to running for congress as running a library in a tiny town, and with all the book-ban bills in this country, those two things are far more related than not. You're pretty sure her cardigans are cashmere. Today's is a dusty rose color.

You give her a hesitant smile before going on with your work.

The rest of the afternoon goes without a hitch, but when you get home, your brain remembers Levi. You hear the bang of his fist hitting the locker beside your head and see that hapless kid he shoved into a car fender.

After heating up your dinner, you sit cross-legged on the sofa with a nature show on, propping the tray on top of a throw pillow so it doesn't burn your knees.

A few bites in, you pick up your phone and text Julian.

This guy at school is going to be a problem, I think.

Julian doesn't answer straightaway, and you're grateful for that because you need a minute to think.

He cornered me twice today and demanded I tell Frances he wants his stuff. His dad's the superintendent and I know he's already gotten off at least two booze possession charges. I literally flushed the stuff down the toilet so it's not like I have it anyway, and I'm starting to get nervous. I don't know what to do.

Maybe you should be telling Hannah this, but your Spidey-sense tells you she'd finally insist on calling the police. The thought of them coming here about illegal substances—no. No way. That will get you thrown back into foster care as the *least* worst option. With your luck, you'll end up in juvie when you didn't even have anything to do with Frances's drug bullshit. You'll wait until you're eighteen, then you'll anonymously call them and let them know about your dead mother's PO box.

Or something. Ugh. Raz would know what to do.

Chapter Eleven

Let's see if we can get ahold of Raz.

When you get Julian's response, you automatically feel better. They have the same instinct you do.

You see the little ellipsis appear that means they're still typing something. Something long from the look of it.

So it looks like I've got this Friday and Saturday off and don't work 'til Sunday night again. You can TOTALLY SAY NO if you want to, but I was thinking maybe I could come your way if we haven't heard from Raz. Maybe chill and decompress? Invite Hannah and her brother (I FORGOT HIS NAME I'M SORRY) for a slumber party. I'll bring the nail polish.

(You can totally say no!!)

This is the best idea you've heard in ages. You've never actually *hosted* a slumber party. It actually makes your fingertips a little tingly.

You text back, *Oh my god why would I say no?? Please come to Bright Springs!*

A moment later, Julian just writes back a *Yaaaaaaasssss.*

You're not gonna lie—it makes you glow a little.

Within an hour, it's all set—Hannah and Julian will come over Friday night, and Matt will join you at some point on Saturday, and then Julian will drive home Sunday.

The idea of a whole weekend with Julian is . . . exciting. Your heart and breath both seem to be doing a tango somewhere in the vicinity of your trachea.

In a fit of excitement and nerves, you spend the next two nights completely cleaning the house all over again. You think you do a half-decent job, too. Despite the way each time you leave and return, it seems like she's been in there the whole time you were gone stinking it back up again, it's probably as good as it's going to get.

You even go outside and tidy up the exterior of the single-wide. The shed out back gets your attention. The dirt around it seems disturbed, scuff marks in front of the double-padlocked door. When you peek through the dingy window, nothing in there seems out of the ordinary. On impulse, you smooth out the small furrows of dirt in front of it with the flat of your shoe and finish taking the trash and recycling to the big cans for pickup.

You go on Amazon when you get back inside and order some posters, mostly *Steven Universe* and one enormous one of Loki, because you're pretty sure he's the only fictional character you've ever had a crush on, aside from Solas from *Dragon Age*. Come to think of it, they're not dissimilar characters. On impulse you search for a Solas poster, too.

The walls in the living room are pretty bare, but the color's not bad now that it doesn't just remind you of the grim sludge of Frances's soul.

You think you're probably going to hell.

A person has to be pretty horrible to think of their mother like that, right?

By the time Thursday rolls around, you've got posters on the wall—you even got some cheap frames for them in Hagerstown!—and you just need to go shopping so there are plenty of snacks. You don't know exactly what happens at a slumber party, but the one thing you're clear on is snacks.

Your phone buzzes when you're gathering up reusable grocery bags, proud for remembering to bring them.

Okay please don't hate me

It's Hannah. You wait for whatever she's going to say next.

. . . Ashton kind of asked me out on a date.

Whoa.

You stare at that for a minute, then start writing back as fast as your still-untrained thumbs can manage.

DUDE why would I hate you? That's amazing!

Yeah, okay, there's a small pang in your chest because you don't really know Ashton, and you're afraid this will upset The Dynamic, but you're pretty sure that's normal, right? As long as you're not a dick about it. And you're not planning to be a dick.

You tuck the phone in your back pocket and grab your car keys. The phone buzzes almost immediately. Hovering just inside the door to the house, you pull it out again.

. . . I know. She wants to get super dressed up and go all out, even! But she wants to do it tomorrow.

Tomorrow's the slumber party. The ellipsis is there, so Hannah's still writing. You should get going, but if you don't wait and answer this, you know Hannah well enough to know that she'll think you are furious. She'll imagine you stewing and angry, and even though it's not true, she'll be super upset and you don't want to do that to her. On the other hand, maybe she's about to ask if Ashton can come too. That sticks in your throat like a pill you tried to take dry.

No. That can't be it. Breathe, Will.

So you wait. Not too long.

I know the slumber party is tomorrow, and I told her I totally want to go out with her but that I might have plans and needed to check. I wanted to talk to you first. I was thinking I could tell her we could go to an early movie right after school in Hagerstown and then I could come over to your place after dinner?? Is that okay? Will you be mad??

Thank god. Plus, Julian is coming over right after school, so that would mean a few hours with just them. The tango in your throat starts up again. Mad? Uh. Not really that.

DO IT, HANNAH

You hope that's enough for her to realize you mean it.

For good measure, you add: *Julian will be here, I'll be fine, and we'll be waiting for you to tell us eeeeeeverything. Tell Ashton yes!!*

With that, you stash the phone in your pocket and hurry out to the car.

You haven't felt this bubbly, sparkly feeling in longer than you can remember. It feels so . . . pure. The whole drive to the grocery store, you blast the *Sense8* playlist you made on Spotify because it's as upbeat as you feel. You're actually feeling *good*. Happy. More than happy.

You're actually *giddy*, Will. Goddamn.

Wegmans is always busy, and you park in the back of the lot. The place is kind of like Disneyland, which you think believing makes you about forty instead of seventeen, but with Frances you were trapped cooking for someone who treated you like something they got stuck on the bottom of their shoe in a public bathroom.

The lights are loud and the people are louder and *everywhere*, but you can do this. Grocery shopping is always overwhelming. Thing is, this time, you call all the shots. You can go hide in the back corner of the vegetable section where it's quiet if you need to without having to worry about being late and incurring Frances's wrath.

You can take care of your own needs how you see fit.

You're a good cook. You've had to be, since you did all of it yourself, but you've never actually cooked for people you wanted to cook for. You look up some recipes on your phone and decide for dinner, maybe you could show off a little. Just a little.

You stop the cart in front of a display of fresh-squeezed juices to text them.

Is there anything food-like you hate or can't eat?

The last thing you want to do is put a plate of food Julian doesn't like in front of them. "Hey, welcome to my home! Toilet's over there if you need to hurl."

Nah. Better avoid that.

I hate mushrooms, but other than that I am a full-fledged omnivore!

Julian's answer comes after only a moment, and you have to try and wipe the grin off your face. You're in public.

Good, you say. An idea strikes you. *Do you like WAFFLES?*

Julian immediately answers. *UH YEAH the more pertinent question is who DOESN'T like waffles because omfg I will eat all of theirs*

Excellent.

"Will?"

Shit. What now? You spin to see Suzie. Suzie the Counselor, from your school.

"Uh. Hi, Suzie," you say.

"Fancy meeting you here! What are you up to?"

Seeing a teacher-like species outside of the school habitat is beyond weird. Today Suzie's curls are freshly rebrowned with no hint of gray roots. She looks pleased to see you.

For a moment, you feel guilty about lying to her. You hate lying at all. You hope she'll eventually understand once you're able to come out of the "Frances's dead" closet.

"Having a slumber party with Hannah and another friend tomorrow night," you say, and your voice sounds almost chipper. "Figured I'd get the good stuff to eat."

"Oh, that's wonderful," Suzie says. "How are you doing this week?"

"I'm okay," you tell her without even having to lie. "Good, actually."

"Is your mom out of town again?" Suzie knows Frances sometimes fucks off.

"Uh," you say again. "Yeah, she's not around."

Smooth.

"Well, I won't keep you. I think if we talk for more than two minutes outside the school, I turn into a pumpkin," Suzie says with a wink. "I'll see you soon, Will. Have fun tomorrow night!"

Dang it. She's too nice. Guilt worms its way through your giddiness. She's been a constant in your life for the past couple years. Kind, earnest. You know she means well, and honestly, you kind of want to trust her with the whole Frances-is-dead thing, but you don't know if you can. What if she calls CPS and it throws your life in the trash compactor again?

You take in and let out a shaky breath, half-heartedly reaching for a bottle of orange juice in front of you. Without meaning to, you bounce a little at the thought of being free.

Out of the corner of your eye, you think you see Suzie watching you, but when you glance her way, she's already gone.

Right. She probably wasn't watching you. You turn back to shopping.

You can do this.

School on Friday seems to take a thousand years.

It's made worse by the strange suspense of not seeing Levi at all. It's like the world's worst game of Duck, Duck, Goose where it's been all ducks and no goose so long that your adrenaline is going wild. After what he said Monday, you fully expected him to turn up and get on your case again. Having any sort of conversation with him is like making out with a face-hugger from *Alien*.

But he doesn't turn up—the morning drags by with no sight of him, and Hannah is so nervous-excited-freaked out about her date with Ashton that the two of you together are two humming strings of yikes, vibrating slightly off-key.

"Are you excited about seeing Julian?" she asks as you walk to lunch. "They seemed to like you. Have you been texting?"

"Yeah, they've been texting me."

There was a message halfway through your last class that was a meme of a black kitten on a unicorn slipper flying into space that just said *I*

RIDE, so you assume that means they're on the way already. It's a long drive, but knowing Julian is en route gave you all sorts of fluttery feelings you're just not used to. Just . . . emotions. What are they?

"You didn't answer the first question." Hannah stops at her locker, shoving her backpack inside and giving the poster of Tessa Thompson at the back of the locker a dreamy stare.

"I'm excited," you say.

"You sound like you're going to the dentist." Hannah closes her locker and fixes you with that smirk of hers that says she knows you're full of it.

The hall is getting louder since everyone is milling about, heading to the cafeteria or off campus to raid the hot cases at the convenience store. So many competing noises that it takes Hannah's sentence a moment to process. Still no sign of Levi.

"Okay, maybe I'm nervous." You lean into Hannah's shoulder and start trudging in the direction of the cafeteria.

"Good, that means I'm not the only one!"

"You're nervous to see Julian?" You can tease Hannah.

"What? No—oh." She actually blushes. "Oh, god. Is this really happening?"

"I think it's really happening." You maneuver through the crowds toward the line. The cafeteria smells like chicken nuggets and pizza, which is, for once, not so promising.

You get your food in a few minutes, sitting down with a chicken burger (not nuggets after all) and a salad. And chocolate milk, because obviously.

Finding a half-empty table, you sit at the empty end, nodding to the sophomores clustered at the other end when one says hi. Hannah sits down across from you a moment later with an identical lunch.

"What movie are you and Ashton going to see?" You haven't asked that yet, and it makes you feel like a bad friend. At least that's how most people made you feel in your life when you didn't ask the right questions at the right time, but Hannah seems unperturbed that it took this long for you to ask.

"Oh, I don't know. I think the plan was to go straight there and then choose. Or maybe be adventurous and see whatever's playing next." Hannah wrinkles her nose at the second idea. "I'm afraid we get stuck with something terrible."

"Terrible isn't always awful," you say. "Exhibit A: *The Room*."

You watched it with Hannah and Matt last year when Frances had vanished for a couple days. The sex scenes were . . . a little awkward with Matt in the room.

Okay. A *lot* awkward. But you're pretty sure they'd be awkward regardless of who was in the room. You're not even certain they wouldn't be awkward if there was no one *in* the room.

There's a philosophical question: if a mortifying film plays in a room without anyone to watch it, is it still a travesty?

"Touché," Hannah says.

Just then, Ashton comes up with a tray and a shy, "Hi. Can I join you?"

You motion at her to sit down just as Hannah jumps and almost knocks over her milk, saying, "Of course!"

Ashton sits. Oh god, she looks as nervous as Hannah. Some of your bristling at Ashton's entrance into The Dynamic vanishes at that. They're both so skittish.

"Hannah says you guys are having a slumber party tonight?" Ashton says, trying to open her milk carton from the wrong end. She finally manages, but the spout gets all mangled.

"Yep," you say. You feel a little awkward, like you should invite Ashton, but she and Hannah haven't even gone on their date yet, and if it goes badly, that would be . . . well. "My friend Julian's already on their way."

You pull Julian's meme up and show her and Ashton, and Ashton makes a high-pitched squeak at the sight of the kitten.

"Oh my god, that is the cutest—*what* are cats and how do they get to be so cute? I want to squish it." Ashton is completely flustered, and her face is flushed, and when she looks at Hannah, Hannah gets this dopey smile on her face and splutters something about wanting to squish the kitten too.

How romantic.

You saw *Bambi* once, and you're pretty certain the technical term for the two of them right now is *twitterpated*.

Ashton starts going on about the outfit she's going to change into after last period, and Hannah refuses to divulge her own except to say that it's blue or green or maybe blue-green, which makes both of them blush all the harder.

You're kind of thrilled for them.

Maybe you're not *totally* a monster.

Chapter Twelve

The rest of lunch goes by quickly, and to your surprise, so do your final couple classes. When you escape to your car, there's a text from Julian saying they're already in Bright Springs, but that they've parked at Wawa.

Eeeeeek sorry! You text back frantically. *Just got out of class, but I'm heading home now!! Head on over! Navigation should find it fine, but if not let me know!*

Your hands are cold and made of nerves when you start the car and place them on the steering wheel. Julian is almost here. You haven't seen Hannah or Ashton since lunch, but you imagine they jetted out of the school with rockets attached to their asses to get to Hagerstown for their movie. What was Hannah's outfit she was so secretive about? You suppose you'll see it.

Thoughts of Julian chase it out of your head.

The drive home takes as long as a whole *week* in your mind, but finally, you pull into the driveway to see an unfamiliar car. It's a little blue Honda Civic, definitely a few years old, but it's a deep midnight color that looks exactly like the color Julian should drive around in.

Julian gets out of the car when you park, and they're wearing a blue unicorn onesie and clunky, unlaced Doc Martens on their feet. You are pretty sure you found someone made of actual magic.

"Are you even real?" you blurt out when you clamber out of the car. "I think that onesie is your actual soul."

"Yassss," Julian says, grinning. They buff their nails against the front of the onesie and go on in a long-suffering voice. "So few people notice."

"I am so glad you're here," you say.

Wow, is *everything* you feel just going to come flopping out of your mouth? Maybe.

Julian just grins wider, though. "I am too."

They open the passenger door to their car and pull out a galaxy backpack that is . . . shockingly similar to your own, and you never remembered to send them a picture.

"Oh my god," you say, turning so Julian can see yours slung over your shoulder.

Theirs is pink and purple and blue—bi colors represent—instead of the range of cerulean to indigo in yours, but Julian's eyes light up like Christmas lights.

"Perfection," they say. "When's Hannah coming over?"

Oops. You forgot to tell them. You motion at Julian to follow you to the front door, fumbling for your keys.

"Hannah got asked out on a date this afternoon, so she won't be here 'til after dinner," you say. Belatedly, you kick yourself for not telling Julian sooner. Now they're stuck alone with you 'til later. "I hope that's okay! If not, we can go into town for a bit or something, get a coffee."

"Pfft," Julian says, motioning to their onesie with a flourish. "This is prime fashion, but it's not for the eyes of the unworthy."

You miss the lock on the door with the key at that. Smooth, Will. Obviously Julian finds you worthy. Your cheeks feel weirdly jiggly, like trying not to grin is exhausting your muscles.

You manage to unlock the door on the second try, asking Julian about the drive while you toss your backpack into your room.

"It was good! Not as long as I thought, and I managed to miss Friday traffic from DC, so I think I need to make some sort of sacrifice to the gods so they don't smite me for my luck." Julian stops in the middle of the living room. "Speaking of, may the Dreadwolf *take me*—these posters are amazing."

"You play *Dragon Age*?" You cannot believe your own luck. In a shyer voice, you venture on with something you normally wouldn't share. "I played them all on an old—super old—360 when Frances let me buy one used years ago. Until she broke the Xbox and wouldn't let me replace it, so I haven't played in ages. Pretty sure she sold the games for cigarettes."

Hannah and Matt would have reacted to the Frances tale—Hannah more than Matt—but just as you expected, Julian accepts what you said in stride.

"*Will*, we will have to fix that. Ugh, I wish I'd known or I would have brought my PlayStation." Julian looks ready to kick themself. "Though that would likely result in the rest of us just watching you play all weekend, which, you know, fine with *me*, but Hannah and her brother might be put out."

Your shoulders relax infinitesimally where they've unconsciously tightened as you braced for your words' impact.

Julian's good mood is contagious, and your smile can't be held back any longer. For a while you just chat *Dragon Age* stuff, which is fun, because you've literally never had anyone to gush to about it, and there's supposed to be a new game soon.

"Ugh, wait!" Julian says as you move into the kitchen to get us drinks. "If you had an old-generation console, does that mean you haven't played the DLC? Meaning *Trespasser*?"

"I've never played it," you admit. "But Hannah lent me her iPad to watch it on YouTube, so I know what happens."

"Phew." Julian leans against the counter while you rummage in the fridge to hand them a Coke. "My older cousin was obsessed with it, so I got obsessed. It was all over for me as soon as that damn egghead elf started talking about the Fade. I had to start over just to romance Solas and go all chin hands when he started talking about being the master of his dreams."

"Oh, my god, I know. I always wished I could lucid dream, you know? Thought if I could learn, at least I could escape while I slept." Again, you've blurted something out without thinking. Usually you're better at staying guarded, but something about Julian is utterly disarming. "I mean—"

Julian's face softens. "You don't have to explain anything to me, believe me."

There's a moment of uncertain silence. "Thank you."

"I have a really good idea. Nay, a *perfect* idea."

They're wearing a unicorn onesie and just said *nay*. You think you might actually die.

"I'm listening," you say, sounding slightly strangled.

"Follow," Julian commands, leading me the fifteen feet back toward the living room, where they dig in their bag and pull out a battered old MacBook Air that is absolutely covered in stickers.

You sit next to them on the sofa, leaning forward to peer at the stickers while they type furiously.

"Wi-Fi?" they ask.

You tell them the network and the password. Man, their laptop looks like you imagine yours would, or could, now that you have dominion over Frances's.

"Ahem," Julian says a moment later, turning the laptop so you're forced to look at the screen instead of the back.

There's an order screen thanking them for buying—

"*Julian*," you say. "Oh my damn, you didn't have to do that!"

They ordered you a wolf onesie. In honor of the rebel god of the elves. The dream walker, the world changer who set his people free.

"It should fit, because you're about the same size as me, and if anything, it'll be a little too big. It should be here tomorrow. Power of the internet, Will. So much power."

"But—" No one has ever gotten you a gift, except Hannah. And Raz.

"No buts. You invited me to stay for the weekend. Consider it a housewarming gift."

"I don't think that's how housewarming gifts work," you say, feeling foolish.

Your cheeks are hot, and your traitorous brain is hearing Julian say *may the Dreadwolf take me* again, and, well. Help. You're also suddenly very aware of how close Julian is, sitting there smirking at you in their unicorn onesie. You just now noticed their silver glitter eyeliner, too, and their blue eyes are dangerously dark and beautiful.

And Julian's looking at *you* that way. Help, indeed.

You swallow. "Thank you."

It comes out hoarsely, and you clear your throat, because yikes. You've never experienced this before. The air itself feels charged with some sort of magic.

"You deserve it," Julian says simply, looking embarrassed all of a sudden. "You should have all the onesies."

"All of them?" you ask. "That wouldn't leave any for you, and that one you're wearing was *made* for you."

You've never heard that teasing note in your voice before, and your cheeks get even hotter. Oh, no.

"Well, obviously," Julian says, grinning. "But I only get to keep it because you approve. The rest are yours."

You meet their eyes. They don't look away.

You jump about twelve feet in the air when your phone buzzes, and you make a high-pitched squeak that causes Julian to burst out laughing.

"It's Hannah. Oh my god, she sent a selfie of her and Ashton. Look." You show Julian the selfie of the two of them outside the movie theater in Hagerstown, and the two of them look so happy you might explode. Ashton is in a sleek black sheath dress or romper, and her lips are silver. Holographic glitter dances across her cheekbones. It's close enough that you can't really see the bottom halves of their outfits, but you do see a flash of blue-green from Hannah's strapless top. The color is vaguely familiar.

"They are too cute! Tell them I said they are too cute!" Julian drums their fingers together evilly. "Did I find the best queers in Bright Springs?"

"Maybe? I don't have anything to compare us to, though one of the football players brought his boyfriend to prom last year. He runs in . . . different circles," you say primly. "Which is to say, he isn't someone I'd consider a close friend."

"So you're saying I'm right."

You grin. "You know what? Yeah. Best queers in Bright Springs, probably."

"If they're just heading into the movie, we've got some time, yeah?"

"Yep." You are not sure why that is simultaneously terrifying and exhilarating.

"Anything you have not seen but want to? I have all the streaming."

For a while, you just watch episodes of shows Julian wants to share with you. Most are on their laptop, so you prop your feet up on the coffee table and sit close enough that your entire sides are touching, and you watch and drink your sodas and laugh until you have tears creeping out of your eyes.

You're not sure you've ever laughed like that with anyone who isn't called Hannah or Raz.

Before long, you've completely lost track of time, feeling the movement of their breathing and spacing out for entire chunks of episodes because you think some part of you was certain Julian would eventually resituate themself, pull away from you. Anything. But they don't, and neither do you. There are moments where one of you will lean forward to get a drink or shift your weight a little on the sofa cushions, and every time, whoever it is comes back.

This is new. You are pretty sure you've never felt anything quite as warm and crackling with energy as the way you're feeling with Julian's body right up against yours. The thrill of it is new and rumbly, like the welcome buzz of a bumblebee. You keep swallowing, and Julian does too.

It's after six thirty when you realize Hannah will be on her way over soon, and you haven't cooked dinner.

"Oh, Christ on a cracker," you say suddenly, your noticeably empty stomach jumping into your throat.

"Raz says that." Julian grins and looks sideways at you. "What happened?"

"Dinner," you tell them. "I mean, dinner didn't happen, and it should."

"Oh! Right. Food." As if to punctuate their sentence, Julian's stomach gives a gurgle that almost sounds like a *harrumph*. "Eesh, excuse me. I did eat lunch on the way, I promise."

"I'm a terrible host," you say, sure Julian'll agree. "I bought a billion snacks and didn't get any of them out."

"Nah," Julian says. "Usually I can be sustained on caffeine and sugar alone."

"I'll start cooking."

"I," Julian announces, "will help. I am certified in slicing, dicing, and pasta-making, and I take direction very well."

You can't help but grin at that. They close their laptop and lean forward to put it on the coffee table next to your now-empty soda cans.

You both stand, but you're standing so close to each other that you wobble, and Julian's hands catch your upper arms.

"Whoopsie," they say. "Gravity, man. What a jerk."

Their words are light, but their hands are firm on your arms, and you're suddenly seeing the entire world through a slight haze of pink, which makes Julian in all their blue look just a teensy bit purple.

They let their hands fall, blushing harder.

"Thanks," you say. "That could have been mildly inconvenient, if not totally disastrous, depending on which way I fell."

"That's me! Here to save the day." A curl falls over Julian's forehead, almost to their eye, and your fingers twitch a few inches upward before you realize you almost reached up to brush it back, and maybe that wouldn't be welcome. It's not like the curl is anything but harmless. It's not going to make Julian suddenly top-heavy, or do anything but make them . . .

Even more ridiculously adorable.

Probably not a danger to them. Might be a danger to your blood pressure.

You are starting to suspect that this press of feeling that seems to be coming from all angles at once and filling you with tingly heat and undirected want might be what they mean when they say *crush.*

You're in deep shit, Will.

Somehow, you make it into the kitchen.

You grab Julian another Coke while you cook, and it's your turn to blush when they are suitably impressed by the mango-salsa salmon you're broiling and the rice pilaf, and the spinach salad. You even got goat cheese to put on it, along with some dried apricot and poblano peppers.

True to their word, Julian wields the knife you give them with practiced ease. When you comment on it, they shrug.

"I've been cooking for myself since I was in fourth grade," they say. "We neglected kids learn all the life skills, hey?"

Some locked-away part of you exults at that. This is someone who *gets* you. That part of you that you usually keep under lock and key—hell, chained and cement-vaulted—gets some air for the first time since you lived with Raz.

"Do you think Raz is okay?" you ask as you put the salmon in the oven and set the jangly timer out of habit.

"Normally, I'd say absolutely," Julian says slowly, "but I don't like that her door was left open. It's not like she tells me when she's taking off for a few days or whatever to go camping, but it's been a week, and I think she would have told me if she was planning to be gone for more than that. To check on the lieutenant if nothing else."

"Do you usually take care of her cat?"

"Nah, she usually gets a sitter, since my work schedule's so unpredictable, but I haven't seen anybody by." Julian leans against the counter in front of the sink, drumming impeccably silver-glittered nails against the lip of it. "But she is an adult. What worries me most is that she's not answering her phone."

"Yeah," you say. "I guess that's weird these days, right?"

"You sound like you don't know." Their lips turn upward.

"I didn't have a cell phone before Frances died," you tell them. "She wouldn't let me, so I'm used to not being exactly easy to reach myself."

"Ah. Yeah, that makes sense."

Your face is hot from opening the oven—or maybe that's just Julian's proximity—but words tumble out of your mouth before you can try to cram them back down your gullet.

"I'm really glad you came, Julian," you say. "I've never really had anyone understand this stuff. Hannah tries, but like, her mom bought her a car. I paid off my mom's car."

"This shit is tough," they say, nodding. "I always got a lot of 'why don't you *just*' do this or that or whatever. Just get born into a family that has money, I guess? Why didn't we think of that?"

"I do not know." You lean on the counter near them, perpendicular to them, your hand bracing against the corner where the surfaces meet. "I'm really glad you came."

"You said that already," Julian says, looking at you sideways with a glimmer in their bright blue eyes.

They're fiddling with their lip ring again with their tongue, again in the way that makes you think it's nerves.

"Oh. Uh. Right, I did. Sorry."

"I definitely don't mind hearing it twice. Sometimes things go in one ear and out the other the first time." Julian meets your eyes, definitely looking nervous now. But not nervous-bad, you think.

It's contagious, the nervousness. You think if you let your hands budge from where you have them gripping the edge of the countertop, they'd tremble like a scared Chihuahua.

"Then I'll say it a third time." Where the *hell* is this boldness coming from, Will? Damn. "I'm really glad you came."

"Me too," they say softly, and then they exhale with a strong gust of breath. "I almost didn't ask. I mean, I know we only met the once, but even where I live, I don't find that many people like me. At least who are our age. I know heaps of queer folk at work, but all of them are in their twenties and thirties, and I'm the tiny baby queer. And I do my own school thing, so it's not like I meet people there."

Your heart softens even more, if such a thing is even possible. It's such a bizarre thing, being at once too old for people your age and too young for people who are older. It makes you feel like you don't fit anywhere. You learn to camouflage, at least as best you can, nodding and smiling when people treat you like a kid even though you're looking at your peers feeling like *they're* kids, simultaneously envying them and resenting them for it.

Something of it must show in your face because Julian goes on.

"And honestly, I think I said it before, but the way Raz has always talked about you, I've always wanted to meet you." Julian says it all in a rush, like this time they're trying to get the words out before they lose their nerve. "For a while I was really jealous of you, which is wicked stupid, because you weren't even there."

"Jealous?" That brings your head up, and you swallow. They said that in Baltimore, but you didn't really process it. "Of me?"

"Yeah. Raz loves you *so* much, Will. Like . . . I always get the feeling she'd catch the moon in a net if it would bring you back to her. She hates that Frances got you back. She feels cheated out of being part of your life." Julian shocks you, reaching out to brush a stray lock of *your* hair back from your face that you barely noticed tickling your cheek. "I guess I kind of do too, by proxy. Especially now that I've met you, because Raz did not exaggerate your awesomeness."

Holy shit. Your face is burning hot now. It might actually combust any second, and Julian is looking at their hand that moved your hair like it did something they weren't expecting, and even though the touch of their fingers on your cheek was softer than a moth's wings, barely even a touch, you are about to fall to pieces.

"I—god, I'm sorry," Julian says suddenly. "I most definitely should have asked before I did that."

"Julian—" you get out.

"No, I made it weird!"

"You most *definitely* did not make it weird," you blurt, and then you're only a bare few inches from them, looking up the short distance into their eyes. Their eyes are *so* blue. So blue you think you could swim in them. "You're perfect."

Their face goes still and shocked, white visible all around the edges of their irises.

Shit. Now you've gone and made it weird.

They're just so damn *pretty*. And they always seem to understand without you even trying to be understood. More than that, they feel *like you*. They react like you, think like you.

You would never, ever think Julian was a monster.

That thought hovers in your mind as you float in the blue of their eyes.

You're both standing there, staring at each other like you've forgotten how to move the inches it would take to get closer, when there's a cheerful knock at the door. You both jump, and this time it's Julian who makes a tiny squeak of surprise.

"Hannah," you half-gasp just as the timer jangles, making you both jump again.

That breaks some of the tension, and Julian bursts out laughing. "I'll get the door, you get the oven."

"Deal," you say, and they slide away on onesie'd feet, leaving you to get the salmon out of the oven and wonder what the hell is happening at this slumber party.

Chapter Thirteen

Hannah bolts into your room to change like a charcoal-and-peacock-colored comet—that's the only glimpse you catch of her when you turn to greet her—emerging in leggings and an oversize black sweater you do not think is hers. She sits with you and Julian while the two of you eat, gushing about her date with Ashton and how she's full because Ashton insisted on getting practically a four-course meal of snacks. Julian asks all the right questions in all the right places, and you sit and eat quietly, marveling at the way they actually seem to know where all those right places even are *and* marveling at how Hannah is beaming. You're not sure you've ever seen her like this.

That thought lodges itself into the seam of your friendship. Has Hannah ever beamed like that at you? You shove the notion from your mind.

The food is good, much to your relief. Julian somehow manages to devour theirs before you're half finished, even though they're talking up a storm, and you're just sitting and watching the two of them.

Julian insists on helping with the dishes when you're done, which is to say they insist on doing all of them. Hannah turns on dance music on her phone, any territorial feelings about Julian apparently forgotten in her haze of Ashton glee, and you show her the new posters while Julian cleans because they shooed both of you out of the kitchen with a snap of a rag.

"Oh my god, you got the egg," Hannah says, rolling her eyes at the Solas poster. "Ugh, I'm going to have to throw you a life vest when that ship sinks, aren't I?"

"I'll go down with this ship," you say, blowing a kiss at your elven AI boyfriend.

You got Hannah into *Dragon Age*, but she was all about Josephine, who is admittedly too pure for this world. Solas is like you. To the point that he ruins everything he touches. To the point that everyone believes he's a monster.

Yes, Solas is the most like-you character in a video game you've found.

Though that's not really saying much, since you really only have ever played three. (You did, however, play those three to death.) You get what others get several years behind, and while they move on, you dig your trenches and hoard what they've left in their wake.

Hannah shakes her head. "Addicted to pain."

Addicted to the idea that the monster can make a world better instead of worse.

"So you had a good time tonight?" you ask quietly, changing the subject as the thought burrows deep into your brain.

Her face softens. Hannah teeters on the edge of one foot for a moment before shifting her weight to regain her balance, and she smiles.

"I really did. She said she's liked me for years, Will. I had *no* idea." Your best friend is glowing softly. Julian grins at her from the sink. "Kind of want to kick myself for not talking to her sooner. Two years of overlapping crush or something. Just . . . ugh."

"Yeah, that's intense," you say, because you don't know what else to say. "Do you know what she wants to do after this year?"

"UMD, I think. Which, cool. That's one of the places I'm applying." This, Hannah directs at Julian, speaking louder so they can hear her from the kitchen over the music. "I don't think Mom wants me to go there, but I don't know. She wants me to apply to Georgetown or something. Or Princeton. She might be happy if I apply to Princeton."

Hannah makes a face. She doesn't have the grades for Princeton—for Matt, college would have been football-focused, so their mom's hoping Hannah wants the academic life—but you're pretty sure Princeton is one of the last places Hannah would want to go. "We'll see, I guess."

It's weird to think of maybe living in a different city than Hannah. If she goes to one of those places, she'll be in DC or New Jersey. You'll be . . . where? No idea. It feels like unknowns are pulling you in a thousand different directions at once.

You don't get it yet, that this is part of grief. You don't understand that it's okay to need support when your mother just died, no matter how much a pile of triceratops crap she was. You don't know how to ask for what you need because you don't know what you need at all. Hell, a lot of adults wouldn't. This shit doesn't really get easier. Nobody knows how to grieve. Nobody knows how it works.

But you think you're broken, because you always assume you're broken, so even being with Hannah and Julian, your mouth approximating the right-ish shapes at the right-ish time and your vocal cords laughing in the right-ish places, you feel like you are made of chunks of lie glued together into a shape no one could ever love.

Not if they really saw you.

"I'm happy for you," you tell her. It's mostly true. You still feel like an asshole.

"Thanks." Hannah's eyes meet yours, and she does the little sideways head tilt thing she does when she's anxious. "You know you're my best friend, right?"

"Yep," you say. It comes out a bit more forlorn than you mean it to.

"I'm not going to up and ditch you for a girl," she says. "No matter how much I like her."

"I know," you say.

You are certain Hannah means what she said about Ashton, nonetheless. You're just not certain she's making a promise she can keep.

There's that gulf that bulges between you, as an unreadable expression crosses over her face. Did she expect you to say it back? That you wouldn't ditch her for Julian? Or Raz? Asking would ruin the slumber party mood, and you can't force yourself to say it. Maybe you would have before Frances died, before you knew how much Raz has loved you all this time.

"Will," Julian calls from the kitchen. "Did you say something about dessert? Because these dishes have been conquered, and sugar overload sounds delicious."

"I definitely did!" You give Hannah a small smile and head to the kitchen, where you pull out a few different varieties of ice cream treats as well as a selection of tarts from the bakery.

The three of you don't make it to bed until four in the morning after watching back-to-back-to-back superhero movies while Julian paints all your nails, and you are pretty sure this is the best idea you've ever had.

You wake up around eleven sprawled on the sofa bed with one of Hannah's arms flung across your face, and when you peek out from under it, Julian is already awake, quietly watching something on their laptop with their earbuds in. Maybe the earbuds are also because Hannah is softly snoring.

Julian smiles down at you when they see you're returning to the waking world, and the smile of your own that immediately answers makes theirs grow brighter. Your heart gives a little *thub.* You slept in the middle, and while the sofa bed accommodated all three of you, it was cozy.

"Morning," you say, stifling a yawn.

"Morning." Julian salutes.

"Not yet," comes Hannah's groggy voice. "Will, I'm going to your room."

She somehow propels herself to a sitting position, squinting over her shoulder at you.

"Wake me up when Matt gets here or when there's breakfast."

"Yes, your majesty," you tease her. A morning person Hannah is not.

She just stares at you uncomprehendingly and shuffles into your room, trailing the throw from the sofa like Linus and his blanket.

When the door shuts, you look up at Julian. Their hair is floofier in the morning, the curls stretching themselves to freedom, and they're wearing black-rimmed glasses. They are . . . painfully cute. They take the earbuds out of their ears.

"Your onesie should be here soon," Julian says.

"Excellent." You sit up, stretching. Scooting backward, you lean against the back of the sofa next to Julian. "Did you sleep okay?"

"Sort of. I'm not the best sleeper." Julian nods in the direction of your room. "What time is Matt supposed to get here?"

"I have no idea. Early afternoon?" You're not quite awake yet yourself. "Do you want some coffee?"

"Yes. The answer will always be yes."

You go into the kitchen to make it. Your mouth is fuzzy with sleep, but your toothbrush is in the bathroom attached to your room (at least you never had to share a toilet with Frances), and you don't want to disturb Hannah. At least this way everyone will be equal in the eyes of morning coffee breath.

As you rummage through the cupboards, it quickly becomes clear that you forgot to get decent coffee when you were at Wegmans, but at least you remembered three different types of flavored creamer, so you can disguise the burnt taste of whatever generic cheap-o Frances got last. Coffee was, weirdly, the only thing she didn't insist you buy name brand for her.

Crap coffee or not, the moment the burbling pot is percolating and coffee smells fill the kitchen, it perks you up.

"Creamer? There are options," you say to Julian. "Amaretto, hazelnut, and pumpkin spice."

"Ooh. I am usually all about that PSL, but I am intrigued by this amaretto you mention." Julian peeks over the unused breakfast bar.

"A lot or a little?"

"I like my coffee like I like my . . . okay, I got nothing pre-caffeine. A lot. Like . . . coffee-flavored amaretto rather than amaretto-flavored coffee." Julian grins.

Their hair is all tousled, and they are too cute.

You pour their coffee and your own, going for the amaretto too since it's your favorite, and you're secretly excited that they picked it.

"Do you think we should try and call Raz again?" you ask when you hand Julian their mug.

You gave them the big mug, the one that's basically the size of a soup bowl, and they look at it like it's the holy grail.

"I doubt it would hurt anything," they say, sipping from the mug. "It just feels like kind of a weird coincidence if she did head out of town or something. Coincidences happen and all, but—"

"But this one feels weird." You perch near Julian's feet so you can put your coffee down on the breakfast bar when you're not drinking it. "Ugh, I hate this. Do you think we should call the police? If something happened to her and we didn't, I'd never forgive myself."

"Give it 'til Monday," Julian says. "If we haven't heard anything by then, we can give them a call. Or I can, so you don't have to talk to them."

"Really?" The thought fills you with relief. "Okay."

Having a plan is better than not having a plan.

"I wish I had her work number or something," Julian says. "If I could call her there, they might not tell me anything, but at least they'd know what to do. I don't even have her email address. We just always use cells. Or like walk the fifteen steps and knock on the door."

"Yeah. We can try and find it Monday," you say. "That can be the pre-police step. If we can call her work and they know something, then we don't have to call the cops at all. If they don't know something, then we at least haven't called the police without exhausting all other possibilities."

"I like the way you think," Julian says.

The sound of tires on gravel reaches your ears. "That's probably Matt."

You get up, marveling that he is turning up before noon, but when you open the door, it's just the delivery guy with a parcel for you. It is most definitely the wolf onesie. You know because you tear open the corner of the envelope it's in before the driver's even gotten back to the truck.

"Oh heck yes," Julian says when you shut the door. "I demand that you try it on."

"You don't have to twist my arm," you tell them, scurrying down the hall to the half bath before Frances's room.

It smells like synthetic fabric, but when you shake it out to get a look at it, you can't help the giddiness that bubbles up inside you. You are in it in moments, zipping it up. You could huff and puff and blow all sorts of houses down in this thing. Awoo, bitches. This was made for you. It has actual feet, and the feet have tufts. Tufts! The hood has a ruff of extra fur around the cheeks, and you look like a big dumb dorky wolf when you look in the mirror. It's so perfect. It's so *you*, Will.

You pad out into the hall again with the hood up, carrying your balled-up PJs with you.

Julian lets out a whoop when they see you. "Oh, my dog, this is so perfect. Yasss, Will!"

You don't even care if Hannah wakes up. You really want to pounce Julian and tackle hug them, but instead you settle for using your words.

"Ugh, I love it so much. Thank you, Julian!"

"It is so good." They are grinning so wide you think you could count their teeth.

You are perfectly happy to settle back down beside Julian on the sofa, picking back up with the show you were watching before Hannah arrived.

You're not sure you've ever been this cozy in your entire life. You're warm without being too hot, the coffee and the layers of plush onesie fabric managing to make the perfect nest on the sofa next to Julian the Unicorn.

By the time Hannah wakes up, it's half past twelve, and she's still barely functional. Hannah zombie-walks half-blinking into the living room, rubbing her eyes. She's like a cartoon toddler when she wakes up. Sleeping is practically her hobby. You wish you were as good at it as she is.

"Coffee?" she asks plaintively.

"I'll start a new pot," you say, reluctantly getting to your feet.

She shuffles after you while you change the filter and dump new grounds into the percolator, squinting at you.

"Did I miss you becoming a furry?" she asks, and you cough a laugh, creating a puff of air that sends a small flurry of coffee grounds to fall on the counter.

"Julian got it for me," you say, peeking at Julian over the breakfast bar, who salutes, pushing their glasses back up onto their nose.

"Awoo," is Hannah's still-sleepy answer, which you take to mean her approval, but it's hard to tell whether the one-word answer is positive or a front for jealousy.

Since everyone's awake, you figure waffles can happen, so you start mixing batter and getting plates out while Hannah and Julian chat over the sound of burbling coffee. Something keeps poking at the back of your brain like an insistent kid, and you keep needing to tell your shoulders to relax. You hold tension like it's gravity, keeping you on the ground. But it's not gravity, not really. You've just spent your whole life bracing for the next meteor to land on your head.

This is the first time you've ever done anything like this, you realize. You've never just had friends over. Ever. Full stop. The few times Hannah ever came over before Frances died were spent half-fretting (or whole fretting, let's be real here) that Frances would just turn up. She never caught you. Lucky for you.

You're pouring batter into the waffle iron, the smell of vanilla and soon-to-be-brunch filling your nostrils, when it finally clicks that she will never just turn up again.

You hurriedly look away on the pretense of getting a mug for Hannah's coffee, even though you probably don't need a pretense with these two. Your eyes sting with the burn of tears on not quite enough sleep.

Relief floods you.

But on its heels is the all-too-familiar guilt. What kind of kid feels grateful and relieved that they'll never see their mom again? How many times did Frances justify herself to you with the words *Blood's thicker than water. Family comes first.* What if she was right? What if you're just that much of a monster?

Much as you try to banish the thoughts, they won't leave.

You mechanically remove the first waffle, putting it on a foil-covered plate into the oven on low to stay warm.

Your phone buzzes.

"Probably Matt," you say, because no one else would be calling you. "Your phone still in my room, Hannah?"

Hannah waggles her phone at you and peers at yours on the coffee table in front of her. "Unknown number."

"Also known as the universal sign of *do not answer*," you say.

But what if it's Raz?

Julian seems to have the same thought at the same time. "Want me to answer it?"

After a moment of hesitation, you nod.

Julian picks up your phone. "Hell-*o*," they say. There's a pause. "Nope, I think you have the wrong number."

You look at Hannah, whose face is stony all of a sudden. Maybe she can hear the voice on the other side.

"Well, perhaps this Frances person you're looking for changed their number in an attempt to find more polite friends," Julian says sweetly and perfunctorily presses the red circle to hang up. Followed by a bit of swiping around. They look at you. "Blocked the number."

"Good call," Hannah murmurs. She's fully awake now, looking troubled.

The phone buzzes a moment later, and Julian jumps, because it's still in their hand.

"Shit," they say.

They hold the phone gingerly, like whoever's calling could reach out a hand through the touchscreen.

"Text this time," Hannah says, leaning over to read the screen. She blanches. "Must be from a different phone. It says they know this is still Frances's phone and that they will find her."

"That's . . . not good." You're not familiar with drug dealers from anything but *Breaking Bad*, but you don't really think *dead* is an excuse they'll necessarily take if they think you stole their shit. Which you kind of did.

"I'll put it on Do Not Disturb for now," Julian decides. "And block this one too. You do not need to deal with this on an empty stomach."

Shit. The waffle. You skid to the waffle iron, opening it to find the waffle just a teensy bit overdone. Julian gets up, to your surprise, and they come in to gather up the plates and set the table. Hannah looks bemused by the action, still perched on the edge of the sofa and glancing at your now-silent phone as if it's a rattlesnake.

Julian starts talking about *Dragon Age* while you finish the waffles, putting butter out on the table and rummaging through the cupboards for syrup. They manage to make you laugh quoting random characters, and you're very grateful for the distraction. By the time the waffles are done, you feel a little better.

Matt turns up while you're eating, and he looks a little unsure about his decision to spend his Saturday night with a bunch of high schoolers, but he settles in quickly enough with a cup of coffee. He's brought a bunch of snack foods—mostly Doritos and a Costco-size box of taquitos—which is touching. Hannah looks at her brother like she's never seen him before.

For a few hours, you forget about the phone. It's not 'til you pick it up absently while Hannah sets up a board game that you remember. The screen is *full* of notifications, one after the other, the most recent only a few minutes ago. When you scroll it with your thumb, it just keeps going.

It feels like tumbling down the rabbit hole, watching the messages—mostly expletives and threats—scroll by your field of vision.

Belatedly, you realize Matt's saying your name. "Will?"

"Shit," Hannah says. "Did they keep texting?"

You hold out the phone for them to see for themselves.

"Will, this is not okay," Hannah breathes after a horrified moment of scrolling. "What if they come here?"

You'd successfully slam-dunked that particular possibility to the back of your mind until now, but it comes exploding back through the wall all at once.

"You have to go to the cops," Hannah says.

"No cops!" you say loudly at the same time Julian says, "Will—"

You look at Julian, waiting to see what they say.

But they don't need to say anything. You see the same fear in their eyes that you feel.

Matt is looking back and forth between the two of you and his sister. "I am starting to think Hannah might be right, at this point. If I can find one of the few I trust—but if we do this, you let me go to them first. No just calling them and playing Russian roulette with whoever gets dispatched."

You and Julian cringe at "Russian roulette," but Hannah doesn't seem to notice. Matt does, though, and he winces at his own choice of words and gives an apologetic, tight-lipped smile, shaking his head as if berating himself inwardly.

"Look," you say, sounding way more confident than you feel. "Frances had a post office box. She clearly didn't do business from the house. They would have no way to find her."

"You think someone would have trouble tracking down someone like *Frances* in a town the size of Bright Springs?" Hannah's incredulity is matched only by the anger seeping into her expression.

"They will punt me back into the system so fast it'll make a lightning strike seem slow," you manage.

"Even if they do, it's better—"

"It is *not* better!" You have to bite back the tide of white-hot rage that floods you at Hannah's words. Your tongue sticks to the roof of your mouth.

"They might not do anything with your birthday so close," Hannah says, and Matt nods.

You know that's true. "But they *might*."

When Julian meets your eyes, you know they get it.

"Let Will be the judge of what they're willing to risk," Julian says softly.

"But these people could *hurt* them," says Hannah, aghast.

"They don't know who I am or where I am," you hear yourself say. "You don't understand what it's like—"

Something dark crosses Hannah's face. But after a moment she looks to her brother, pleading written in her eyes. You feel a pang at that. If it were her, if your places were reversed, what would you do right now, Will?

You have no way of knowing, because just as Hannah does not understand your life, you sure as hell do not understand hers. She's always been protected. She's always had someone protecting her. And she's never *needed* that protection the way you have. She doesn't know.

Matt shakes his head. "I can't make any decisions for you, Will. I don't think you should let this go, though. You don't know what Frances was into."

"Yeah, we do," you say. "We didn't find anything harder than oxy."

After a moment, Hannah lets out an explosive sigh.

"Okay," she says. "But we're going to screenshot every one of those texts, put them in a file, and catalog anything else that comes through this phone until Monday, and you're going to change your number as soon as humanly possible for real."

"Okay," you say. You can handle that.

Julian looks relieved. You give them a small smile.

"Not a high school sleepover without some drama, right?" you say.

To your surprise, Matt bursts out laughing. "Most people do not start by cranking it up to eleven, Will."

"I'll try to remember that next time."

You sit there, then, while Hannah and Julian go through all the texts and put them in a folder in the cloud, sharing the link among everyone present.

You're thankful for all of them. Matt and Hannah might not understand, but they care. And Julian, well.

People like you and Julian, you have reasons behind the fear.

You hope Hannah and Matt never do.

Chapter Fourteen

The rest of the slumber party goes smoothly and Matt leaves on "an errand" and returns forty minutes later with an iPhone he kept as a backup when he last upgraded, handing it to you with a crumpled Christmas bow stuck to the otherwise-pristine box.

"So you don't have to deal with any of that texting bullshit," he says.

That mollifies Hannah a bit, though she is quieter than usual for the rest of the weekend. You catch her looking at the iPhone after Matt gets it set up for you and connected to Wi-Fi—you'll get it added to Frances's plan tomorrow—and she looks almost . . . hurt. Even though this one is two generations old, and she's got the newest model. And when you go into your room with Hannah as she gathers her stuff, you catch a glimpse of something blue-green and sparkly that vanishes almost immediately under a pair of leggings before you can dredge your brain through making sense of it. Hannah turns her back to you as she packs.

You hate this gulf that has sprung up between the two of you. It never used to feel so big. You're not sure what has changed, besides the obvious. Rather, you're not sure what *about* Frances's death changed your relationship with Hannah.

It comes to you when you're driving to school Monday morning.

Hannah is so used to being taken care of that she is trying to take care of *you*, and she doesn't see that you don't need it. Or maybe you do, but she's realizing you're *okay* living alone and without a parent of any kind, and it's so foreign to her that she doesn't know what to do with it.

That and the fact that Frances was a drug dealer is making this experience a lot more nerve-racking than it should be.

You do feel a bit better today, though. There's some hope, you think. Hope that you'll make it through this mess. Tangled up with the hope is the knowledge that today's the day you will have to decide whether to call the police about Raz, though, and you aren't ready for that.

It's strange at school on Monday. No Levi again at first, which is weird and dread-inspiring. You're relieved when you see him on your way to the bathroom—for precisely five seconds until you remember his presence is worse. One glimpse of greasy hair and glassy eyes is all you get.

Because instead of just passing you in the empty hallway, he shoves you. Hard.

You're more startled than anything as your shoulder collides with a locker, the *clank* loud enough that it sounds like a report through the hall. By the time you spin around, rubbing your shoulder, Levi has turned the corner and is nowhere to be seen. Not a word, not a glance, just a very unrandom act of violence.

For the rest of the day, you keep a lookout for Levi, unease roiling through your belly, but Hannah and Ashton are so awkward and blushing and cute when you get to the cafeteria that you spend your lunch watching them go back and forth accidentally interrupting each other and getting embarrassed every time.

Neither of them seems to notice that you don't actually eat, only push your food around your tray with your fork until it's mushy enough that it looks like you chewed it only to spit it back out. As much as you're happy for Hannah, you can't wait for the bell to ring.

You hanging in there? The text from Julian comes out of the blue. You're working in the library, and it's slow, so you have nothing to do.

Trying to, you write back. *I guess today's the day we're supposed to decide about calling the police about Raz, isn't it?*

The ellipsis immediately appears, and you wait, absently gathering up some books to shelve while they type.

That's the thing, Julian says when you look at your phone again. *I went over to check on the lieutenant, and there's something weird going on. I've been super careful about how much to feed her, but she's looking . . . rotund.*

Huh. The cat's getting fat? That means either Julian's feeding her too much or—

I think someone else has been feeding her, but if it's not Raz, that probably means a sitter. Maybe there was an emergency and Raz had to leave in a hurry? I don't know. You can almost see Julian fretting. *I'm going to try and leave a note on the door and see if anybody responds, but I'll be at work late tonight. I'm closing.*

Okay, you tell Julian. Part of you calms with the evidence that Raz really did plan this time away, even if you can't reach her. It's just so unlike her to be careless about leaving a door literally open if she were going out of town.

Your thumbs hesitate on the screen long enough that Mary looks over at you with a wry smile from behind the circulation desk.

"Once you start, it's hard to stop, right?" she says.

"Yeah, sort of," you tell her. "Sorry."

"It's slow. Don't worry about it, Will."

Your boss is too nice to you. You're pretty sure she should be yelling at you or something. Because of the tidy weight of guilt that weighs down your chest about it, you busy yourself doing library things. You dust some shelves, organize others, and by the time you give in to looking at your phone again, there's another message from Julian time-stamped twenty minutes ago.

I think Raz is probably okay but out of service reach somewhere. I'll let you know as soon as I know anything else! Btw, thanks again for the fabulous hospitality this weekend. We should do it again sometime.

The message makes your heart give a little spasm of a flutter. *I'd love that.* You hit Send before you lose your nerve and shove your phone into your back pocket again.

There weren't any more overly warm moments between you and Julian over the weekend after the threatening messages, so you firmly clamp down on the little tendril of hope that wants to reach upward into your chest. Part of you wants to write it off as Matt and Hannah being present, since the capital-M Moments that happened with Julian mostly happened sans the siblings, but also you are pretty sure there's no chance of Julian actually liking you. That way, anyway.

You don't know why you're so bothered about it. Maybe because it's the first time you've ever actually had a crush on anyone who wasn't a fictional character.

The rest of your shift at work goes by slowly, and even though Mary offers to let you go early, you insist on staying until close at eight thirty. You're going to need the money.

When you say goodbye to Mary, she walks you to your car and she waits for you to start the engine and pull out before she leaves herself.

It's a strange act of caring.

When you get into the driveway, you take a quick circuit around the yard, more out of habit than anything else. You're so used to Frances replenishing the crushed beer cans littering the ground that for a moment, you're shocked into stillness that they're not there.

The shed in the back remains undisturbed but still somehow unsettling. You shake off the feeling.

Not ready to unpack *that* particular sensation, you make your way inside.

With nothing else to distract you, you mill aimlessly around the house. After three days of it full of laughter—and some panic—you aren't sure what to even do with yourself.

Julian won't be done with work until midnight, and there is no way in hell you're sleeping before you hear from them. To cope, you check your bank balance. It's still higher than usual since Frances died before she could smoke and drink away your last summer paycheck, but it makes you nervous. You're working fifteen hours a week instead of forty, and you've got to last until summer.

Given something tangible to worry about, you start scribbling budget stuff on one of your new notepads with one of your new pens, adding up the monthly expenses. You could live on your library money if you completely ran out of the bank funds, though it'd be tight.

But then you realize you can cancel your cable and just keep internet, which will save you easily a hundred bucks a month.

Relief floods you at that thought.

Look at you, surviving.

Once you're content that you will make it at least through the next year, you guiltily click over to Amazon.

You know you shouldn't do it, because it's expensive, and you have just spent three hours looking at money, but . . . it's for you.

You order a used PlayStation 4 and *Dragon Age: Inquisition*. The ultimate edition that comes with all the extra content.

Glancing up at the poster of the egg himself on the wall, you give him a sheepish smile. "Just this one thing, right?"

You're pretty sure he'd approve of finding some sort of solace in a world of wrongness.

It occurs to you that this is your act of being a kid. You think of Hannah with her Jeep and her gadgets she gets under the tree every year, always the latest model, always brand new.

When you get the email confirmation of your order, you almost panic and cancel it.

But you don't.

Just this once, you decide it's yours.

I know phones are the worst, but can I call you? This arrives from Julian at quarter past twelve.

You've been talking about the PlayStation (they've told you you're allowed to get something for yourself, and you appreciate it even if it might be what Suzie the Counselor calls "enabling"), so they know you're awake.

Sure, you say.

You're perched cross-legged on the sofa with a blanket around your shoulders and your wolf onesie on. It's going to need to go in the laundry sometime this week. Right now, though, you kind of don't want to wash it. It's like those stories of people not washing their hands after someone famous shook it.

You're being silly.

A moment later, your phone rings, and Julian's face with their unicorn hood pulled up flashes on the screen. You took a picture of them before they left yesterday, and they did the same, so you're a wolf in their phone.

"What happened?" you ask without preamble when you answer.

"So Raz is fine," Julian says immediately. "The sitter left a note in my mailbox. Said she felt like a total buffoon when she read she'd left the door open that day and the lieutenant had gotten out."

"So why isn't Raz answering her phone?" you ask.

You immediately think it's because she doesn't want to talk to you. Why would she, really? She probably realized it was a mistake to write to you at all.

"She's backcountry camping off the Appalachian trail like she told us, I guess, with family? I think the cat sitter said Raz's brother's ex and kids went with her, but she's totally off the grid." Julian doesn't sound sure.

Your brain's an asshole, Will. Raz has contacted you for literal years—it's illogical to think she'd stop now.

"The sitter said she only expected to be gone a couple of weeks, so she should be back soon. There's a landline the sitter said she could call to try and reach her in case of emergency but that last she'd heard, Raz was calling from the last place she'd have service. Sitter said she wasn't comfortable giving that number out but that she'd leave a message on our behalf."

"That's good, right?" You think that's good.

"Yeah, except I didn't give that many details in the note I left," Julian says. "Ugh. I wish I had said more, but I didn't know if there actually was a sitter coming by, so I just said that I was worried about Raz and she wasn't answering her phone and asked someone to respond or pass on contact information. I'm sorry, Will. I'll leave another note tomorrow."

"Did the sitter give you her number?"

Hope flickers and goes out the moment the question leaves your mouth.

"Nope. Can't say I blame her, though. She's never met me. I did leave mine," Julian says.

"Thank you for trying. At least we know she's not dead or anything," you say. That is a relief. You just wish you felt more . . . relieved. Backcountry hiking is more adventure than you've ever had, that's for sure. Jealously prickles at you once more like little needles.

"Hopefully we'll get hold of her this week, and if not, she should be home super soon," Julian says. "So that is definitely a plus."

"Yeah," you say.

"Any news about the Frances fiasco?" Julian asks. "I didn't really want to ask about that over texts."

"Not since I blocked everything and let her phone die," you tell them. "Thank god for Matt's spare. Hopefully there won't be any other issues. Though I keep worrying about stupid things, like if I'm breaking the law by not going to the cops with what I know."

"I—" Julian breaks off. "Shit. I don't even know. Is there anyone you could trust to ask?"

"Raz," you say wryly. "I don't know. Maybe the counselor at my school if it came to it, but if she finds out about Frances, she has to run it up the chain, by law."

"This whole thing is a mess."

"You're telling me." You almost can't think of it too closely, the way you can't look directly at the sun. It's too much, too bright, too potentially fatal. "I think Hannah wanted to talk more about involving the police, but thankfully, her new date-person was there at lunch today, and Ashton doesn't know."

"Woof," Julian says. "I wonder what it's like to like, be able to just intrinsically trust the cops."

"No idea," you say. "Must be nice."

There's a long pause. Part of you wants to wonder what made Julian not trust cops, but you don't want to pry. Well. You sort of want to, but you won't.

Yeah. Too much risk you'll get a bad one, or an apathetic one, or one who would rather put you in jail than the folks Frances worked for because you're present and easy and scared.

Nope.

"I should probably get going," Julian says. "It is a school night for wolves."

You glow a bit at that. "It is, but I'll be up a while anyway."

"I should probably attempt to sleep myself soon," they say. "We unicorns may not go into school, but hauling dirty dishes around for customers all night is hard on the mane and muscles."

"I can let you go," you say quickly.

You always miss social cues like that, the way people sometimes try to make it sound like they're bowing out for your sake so they don't feel rude about needing to bow out for their own.

"Please don't," Julian says, and then you hear a slight rustle on the other end that sounds ever-so-slightly like panic. "I mean, I'm happy to keep talking if you want."

"Er, yeah!" Yikes. Yikes, Will, what have you done?

"You should tell me what your plans are for saving Thedas, then," Julian says, a touch of embarrassment still coloring their words.

So you do, nudging into an easy topic for the both of you where you can leave Earth and Earth problems behind. You usually hate talking on the phone, but Julian is nice to talk to.

You never really thought that a world of magic and danger and demons and ancient gods and sentient tectonic plates would be a place you wish you could literally escape to, but hey, at least in fantasy worlds, your choices seem to matter and actually change things.

By the time you get off the phone, it's almost two.

You collapse into bed, dreaming about wolves and unicorns and setting yourself free.

You're not sure you've ever hated your alarm as much as you do Tuesday morning when it goes off at six thirty.

Even worse is that Frances's phone is lit up with messages next to your iPhone, and zero of them are from friends. The friends all have your new iPhone's number.

And Frances's phone is supposed to be dead. It's fully charged somehow. It's not even plugged in.

With your pounding heart in your throat and your stomach churning, you scroll through the messages on France's Galaxy. Your memory is not a fully eidetic one, photographic, but you're ninety-seven percent certain that the few numbers that are not hidden are ones you already blocked.

You scroll past all the *You'll be fucking sorry* ones and then your eye falls on one that makes your stomach acid curdle.

The kid knows where you live.

You know exactly who "the kid" is.

Block, block, block.

You work your way through all of them, blocking the numbers after screenshotting all of the abuse. You feel like you can't trust your own memory right now. Surely you blocked all these numbers before, right? That one that ends in 7733. That's kind of memorable.

A whiff of cigarette smoke makes you feel even sicker. You're probably still half asleep due to exhaustion—the combination of the near-dreaming state and barely plural hours of sleep are not a good recipe for a clear mind.

You'll figure it out later.

Stumbling bleary-eyed into the shower, you stand under the hot stream of water for a solid half hour before you manage to stuff yourself into a pair of jeans and your binder and a black T-shirt. You tousle your hair with a bit of pomade, and it'll probably be a shoulder-length frizz-show by the end of the day, but you do not care.

You're never hungry first thing in the morning, but apparently the lack of sleep has confused your belly. You practically pour the Lucky Charms down your throat.

Hannah texts you at seven to say she'll meet you for coffee.

Coffee sounds like the best invention at this moment.

By the time you make it to school, you are still fuzzy round the noggin and only half-listening to Hannah and Ashton (Ashton, of course, met you at the coffee place too).

Levi's not here.

Your shoulder twinges at the thought of him as your eyes scan his crowd of friends, seeking him out. He's almost always in an eddy of them, like the current exists to flow around his presence, but there's no sign of him, and the group's dynamic feels more frenetic, more chaotic. Like they lack focus without him.

You do not like the implications of that, even though he's probably just faking sick or something. His absence today has the feel of the calm before the tornado that tears your town in half.

A note arrives just before lunch with a request for you to go see Suzie, so you tell Hannah you'll meet her in the cafeteria and make your way to the counselor's office.

Suzie looks up from her computer when you walk in, taking off her glasses and letting them fall to hang round her neck on a little gold chain.

"Will," she says warmly. "I won't take up much of your lunch. I just wanted to check in and see how you're doing."

Belatedly, you remember that the last thing you talked to Suzie about in this office was Raz's letter.

"I'm okay," you say, which is pretty much true. You don't sit down, instead choosing to stand up and fiddle with the zipper on your jacket. "Tired, but caffeinated at least."

"I wanted to check in with you about the letter." Suzie holds up her hands as if to say you don't have to before actually saying it. "You don't have to, but if it was something important to you, you can always talk to me."

"Thanks," you say, doggedly staring at the shelf behind her and hoping that's close enough to eye contact to not look too suspicious. "It's fine. An old friend wanting to make sure I'm okay."

"I'm glad you have someone like that, Will." You are pretty sure Suzie means that.

"Thanks." You also have no idea how to respond to it.

"There was something I was hoping to talk to you about at some point. It's nothing bad, and you're not in trouble—it is something purely for your own personal development. Would you be willing to get a form signed by your mother sometime soon so we may talk it through?"

Her words take you aback, and suddenly, your whole exhausted body feels rigid and tense as your shoulders creep upwards toward your ears like someone's tugging on marionette strings.

"Sure," you say after too long a pause. Personal development? Is that a euphemism for something you don't know? "Sure thing."

Suzie nods.

"I'll let you get to lunch, but please, feel free to stop by and talk to me. About anything," she adds insistently. "I know I say it a lot, but I'm here for you, Will. I'm on your team."

"Go team," you say with a small smile. "Thank you, Suzie."

You really want to believe her.

Maybe you would if it didn't always feel like she was studying you. Even as you leave, even without making eye contact, you can feel her gaze on you like a blowtorch aimed between your shoulder blades. Why do you always get the feeling she's not saying something important?

Because she is. She just told you that. Suzie wants to talk to you about some unidentified topic big enough to need permission to bring up but "not bad." Any hope of trusting Suzie with Frances's death vanishes. Can't get parental consent from a corpse.

Suzie has had ulterior motives all this time. You can't trust that, no matter what she said just now about being on your side. You'd thought maybe she could be an alternative to going to the cops if it became necessary.

Now? Now you don't think you can.

You make your way to the cafeteria, feeling numb and adrift.

Hannah herself is sitting with Ashton with their backs to you when you get your tray. You stop at the condiments table to pile extra pickles onto your flimsy school burger, and when you approach, you can hear them talking.

Your greeting dies on your lips.

"I don't know why they just won't get help," Hannah says. "Like, the cops wouldn't do anything to hurt them. Most people would want to murder Frances if she wasn't already *dead*, and the rest is just bonkers."

"Yeah," Ashton says, sounding awed. "Seriously. What a terrible excuse for a human being. Poor Will."

Poor Will.

You turn on your heel, almost bumping into a sophomore whose name you don't know.

"Shit, sorry," you say.

"Uh, it's okay," the kid says, scurrying away in a cloud of body spray that prickles at your nostrils the way raw onion burns your eyes.

You glance back once, just in time to see Hannah's wide eyes staring after you.

Shit. *Shit.*

Chapter Fifteen

It's only lunchtime. You've never cut class before, but you are tempted. The only thing that keeps you is the cremated skeleton in your proverbial closet. Cutting risks someone asking questions.

You hide in the library until seconds before the bell and scoot into class just as it rings, taking the last seat, which is thankfully at the back of the room where Hannah isn't.

Avoidance isn't the healthiest coping strategy in your arsenal.

But for all that, Hannah catches up to you in the parking lot at the end of the day. She must have bailed from class early. You see her head twitch once, one of the physical tics of her Tourette's. She's holding her hands in front of her, clearly trying *not* to pick at her cuticles like she does when she's super nervous.

Good. She should feel like a jerk, but you do not want to do this right now.

Or at all. You wanted to not do this *ever*, but she had to go and spill your most personal business to someone she's had a close relationship with for what, a pair of weeks compared to literal years? The fear of

Hannah slowly slipping away to be with Ashton has been replaced with something somehow sharper, hotter, like a brand on your skin. *Poor Will.* You are vibrating with anger. You might actually start bouncing across the pavement. Emotion identification doesn't come easily, but this one? This one you know.

"Will," she begins.

"Stop," you say flatly.

"Can we talk about this? I needed someone to talk to about all this. It's a *lot*."

"You have a brother who knows everything and lives with you. You told Ashton because you wanted to tell Ashton, because it's big and juicy and dramatic, and *poor Will* is having a hell of a time." The words pile out of your mouth like they've been dipped in spite and plunked onto an assembly line. "You should have asked me first. I would have said no, but you should have asked."

"Julian knows," she says.

"Seriously? Julian knows because they are Raz's next door neighbor and already knew about both me and how terrible Frances was. Try again."

Ugh. There have been a few arguments with Hannah over the years, but nothing like this. This is a . . . you fish around in your brain for what this is. Betrayal. It's a betrayal.

"She's not going to tell anyone," Hannah protests.

"That's not the *point*," you say, louder than you mean to.

She came here to talk about this and she's not even willing to say she did something wrong? She's just making excuses?

You unlock your car with a click of the button on your key ring, and the little noise it makes is nowhere near satisfying. You want a really loud, really crash-y noise right now.

Hannah is just standing there looking like she's going to cry.

Maybe a good friend would just hug her and tell her it's okay, that they just want her to be happy, and they'll deal with whatever fallout comes from this.

You are pretty sure you're an asshole friend, though, because you're not going to do that. She doesn't get to hurt you and then have your comfort. Maybe before Frances died, when you were caught between Frances hurting you and the fear of losing your only friend, you would have given that comfort to Hannah like you did with a hundred tiny hurts before. Hannah's feelings have always come first.

Fuck this. Fuck all of this. She doesn't get to tell her brand-spanking-new girlfriend about your life's trauma and then come to talk about it and make *you* feel like the monster. Because you are, and the reminder does not feel good.

Yanking open the door, you get in the car without another word. Hannah is still standing there looking utterly lost, like she doesn't understand what is happening or why. Like she expected the comfort. You know she did.

"If you want to figure it out," you say coldly, "ask Matt. He can probably tell you."

You slam the door and start the engine. She's still standing just a few feet away.

You don't look at her as you drive away.

Part of you wonders if she's really always been like this and you just never noticed. Is she really that oblivious to what your life is like? You're starting to think she might be. It's true that you kept the worst stuff from her, but it's not like the middle of the road in the Life of Will was anywhere but a dump.

The car's running low on gas, so you stop at Wawa. Your stomach is growling, and you have to go to work for a few hours anyway, so while the gas is pumping, you go inside and splurge on the cheesiest, greasiest, most delicious sandwich and fries combo you can find along with what is probably the equivalent of a two liter of soda in one enormous cup.

You pull your car around the back, crank up the local rock station as loud as it can go—which is poorly timed since it's a commercial, but you still haven't figured out how to get your new phone hooked up to your car, and she only had country on there, anyway.

There's a beat-up red sedan a few spaces down, and it's packed with grungy-looking white men who look over at the sound of your blasting payday loan commercial playing at high volume. For a moment, something inside your stomach clenches as the sight of them tickles a memory. Maybe one of them was among Frances's conquests over the years. You don't know, and when they lose interest a moment later and go back to whatever they're doing in the car, you stop caring.

Eating is a sorry affair. Everything tastes delicious, but your stomach is roiling with anger and anxiety, and if hunger's the best sauce, this is kind of like pouring antifreeze over your food.

When you get to the library, your body's making some very confused and unhappy sounds round the middle, but you don't care.

Mary waves at you when you come in.

You give her a polite hello, tucking your vat of soda under a shelf with your backpack.

Usually, the quiet of the library is soothing to you. But today it's too silent. Even the few people who are milling around asking Mary for things seem like they've been muted.

You're bad at this. Part of you wants to text Hannah and tell her she's forgiven, but you don't have it in you. You know you need her; she's your best friend.

But you also know that when you need something, you don't get it. That's how life *works* for monsters. Some previous you must have stacked up some majorly crap karma, because you, clear-eyed and realistic, know that you deserve whatever comes trundling your way. You probably did make Hannah tell Ashton. She deserves to confide in someone about all this. She was right about that.

Then you remember her throwing Julian at you like evidence, and something sharp and white-hot cuts through your thoughts as you roll a cart of returns out into the children's section.

That hot, tight ball of ouch in your chest, Will? Yeah. That sucks. It sucks a lot.

You can hear Frances as if she's standing right beside you—also as if she'd ever willingly set foot in a library instead of just making you pick up books she wanted—knowing every thought going through your head.

You think you're hot shit, don't you? News flash, Will, you didn't spring into being because of your own perfection. You're a selfish, spoiled, cruel little princess. But why would you listen to me? You damn well never do unless I'm kissing your ass.

Frances did always call you by your name, but she never hesitated to misgender you.

For a moment you're almost bowled over by the tangled web of mind games Frances always played with you. You're aware enough to know that this isn't *normal*, and maybe even aware enough to know that it's not healthy, but you are a monster, so you figure she's right anyway.

You spent the rest of your work shift going from task to task as if the next one will be the one to fix all your problems.

Before you go home, you go by the post office to check Frances's PO box again. Something Matt said made you feel like you need to make sure of what you assumed—that weed and oxy were the extent of it. There are two more envelopes. With a sick feeling in your stomach, you take them both.

Julian texts you just as you're walking back to your car. *Doubles should be illeeeeeeegal.*

Agreed, you reply. School and then work definitely feels like a double, especially on four hours of sleep. It's not even nine o'clock, and you're ready to pass out.

It's nice hearing from Julian. From someone who understands you.

How was your day? And they even ask about your day.

Kinda crap tbh. To understate it properly. Especially with an armful of drugs you have to decide what to do with.

You send a quick *Brb, driving* to Julian and hop in the car.

You're ravenous again. How is it possible that gorging yourself on junk food just makes you hungrier faster? You consider another round but make yourself drive past Wawa instead of stopping.

What happened? is the text from Julian when you get home and kick off your shoes.

Hannah told Ashton everything, you say, and you quickly explain what happened.

You've literally never talked about Hannah to anyone and it feels weird and kind of wrong, but it *hurts* that she told Ashton without asking you first, and it hurts even more that she didn't even apologize. She just excused.

Dude, Julian says when you've plopped yourself on the sofa with a microwave dinner and a giant cup of orange juice. *That's . . . ugh, I'm sorry. Even if she meant well, that wasn't hers to share, and you don't have to feel bad about being angry about it.*

I do feel bad though, you say.

It takes a while for a response to appear, so you pick at your dinner. You wish you'd given into the urge to get junkier food again.

I know you do, because you're like me. You've been taught that everything's always your fault, but it's not. You didn't deserve to have a parent like Frances, you didn't deserve to get taken away from Raz, and you don't deserve having your very personal business shared to someone you barely know without your permission.

You stare at that for a long moment before you respond. *You feel this way too?*

Waiting for the reply seems to take a decade.

My Frances was my dad, Julian replies at last. *Told me every day I was dirt. He never hit me, but he hit things near me. Just to show he could, just to remind me I was only ever an inch away from his fist.*

There's another stretch of silence. Would you ever tell Julian this was their fault?

I don't like to talk about it, so that's all I'll say. It took me a long time—like two years, idk—to believe I didn't deserve how he treated me. Sometimes I still don't believe it. I can believe it about you a lot easier than I can believe it about me.

It's so close to what you were just thinking that you just stare at Julian's words for a minute.

You didn't deserve to be treated that way, you tell them.

Will? Neither did you. Julian's answer comes almost immediately.

You don't know this feeling. Sure, Suzie the Counselor has said stuff like this to you before—that you didn't deserve what Frances did—but she's paid to try and help increase your self-esteem, and she never really knew the whole story anyway. You very carefully hid your monster face from Suzie, and it's not her fault she doesn't really know how to help you.

But Julian does know. For just a flash, you see a picture of what you could be. Confident like Julian, or maybe just at peace.

Julian is not a monster.

The thought comes to you unbidden, so vehement and bright that it shines like a star in your mind.

Julian is not a monster.

There's a logical next step to take after that thought, but you can't take it. Not yet.

You don't know how to reply, so you scrape the mashed potatoes from the plastic tray with your fork and think.

What if Julian's right?

There's a thought you haven't had before. It's foreign and too bright, and it flashes against the inside of your skull like a supernova going off behind your eyes. It's too much to think of right now. You *have* to believe this is your fault, like Frances said it was. You have to believe you did *something* to deserve this life, Will.

You have to.

Because if Julian's right, if they're right and if you didn't, it means . . . well. It means there is no reason for you to have been literally thrown in the trash as a toddler. It means there is no reason for terrible foster parent after mediocre foster parent after rotten foster parent up until Raz. It means there's no reason you'd find someone like Raz only to be ripped away from her just when you were starting to believe you could be happy.

It means this sort of shit just *happens*, that people like Frances are like that because they *are*, and that they hurt people who don't deserve it.

That's too much.

Your hands feel tingly, and you chug half your orange juice until it sloshes inside your stomach.

Thank you, you write back, even though you don't believe Julian is right. *I just wish I knew what to do.*

Raz'll be back soon, Julian says. *It's gonna be okay.*

It's gonna be okay.

Huh.

That's a thought.

Your conversation turns lighter after that, but Julian's words stick in your mind. Before you go to bed, you open the two new envelopes. One has a single small bag of weed and a note that just says "XOXO"; the other is cash. Putting the cash in your wallet to deposit later, you flush all the drugs down the toilet, even the pot from the first batch. The note goes in the trash. Whether a bonus or a secret admirer, you don't want to know.

France's phone is clinging to battery, so you put it on the kitchen counter, open every app you can, turn the volume off, and turn on a twelve-hour YouTube video.

You leave it there to die.

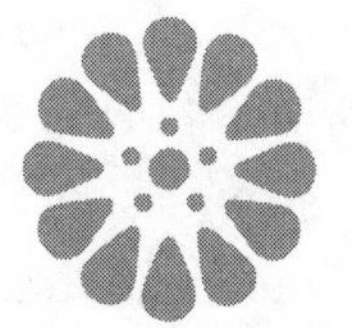

Chapter Sixteen

Hannah isn't at school Wednesday. Ashton isn't there either. But Levi is.

What was a stormy, clashing ball of anger yesterday settles into a slimy, congealing ball of anxiety today. You pass Wednesday in a blur, hiding from Levi—the one glance you get of him is enough to convince you to dive into the nearest bathroom. Though the bruise on your shoulder has faded, you're in no hurry to replace it. It twinges anyway at the very sight of him. You even skip lunch altogether.

You don't get a text from Hannah. You're pretty sure this is the longest you've gone without speaking to her in the entirety of your friendship. It sucks. You hate it a lot.

You don't want to fill that gap with someone else, especially not Julian, because Julian deserves to have their own Julian-shaped unicorn place in your mind. Just because they understand doesn't mean you want to build this friendship on shared pain. They told you last night that they don't like to talk about their own trauma, and you don't want to constantly shower them with yours.

You can't tell Suzie the Counselor about Frances or the drugs, and no way are you opening the Pandora's box of whatever she wanted to talk to you about, but there's one thing you can trust her with, and that's normal high school troubles.

So you do something you've never done before: you ask to go to Suzie the Counselor on purpose, without being prompted.

Your teacher excuses you from last period at your request, and you head for Suzie's office. Superintendent Strand strides toward the principal's office just as you get there, coming this time instead of going. He again seems to not even see you, but from the way his face is a mask of tension and a visible vein on his forehead, that's a good thing. *Someone's* gone and pissed him off. You're just glad it's not you. Maybe a teacher dared to give Levi a B. It's weird that Strand's been here so many times lately.

He almost throws open the door to the office to a startled "Superintendent!" from one of the administrative assistants, and before the door closes with a heavy thud, you hear his answering "What has he done now?"

Is—is the superintendent angry at *Levi*?

Before your world completely spins out of place, you remember why you're here. Right. You better do this before you completely lose your nerve.

You knock on Suzie's door just as she's squinting at her computer screen, her glasses sliding down her nose far enough you wonder how she hasn't realized she has to scrunch up her neck to look down her nose to see through them.

Suzie actually jumps when she sees you, and she hurriedly pulls her glasses off to dangle at her chest again. "Will! What a surprise! Come in, please."

You shut the door without prompting, and you sit in front of her, wondering what you're going to say.

"I think this is the first time you've ever come to see me like this, Will. Are you okay?" Her face is . . . really kind.

You like Suzie, you think.

"Kinda not okay," you hear yourself saying. "I got in a fight with Hannah."

"Oh, Will," she says. "I'm sorry to hear that. I know how important her friendship is to you. Have the two of you talked about it?"

You shake your head. "She wanted to talk about it, but she didn't apologize or anything."

"Do you want to tell me what happened?"

You like that Suzie does that, that she gives you the space to decide how much to tell her.

"She started dating Ashton, and she told Ashton some stuff about me that's private," you say.

When the counselor nods, making her brown curls bounce, you feel a tendril of relief unfurl.

"I can see how that would feel like a betrayal," Suzie says. "When someone shares something with another person, something we told them in confidence, it can be really confusing, especially when we know that person cares about us. She didn't have a right to do that."

It's close to what Julian said. Julian, who is probably half Suzie's age and definitely not a counselor.

You realize then that Julian probably has *seen* a counselor. Maybe even a good one.

"Yeah," you say. "My friend Julian said that."

"They sound wise," Suzie says. "How are you feeling?"

"I don't know. Angry. Really angry. I didn't think Hannah would do that." It might be the most honest thing you've ever said to Suzie about your feelings.

"That's understandable. How did she react when you said you were angry?" Suzie asks.

"She said that Julian knew," you say.

"Julian knowing doesn't mean everyone is allowed to know. I take it you told Julian yourself?" Suzie sits back in her chair a little. There's a small line off-center between her eyebrows, just a dimple of concern.

"Yeah. I told them, and Hannah thinks that means it was okay for her to talk to Ashton about it. She said Ashton wouldn't tell anybody, and that made me even more angry." You feel like you're younger than almost-eighteen. Your words, your voice, they all sound like a kid's voice and words.

"I can see how that would feel frustrating," Suzie tells you. "You thought *Hannah* wouldn't tell anyone without your permission; it stands to reason that someone you trust as much as you trust Hannah, that person's benefit of the doubt does not extend to the people they've decided to include. Does that sound familiar?"

You nod. Suzie actually seems to get it. Your shoulders lose a little of their tension, and you shift in your seat.

"I don't know how to explain it to her if she doesn't already understand it," you say dubiously. "But like, she knew it was wrong. She realized I'd overheard her talking to Ashton about it, and she looked like she'd swallowed a tooth. But then when she came to talk about it, all she did was try and make it sound like I was the one overreacting."

"That's not okay," Suzie says, and you jump at the tone of her voice. "Will, that's called gaslighting."

"I know what gaslighting is." On an intellectual level, anyway.

"Is this the first time something like this has happened?"

"I—I guess so. I don't know. She doesn't always understand why some things are a big deal to me. It's like . . . her family has everything. Her mom makes a lot of money, and she doesn't have to work or do anything but be a kid, and sometimes I feel like she thinks I'm the one who doesn't understand how the world works." It all comes out in a rush. You stop at the end, feeling like your tongue has burned you.

"That sounds really hurtful," Suzie says.

"She's my only friend," you mumble. Shame coats you now, hot and heavy and thick. "I shouldn't have expected she wouldn't need someone else to talk to too."

"Will, your friends should listen to you and be willing to admit when they're wrong," Suzie says gently. "That is the bare minimum of a healthy friendship."

"What if I'm wrong?" You are confused now. Why did you come here?

"I can't speak for all of your friendship, but very simply, someone betraying a confidence is wrong. I hope you will be able to work things out and that she will apologize properly," Suzie says. "This isn't your fault, Will."

The bell rings loudly, and while you don't have to work today, the sudden sound is a reminder that you're at school.

Your lips feel a little numb. "I hope so too."

"Thank you for coming to talk to me," Suzie says, and weirdly enough, you think she actually means it. For a moment, she opens her mouth again, but then she closes it, and you think she changed her mind about whatever she'd been about to say and decided on something else entirely. "I mean it when I say any time. If there is anything you need to talk about, I'm here."

"Thank you," you tell her, meaning it.

This is a new feeling, and one you're really not used to. You walk out of Suzie's office feeling very alone, but for maybe the first time in your life, you feel a little confident that you're not the one who messed up.

Feeling a little confident lasts only until you get home.

With no work to distract you today, the house feels too empty for the first time.

But—and this is no small but—the delivery truck shows up with your new purchase.

That is the distraction you need.

You put your phone in your room and spend the next hour setting up your new PlayStation. It's yours, and if Earth sucks today, at least you can escape into Thedas.

There, you can be exactly who *you* want to be.

It takes you almost an hour just to get through character creation, because you are so hung up on the fact that you get to make someone who can be what you want them to be without worry Frances will see your character and make fun of them that you take way too long.

You make a female elf, but you decide she's trans and give her an Adam's apple, because the nice folks at the game studio made that possible. She gets Mythal's vallaslin in pale, pale blue. Eyes that are pink in their inner ring and blue in the outer, because you know that's how Solas's are. She gets the intricate braided updo for hair and soft, full lips, and she's so perfect and so yours.

Just the sight of the characters on the screen makes you tear up, and you let yourself because this is exactly what you needed.

Time soars by. When you finally break because your bladder's about to burst and your stomach is about to devour itself, you've already plowed through a chunk of the starting area and are already level seven.

Your iPhone is flashing on the corner of your bed. You pick it up after you pee, with a new knot in your gut.

Ugh. This is one part of not having a cell phone you don't think you missed. The anticipation of whether it's going to show you something you want to see or something you don't want to see. How do people do this?

You turn on the screen. There is a text from Hannah, but it's buried under texts from Julian, so you look at those first.

Yoooo I hope your day is going okay! Did you get your PS4??

Omg you made me want to start a new play through, so BEHOLD MY LAVELLAN.

Ugh I was going to do a Dorian romance for realsies this time, but the call of the egg is TOO STRONG

I blame you, wolfy

There's a picture of a Dalish elf—you grin a bit dopey at the sight of Mythal's vallaslin branching up the bridge of her nose just like you chose for your character, but purple on Julian's.

You hurry into the living room and pull up the character screen so you can get a good shot of your Lavellan, and you send a picture back to Julian.

She's perfeeeeect, you say. *He's gonna lose his mind when he sees your Inquisitor!*

You've never really been able to share this game like this with someone. Even with Hannah. She doesn't get the egg love, which, fair.

Dinner. You need dinner. Much as you wish you could subsist on the high of playing your favorite video game alone, you can't.

In the time it takes your food to microwave—you should at least buy a vegetable sometime soon, or you will turn into a walking ball of cheese—you work up the courage to look at the message from Hannah.

I talked to Matt. Will, I'm so sorry. I shouldn't have told Ashton your personal business at all without your permission, and I know I'm excited about finally getting to date her, but that doesn't mean it's okay for me to give her a full backstage pass into your life. I am so sorry. Can I take you out for coffee after school Thursday to apologize properly?

Your stomach does an awkward cartwheel.

Does this feel better? You don't know. Maybe?

It's a real apology, at least. You're not thrilled it took a Matt explanation for it to make sense to her, but you make a mental note to send him a thanks anyway.

Coffee sounds good. Thank you. I'll see you at school tomorrow.

Hopefully Hannah will cope 'til then.

She sends one message back almost immediately. *Phew. Okay. Thank you. Love you. Xoxo*

Okay, that stings, but not in a bad way.

Love you too, you write. Because it's true.

Ugh, this sucks. Is this how it's going to be now? Constant tension of waiting for another Ashton shoe to drop? You hope not.

Then a phone buzzes, but not in your hand. It's Frances's, which you put on the kitchen counter away from any possible power outlet. Despite yourself, you look at it immediately, hoping it's some pointless push notification.

But it's not.

It's a text from one of the blocked numbers. The one that ended in 7733.

You're going to be sorry you fucked with us, bitch.

With your heart pounding in your chest, you screenshot it. Then you write down the number on a notepad and block it for what your gut tells you is the third time.

This shouldn't be possible. The phone is charged again, despite everything you did to kill it. Your throat is dry, so dry it feels like your mucus membranes are just dry, paper-thin layers of cells.

Your brain is full of words, mostly not your own.

Chapter Seventeen

Thursday passes with a frisson of nerves throughout the day. You see Hannah and Ashton both, but after a shy smile, Ashton removes herself. You think it's to give you and Hannah some space, which you appreciate.

Levi is here too. He looks like he's on edge when you catch a glimpse of him, exhausted at the same time. When he sees you, his glassy eyes go flinty, and he makes like he's about to jump you anyway—it's a feint, but several first-years startle around you at his movement, one letting out a squeak. You don't. You stand your ground as they scurry away, and Levi takes one more look at you and punches the nearest locker.

"Strand!" A teacher calls out his surname in exasperation. "Inappropriate! Your father was just here again—do you want me to call him back?"

You dart a glance upward at the ceiling to check for flying pigs. Has any teacher ever chided him publicly before that you know of? And—almost the more unbelievable aspect of this surreal moment—why does it actually sound like Levi's dad coming back to the school would be *bad* for Levi? It's always been Superintendent Strand getting him *out* of trouble, not the other way around.

Levi looks like someone just gave *him* a jump scare, for all of half a heartbeat. Then a wild, rakish grin peels his lips back away from his teeth, and he looks at the teacher, who is half a head shorter than him and has a shaving cut healing on one cheek.

"Just playing percussion," Levi says with saccharine sweetness, eyes unblinking.

The teacher actually takes a step back, and you honestly cannot blame him.

It's enough of a distraction for you to escape.

Your last class is stressful and all about an upcoming test—*already?*— and you shoot out the door like you're propelled by the world's strongest slingshot as soon as the bell goes off, hurrying out to your car.

It's snowing.

You step outside the door of the school in disbelief. It's too early in the year for this, mountains or no mountains.

It's warm enough out that the flakes drop from the sky in thick, heavy clumps. Most of the cars already have a thick layer of white on them. This is going to be atrocious to drive in. You look at your phone. Nothing from Hannah, so you send her a message asking where she wants to meet since you were too jangled to ask.

You pick your way gingerly across the parking lot. Your knockoff Chucks are not cutting it. Moisture seeps through the soles before you've gone more than ten steps. You open the door to your car and turn on the ignition with the defrost on high, since your feet are officially wet and cold. Digging around in the back seat until you find your windshield brush wedged under the back corner of the passenger seat, you tug your sweatshirt over your hands as much as the sleeves will stretch.

It's sticky, wet snow that clings to the bristles of the brush and to the sleeves of your sweatshirt. You do have your coat, but it's just the thin pleather one and doesn't do that much.

You don't notice the footprints in the snow until you are batting snow off the passenger-side mirror.

Weird. There's a depression in the snow in front of each wheel, and—

What. The. Hell.

Your heartbeat leaps into your throat. With the inch and a half of snow, you didn't notice, but the rims of your wheels are resting on the *ground.*

You make your way back around the car in disbelief. All of them. Every single one, flat. When you crouch to take off the caps on the air intake valves, they're secure in place, but when you press on the edge of the tire, air gusts out of a crack in the rubber.

Not a crack. Someone slashed your tires.

It feels like your molten rage boils up from the earth's mantle. You stand there for a moment in the densely falling snow, afraid to move because if you do, you think you will throw back your head, open your mouth, and erupt like a volcano.

Levi.

It had to be Levi.

He threatened you, and now he pulls *this.*

You actually put your fist in your mouth to avoid screaming in pure fury.

You need your car to get to work. You need it to get home. Tires are expensive.

You've got lungs made of starlings in flight, an entire murmuration of them rising up enough that your heels actually leave the snow-covered asphalt. You can't breathe.

Beating in your chest like wings, that flapping might be your heart. It might be. You don't know. You can't think of anything right now, nothing except the cold kiss of fat, sloppy snowflakes landing on every inch of exposed skin. It sticks to your hair, melts into the waves, dips its melting, frozen drops all the way to your scalp and runs in rivulets through the strands there.

In this moment, you think you might dissolve into nothing but lava and feathers and fractal bits of ice.

You're officially the last person here except for the athletes, and there is no way in this frozen-over hell you're going inside to ask any of them to help you. Levi's got to be in there.

The urge to march in there and put your fist all the way through his chest sends you reeling. You're not a violent person. You've never wanted to physically harm someone before.

It's such a . . . *Frances* impulse that you clench both fists, digging your nails into your palms until you can draw more than a ragged breath.

None of this is helping.

You close your eyes like Raz used to tell you to do. A breath in brings winter air when it's only autumn. There are still leaves on the trees, but they're going to fall in enormous clumps with the weight of this icy press upon them.

When you open your eyes again, you fumble for your phone. Still nothing from Hannah. You hate calling, but you have to. Finding her number, you hit the Call button.

It rings, but it keeps ringing. Just ringing and ringing. When it goes to voice mail, you realize you've never actually left Hannah a voice mail before.

"It's Will. I—was ready to meet you for coffee, but I got to my car and fucking Levi slashed the tires, and it's snowing like blizzard-level proportions, and I am stuck at school. Can you come and get me?" You hang up, feeling rotten and cold and burned out.

Now that the fire of the rage has passed, you just feel like ash. You get into the car where it's at least warm, sitting there with the heat blasting until you warm up. It's too quiet, but you can't bring yourself to turn on the radio. There's just the squeaking *fwap-fwap* of the wipers and the tiny pats of snowflake clumps hitting the car's roof.

You lose track of time just staring out the window.

Your phone doesn't make a peep. It's been twenty minutes but the snow is coming down even harder. Every minute you waste makes it deeper to walk through. You turn the car off. Lock it. Sling your backpack over your shoulder where it's almost certainly going to get soaking wet in this snow, including your books and notebooks and stuff.

If you're going to have to walk home, you better get started.

You tuck your iPhone into your binder, facing away from the school to wedge it between your smushed boobs and the tight fabric, because you'd rather have it a little sweaty than soaking in melting snow in a pocket the whole way home.

Your feet are cold again before you even reach the road outside of the school.

Steeling yourself, you start walking.

You know, there's a part of *Inquisition* where your character trudges through knee-deep snow escaping from something that wants her dead.

You're not quite melodramatic enough to think Levi will kill you, but you gain a whole new appreciation for that scene. You are shivering and soaked from head to toe when you get home, and your fingers fumble on your key ring. Getting the door open is a miracle.

It's warm inside the house at least, and you drop your sodden backpack just inside the door and kick off your sodden shoes.

Shedding clothes as you walk, you make a beeline for your room and your bathroom, grabbing your onesie and a pair of long johns from your drawer as well as a thick pair of socks. You turn the shower on as hot as you can stand it and pull out your iPhone.

Still nothing from Hannah. Unbelievable.

You send a curt *Nvm, I walked*, and it takes every ounce of remaining self-control you have to not throw the phone across the room.

Instead, you put it on your dresser and shut the bathroom door behind you.

You're still shivering.

You fight back tears as you climb into the shower. The water is hot, almost scalding. Your skin turns from too-pale, sun-deprived olive to ruddy pink in instants, and you don't even care.

You stay there a long time. As long as you think you can risk it. The water heater isn't the best in this single-wide.

The shower doesn't fix much but your temperature. You're exhausted.

At some point, you need to think about your options, Will. You can't just pretend none of the last hour and a half happened. Something in the attic of your mind knows you should probably tell Suzie about this. Or hell, at this point call the cops because someone maliciously slashed your tires.

Like they'd do anything to the golden boy football star whose dad is the superintendent.

Brain fuzz claims you before you make it out of your room. You collapse on your bed in your wolf onesie, curling up around your body pillow. You think you could go to sleep right now, right here, but you should probably do the grown-up thing instead, because that's what you generally do.

So you get up.

You pad out into the living room to grab the laptop. It's sitting where you left it on the kitchen counter, and as you approach, the security light in the back yard turns on.

Your shower-wrinkled fingers freeze on the cool metal of the MacBook Air.

Deer, raccoon, opossum, squirrel, elk—there are any number of creatures that regularly trigger that light, but when you move around the peninsula of the counter to peer out the kitchen window over the sink, it's not animal prints you see in the snow.

Footprints.

Not yours.

They lead away from the seldom-used back door on the rickety porch, toward the shed, where they seem to crisscross in front of the door.

A rushing sound begins in your head, and you react on pure instinct, throwing yourself away from the window. Scrambling down the hall into Frances's room, you don't even bother to turn on the light as you go to the top drawer of the bureau where Hannah put the Colt .45.

You don't know how to shoot it; of course you don't. But if someone's out there . . .

Ears already hot from the shower, they start to tingle with adrenaline and the newer inrushing of blood.

The gun is heavy in your hands when your fumbling fingers find it, and you make your way back down the hall on teetering feet.

What are you even going to do, Will? Shoot someone? Like you'd even hit them.

But when you get back to the window, the light is still on, and you see something you didn't notice before in your panic.

Throwing the door open, you ignore the blatant danger, hand holding the Colt tight.

Sure enough, they *are* footprints. But they're not just any footprints.

They're fucking boots. *Boots*. Big ones, too.

That's not even the weirdest part.

The footprints start at the door. Like—like someone just stepped out over the threshold and into the snow.

You're losing it. The walk home froze your brain.

Closing the door with a thud and locking it, you set the gun down on the edge of the counter, tucked into a fruit bowl that has never actually held fruit in its entire existence. It's full of mail and random condiment packets instead, and now a firearm.

It takes maybe ten minutes for your heartbeat to settle down into your chest where it should be, slowly working its way downward from where you were about to choke on it. You take long, steady breaths, reaching for the MacBook now with shaking hands.

You Google what to do about hypothermia just in case.

Shower, check. Warm clothes, check. You get up and put water in the teapot to heat.

You vaguely remember there being booze somewhere in the house.

You've literally never drank anything alcoholic in your life. It's not the best sign of your mental state that it sounds almost like a good idea now.

Still, you fight it back. Frances gave you a tour de force of alcoholism firsthand, thank you very much, and it's never held allure.

In the recesses of another cupboard is a nearly empty bag of stale mini marshmallows, which settles you on hot cocoa.

You take your steaming mug into the living room. Exhaustion tugs at the sides of your mind.

When look at your iPhone again, a message from Julian pops up.

How are you today?

The simple question is so welcome, but you are such a wreck you're afraid to answer it. A panicked laugh bubbles out of your mouth at the thought of telling them about the footprints. Julian's going to think you're a hot mess.

Well. You're kind of a hot mess, Will.

You tell the truth anyway.

Uhhhh so I think Levi slashed my tires, and it's a fucking snowstorm, and Hannah stood me up, and I had to walk home in the snow. And there were some weird footprints around the house in the snow. I just got out of the shower and made an enormous vat of hot cocoa, and I'm just going to sit here and feel sorry for myself.

You hit Send before you lose your nerve. The omission burns worse than the scalding sip of cocoa. It feels like lying, and you have never liked anything resembling that feeling.

For a while, when Julian doesn't immediately reply, you just watch mind-numbing YouTube art videos.

When was the last time you drew anything?

Fuck. Your sketchbook.

You jump up from the sofa and bump the coffee table, sloshing hot cocoa over the surface, but you don't even care.

Your backpack is lying where you left it in a soggy lump of blue stars. Unzipping it, you pull everything out and spread it out on the carpet around the floor vent.

Your textbooks, your brand-new sketchbook, your new notebooks—they're all *damp.* The textbook pages have swollen enough that there's a chance the school will charge you for damage.

You just did your school shopping to have a fresh start, and now they're bloating up like paper corpses.

For a moment, you can almost hear Frances's laughter.

This day is the worst.

You kind of want to scream.

A *ping* on the iPhone says someone sent you a message.

You can't do anything about the books now, so you leave them after draping a blanket over a stool to try and keep the heat in and dry them out in a makeshift tent.

Whaaaaaaat is all Julian's said, but they're typing more.

Will, that is messed up. Ugh, Levi's the one whose dad's the . . . principal? Something? Small towns, man—would they even do anything to him? Are there cameras that show the parking lot at all? And the footprints??? That is not good. Can you tell Matt or something?

And that just . . . really sucks about Hannah. Maybe she had something happen or something??? I'm worried about you. You walked all the way home in the snow? Isn't it like a fifteen-minute drive??

So many question marks.

For once, it's you who asks to call. Julian immediately agrees, and you video-call them.

"God, Will, you look exhausted," they say, looking a bit rumpled themself. "Ugh, I am so, so sorry. Are you okay? Is there anything I can do?"

What a bittersweet pang. You are so thankful for them asking, but this should be Hannah caring, Hannah worried, Hannah giving a flying fuck whether you made it home safe or not.

Still, Julian cares. Julian *understands* in a way you've never felt understood by anyone but Raz. You are dying of thirst in the middle of the ocean, and Julian is fresh, sweet rain.

Chapter Eighteen

It takes approximately fifteen seconds when you wake up Friday morning to decide not to go to school. Your head is fuzzy and thick, and it feels enough like an oncoming cold that you are not risking it. You'll forge a note from Frances if you have to, which'll cause problems if anyone ever finds out she's dead, but you'll risk "my zombie mother excused my absence" to not have to get out of bed.

You have Frances's car at least, so it's not like you'll have to walk to work tonight—you will still go to work—but the thought of getting into it and its sharp rose-scented interior is too much.

Staring up at the ceiling, you hope Raz gets home soon. Julian said they hadn't heard back from the pet sitter (who, frankly, seems like just a bit of a flake to you), but they promised last night they'd leave another note saying it's urgent that they get in contact with Raz, so hopefully this person will pass on the message.

When you pry yourself out of bed at eight, you make coffee and some scrambled eggs and check your email.

You haven't looked at your iPhone since last night, and when you screw up the courage to plod into the bedroom and do so, not only is it almost out of battery, but there is a whole slew of missed calls from Hannah. Even a couple from Matt, one from only ten minutes ago.

Raz used to tell you that if you have something unpleasant to do, sometimes setting a window of time for yourself to not do it can help you work up to doing it. You plug the phone in to charge and decide that when the phone's battery is at fifty percent, you'll deal with it.

Just doing that reminds you of Frances's phone where you shoved it behind the fruit bowl full of mail and ketchup—the one with the Colt .45 in it—and a tinny panic sparks in your heart.

Breathe, Will. Fifty percent and you'll deal with it.

Until then, you're going to eat your eggs and play *Dragon Age*.

Well. After you email Suzie. You figure you can fudge the Frances thing a teeny bit with her, and you temper it with a bit of truth.

Suzie,

I had to walk home in the snow after school yesterday (flat tire) in the snow, so I'm not feeling so well today. Frances isn't around to call, and I probably can't excuse my own absence, but I thought I should let someone know, I guess.

Will

Hopefully she'll get it.

After that, you also open the back door to see the footprints again. They're nowhere to be seen—either the wind blew the snow over them or you imagined them in your hypothermic haze.

Never in your life did you expect you'd hope to have hallucinated.

You settle in to play some *Dragon Age*, losing yourself in gathering random herbs, because at least you can help some fictional refugees even if you can't really help yourself.

You don't realize that helping yourself is exactly what you've been doing all morning.

When someone knocks at the door, you almost jump out of your skin.

You put down the controller, your heartbeat palpable in your teeth.

Has one of Frances's people found you? You don't know. The phantom footprints from last night seep back into your memory. You slowly edge back from the patch of carpet where you've been sitting to play—the sofa's too far back for you to see—and look at the door. The blinds are closed on the window, so you can't see who's out there.

The knock comes again, insistent.

"Will? It's Matt."

Oh.

You get up and go to the door, opening it. Sure enough, Hannah's brother stands on the doorstep all bundled up in a hat and scarf and Timberlands. Breath makes puffs of vapor in front of his face, indicating that it's still damn cold out there.

"Hi," you say. You don't know what else to say.

Holding the door open for him to come in, he kicks the doorjamb a couple of times to shake the snow loose from his boots and steps inside.

You shut the door behind him.

"Uh. Want some coffee?" you ask.

"Sure," he says. "Are you okay? We've been worried sick about you."

"Sorry," you say. "I'm fine, but I couldn't face school today."

"Hannah said Levi slashed your tires? I drove by school on my way here, and someone definitely did." Matt bends to unlace his shoes, wiggling his feet out of them while you go into the kitchen to pour him a cup of coffee.

"It had to be Levi, unless I'm collecting enemies the way some people collect secret admirers," you say.

"I've got AAA," he says. "I can get your car towed to the shop if you want. It's no problem."

"I don't have the money for four new tires," you say bluntly. "But thanks. I guess if you want to just have it towed here, that'd work until I can figure something out. I can change a tire myself, and I have one spare. So I guess I only need to save up for three."

Matt just stares at you for a second, but then he nods. You hand him a mug.

"Don't you have to work?" You pour yourself some more coffee while you're at it, dumping in a bunch of pumpkin spice creamer this time.

"I'm off 'til three today," he says. He hesitates, lifting the mug to his lips. "Will, you're not alone."

You return his stare, and he shifts his feet uncomfortably. Leaning against the counter, you feel awkward. What do you say? *I wasn't alone until your sister stood me up and left me to walk home in a damn snowstorm.*

"Hannah's really sorry," he says after a beat. "She feels terrible."

"Good." It leaves your mouth before you can think. You wince. "Shit. I'm sorry, Matt. I'm . . . really upset."

"You don't have to apologize to me," Matt says softly. "Hell, in your place I'd be spitting gravel. I came over mostly to check on you. Mom doesn't know you walked home yesterday or she'd probably be here herself with a cauldron full of soup."

It's . . . a weird thing to say. Weird mostly because he means it. The words bounce around your skull like they're in a completely different language, and maybe they are. Is this what moms do? It's what Raz would do, you guess. You always just thought she was the exception and not the rule. The sudden confusion that accompanies the bloom of doubt nearly overwhelms you. You cannot think about this right now, the "what if people like Raz *are* the rule and not the exception" thing.

"Thanks," you say, for lack of a better idea.

"For what it's worth, Hannah said that missing Wednesday at school's why she messed up yesterday. She says she thought it was Wednesday all day, not Thursday," Matt says, stopping to sip from his coffee. "But since Ashton came over while Mom was at work when Hannah was home 'sick' the day before, it's not the best excuse, as far as excuses go."

That—you'll try to process that in a minute. For now, it chases away the remainder of the existential crisis you punted into the back of your mind. You're surprised to hear that note of annoyance in his voice. "Matt?"

He sighs. "I'm a little unnerved that she's so infatuated with someone she just started dating that she's risking fucking up her oldest friendship."

Whoa.

"Uh," you say because you don't know what else to say. Finally, you shrug. "I mean, same."

"I know you already know this, but my sister doesn't quite see how good she has it sometimes," Matt says then. "She knew Jacob, obviously, but she—"

"You don't have to explain it to me, Matt," you say, and he looks relieved. "Part of it's kind of my fault anyway. I never really told her how bad it was with Frances. She knew about me paying some of the bills and knew Frances was big into the booze, but some of the rest . . ."

You trail off, because even Matt doesn't know. You think he's guessed some of it.

When he meets your eyes, he just gives you a noncommittal look as if to say you can tell him and he won't judge.

"When she'd get really drunk, sometimes she hit me," you say softly. You've never said these words out loud. "Less the last couple years, but last year she went on a bender and hit me with a chair in the spring. But I'd almost rather she do that than the rest. The mind games, the constant flipping of the script. You know she used to tell me I should be grateful? Told me I was selfish and spoiled all the time."

Matt's face takes on a tinge of horror. "Will, I'm so sorry."

You wave your hand. "She is literally dead now."

"Well, yeah, but like . . . that doesn't just fix everything."

Doesn't it? Something of your confusion must show in your eyes.

"Jacob's dad was abusive like that," Matt says after a minute, and whatever you were going to say vanishes. Abusive. "He used to just put Jake down all the time. No matter what he did. No matter how good his grades were, no matter how many touchdowns he got. Like, Jake was all-state. Over two hundred pounds of muscle, but his dad would look at him, and suddenly he was a kindergartner with skinned knees."

"Shit," you say, because you had no idea.

"Yeah," Matt says. "People use for all sorts of reasons. A lot of the time I think it's self-medication. Something's wrong, and they try to fix it that way. Some people, like Frances, deal with their pain by causing more. Other people, like Jake, try to numb it away completely. And then there's you."

Well. This is not where you thought your morning was going. You take a gulp of your coffee because this is getting real.

"I'm going to say something I had to tell Jacob a lot, okay? And you're probably not going to believe me, but I mean it, and it's also objectively true." Matt looks at you with the kind of intensity you've seen on TV, a protectiveness. He looks like . . . a big brother. "It's not your fault. You didn't do this. You didn't cause it, you didn't deserve it, and you couldn't have stopped it. Frances did this to you. She was a monster, and it's okay for you to feel glad she's gone."

She was a monster.

The words are so alien because they clash with everything you know. You are a monster, right? You are.

You can't manage to make any sounds happen, but Matt doesn't seem to expect it.

"I spent a long time last night talking to Hannah. I didn't know for sure about Frances until you told me just now, but Jake was my best friend," Matt says quietly. "I knew him better than anyone else did. I learned his signs pretty well. After Frances died, I've spent more time with you. I've guessed that Frances might have been a bit like Richard. I was the only one Jake let see what his dad did to him, and it eventually killed him."

He says it so simply, something in your heart breaks.

"You're not alone, Will," Matt says again. He slurps down the rest of his coffee and sets the empty mug on the breakfast bar. "Even if Hannah can't get her shit together and step up for you, you're not alone. You've got me, and I don't want to make it weird, but you're like family to me too. Whatever you need."

Something hot burns at your eyes. This feeling is utterly foreign to you. Like something remembered from a good dream you woke up from into a nightmare. But real.

It's a Raz feeling.

"Thank you," you say to him. Your voice is all crumbly round the edges. "For everything."

"That's what brothers do," Matt says.

He leaves then to get your car towed, saying he'll be back later. You give him your spare car keys and tell him if Hannah wants, she can stop by after school.

You're not sure you believe him, that it's not your fault, but he said it anyway.

That, at least, is real.

You're feeling wistful and a little achy when Hannah arrives.

This time you actually hear the tires on the gravel outside, and you pause your game and get to the door, opening it when her hand is raised to knock.

Hannah looks awful. Her red hair is in a sloppy bun, and while she's wearing makeup, her eyelids have that puffiness to them that says she's been crying. Her freckles are the only spots of color on her face.

You step back for her to come in.

"Will, I'm so sorry," she says, all in a rush when the door closes. "I fucked up. I hurt you, and I made Matt mad at me, and—"

She drops off when you give a small shake of your head. You don't really want to hear about how bad she feels, which surprises you.

"You've never done that before," you say after a beat. "You've never like . . . completely disregarded my feelings before, not to that degree. Where even were you?"

She winces, her jaw twitching with her tics. "Ashton and I kind of stayed up until five in the morning texting Wednesday, so Thursday I went home and fell asleep."

"You fell asleep." You repeat the words like they don't quite fit in your mouth. "You just forgot about me and fell asleep. And this is after like what, one date with Ashton? I get being excited over her liking you back, but *Jesus*, Hannah."

"I know. I'm sorry." Hannah glances at the Pause screen on the television and goes to perch on the edge of the sofa. "She just seems to *get* me."

That brings a pang with it, the implication being that you don't. But isn't that what you've thought about her? Julian understands you in ways Hannah doesn't.

Hannah seems to sense it after a second. "Sometimes lately I feel like there's this gap between us. I don't know why it's there or why it started."

She looks confused, like she's thinking back over things but can't see the pattern in the chaos. Her knee bounces, and she stills it when she notices.

"Matt said he talked to you," you say hesitantly.

"Yeah," she says. The word sounds dubious. "I don't know if he was right about everything, but—"

"He was right," you say. Flat. Unwavering. "Probably barely scratched the surface if he was guessing, but he was right."

Her head snaps up, and she chews on her lip. "He said a lot of stuff. About Frances. Matt thinks Frances was like—like Jacob's dad. Who used to hit Jacob."

"I know. Matt told me."

Hannah waits for you to go on, like she's bracing herself.

You really hate this whole conversation. You kind of wish you could just jump through a portal into another world, but none opens up to take you.

"Remember last year when I said I tripped and fell against a table?" you ask. When Hannah nods warily, you go on. "I had that nasty bruise for weeks. Yeah, that was bullshit. Frances got drunk and hit me with a chair. Real hard."

Hannah stares at you.

Something kindles in the void of your chest. "On my fifteenth birthday, she brought home a guy from a bar, and he called me a freak when he saw me. Frances wouldn't let me go to my room. She grabbed my shirt when I tried to get away and wouldn't let it go. They both just laughed and laughed at me, and he went into my room and tore up my sketchbook. The one with my pictures of Bull and Dorian."

"You said you just lost that sketchbook." Her voice is so small, so fragile.

"Yeah, I did," you say. "He didn't like . . . actually hurt me. I was grateful. Can you believe that? Grateful. I got off easy that time."

"Will—"

"You know what Frances said right before she died? She literally pointed at me and said *this is your fault*," you say. The words are just pouring out of you now. "She used to say shit like that all the time. One time I was a couple of days late paying her cell phone bill, and when she got the reminder text about it, she told me I was an ungrateful piece of shit who couldn't tie my own shoes. And then she told me it was my fault we didn't have a normal life, because I was an *ungrateful* daughter who had never really loved her."

Hannah's mouth is hanging open like a baby bird's. It moves a couple times like she is trying to say something but is too shocked.

You pull up the sleeve on your onesie. "This scar? Not a fall in the shower. She pushed me into the screen door a couple summers ago because I wasn't fast enough with her beer. That time I missed school last spring? She found out I went to see *Captain Marvel* with you."

"Will, why didn't you *tell* me?" Hannah bursts out. "You shouldn't have had to live with her! You—"

"What, could have gotten put back into the system again? Risk landing with someone worse?" You're crying now, angry tears. "At least she called me by my *name*, Hannah. A queer nonbinary trans kid getting put in foster care in *this* Fox News–loving county? I was just trying to *survive*. And I have. I did. She's dead, and I'm alive."

It's the first time you've ever said anything like that, and you realize it's absolutely *true*. True down to your marrow, in every cell and every bone of your body. You feel it ring through your damn fingernails.

You might be a monster, but you are still standing.

"I just have to get to my birthday, and then I'll be an adult, and *no one* will ever make me feel that way again. No one will be able to force me to live with someone like Frances ever again." It comes out of your mouth quietly, but with the force of mountains behind it.

"You should have told me so we could take *care* of you," Hannah says.

And that knocks you sideways.

"What?"

"My mom's a lawyer, Will. A good one. If she'd known, she would have had you out of this dump so fast, it'd leave a dust trail. She would have had Frances behind bars," Hannah says vehemently.

Naturally, out of all that, your brain fixates on the word *dump.* It hits you like a needle to a bruise, small and sharp, and you can't help but look around the single-wide. The thing you've spent the last weeks cleaning incessantly, putting up posters and framing them. Making it smell nice, or at least like things you like.

"Your mom is *yours,*" you say instead. "There's no way of knowing what even would have happened if she'd tried."

"I know my mom," Hannah insists. "She would have—"

"You can't fix everything just by throwing money at it!" you say, louder than you meant to.

"Is that what you think I mean?" Hannah is very still now, everything but her face, which is twitching just a little.

"Yes. No." You clench your fist and unclench it a bunch of times, almost drumming your nails against your palm. "I don't know. Fuck, Hannah, you have a mother who fixes things. I had pretty much the exact opposite. You can't just walk up to someone and be like, hey, my life sucks, can I join yours? That's not how life works."

"No, it's not," Hannah agrees. "But people help each other when they care, and I care."

There's silence for a moment.

"I wish you'd trusted me," she says.

There it is. That's the crux of it, the place where the wedge got driven in.

Because you didn't. You couldn't. You knew she wouldn't understand, and everything in the past few weeks has been like that, proof.

"I need you to understand something," you say. When you meet her eyes, she gives a small nod as if to say she's listening. "You trust authority figures. You have a mother who helps make sure the law serves the people. Every time something's gotten worse over the past few weeks, you've suggested going to the cops, because you trust them to help."

Hannah nods slowly, waiting.

"You know what authority figures have done for me?" you ask. "Once I called the cops on a foster parent who hit my foster brother. You know what they did? Nothing. Didn't even believe me. And the kid was so terrified that he denied it, because he'd already learned what I hadn't yet. They took me away from Raz. They gave me back to Frances. Why in the fucking hell would I trust them to do anything but ruin my life more?"

You watch as she processes that. You half-expect her to argue, but instead she just sighs.

"I'm so sorry, Will. That's not how it's supposed to work."

"I know. At least in theory. You don't see what's broken because it works *for you*." You see as it clicks for her, almost an audible snap of ideas coming together like magnets.

"I'm sorry," she says again. "I was—I messed up. You want to know something absolutely ridiculous?"

"Sure?" You really aren't sure.

"I was jealous of you."

"What." That cannot be what she just said, but it is.

"Yeah. You've got a place of your own, can come and go as you please. You're free, and I like . . . can't wait for that." Hannah shrugs, looking uncomfortable.

"This is not freedom," you say flatly. "You know what happens if I don't work? I don't eat. You will always have a net to catch you if the ground gives out underneath you. I never will. Do you know what that's like? Watching your life spread out before you and knowing that every month is going to be spent wondering if some disaster is going to befall you, like some piece-of-shit bully slashing your tires when you don't have a grand to replace them?"

You're angry again because this is ridiculous. You think you're also angry that she knows it's ridiculous, because it's like her using the word *dump* again.

"What can I do?" she asks quietly. "How can I fix this?"

It's the right question, or the right pair of them.

"I don't know," you say. "Maybe try and figure out how to reconcile the fact that you just called my house a dump in one sentence because you know how good you've got it, but then say you envy it in the next."

You think she might clam up at that, but to your surprise, she nods.

"That is . . . a good point," she admits. "I'm sorry I called your house a dump."

It's close to *trailer trash*, which she did once say, back in the early days of your friendship before she knew you lived in something very close to one.

Hannah takes a shaky breath. "I think like—I don't know. I knew it was bad with Frances, but I didn't know how bad. I assumed you'd tell me if it was worse, but I think I understand why you didn't. I should have been a better friend."

You're quiet, because she doesn't sound like she's done.

"Not just this week," Hannah says dryly, "because obviously. But before. If I expected you to trust me, I should have tried harder to be someone you could trust."

You swallow. You're tired of standing up, but you aren't quite to the point of being comfortable going to sit beside her yet, which stings a little.

Hannah takes a deep breath, looking around as if she can't believe what she's about to say. "I took one of Frances's dresses," she blurts out.

"You *what*?" Your voice is a crack of thunder in the sudden silence after her words, but then you see that flash of peacock blue-green again, first as she breezed past you after her date—she wore one of Frances's dresses on that fucking date!—and again when she was packing at the end of the weekend. She clearly hadn't wanted you to see it; Hannah had shoved leggings on top of it the moment you came into the room.

For some reason, a laugh cracks open your throat and pours out, brittle and helpless.

Hannah just stares at you, bewildered.

"You were going to donate it, and it's—it's my favorite color, and I don't know what came over me. I just had to have it, had to wear it." She shakes her head. "That's not even an excuse."

"God, you can keep it," you tell her, and you think you even mean it. Your throat feels raw from the sharp report of your sudden laughter, even as brief as it was. "I'm not going to wear it."

It is kind of fucked up, though. To your surprise, Hannah opens her mouth and says exactly that.

"It's fucked up," she says all in a rush. "I was just—I don't know. It was just my size and I looked perfect and it wasn't until that Sunday after the sleepover that it hit me what I'd done. Frances stole your money from you, and I just . . . took advantage of it myself."

"Yeah, you did," you say, because you don't really know what else to say. "But seriously, it's almost poetic, in a way. Frances would hate knowing it looked that much better on you."

It's the truth.

God, she'd be pissed.

Hannah cracks a broken smile, but it doesn't reach her eyes. "Are we—are we okay?"

You let out a breath that sounds more like releasing the steam from the Instant Pot on manual, a hiss.

"We're not *not* okay," you tell her slowly. That's about as good as it's going to get for now. Your smile feels every bit as broken as hers. "I think we can be okay."

Hannah nods, letting out her own breath.

You have to go to work. When you say so, Hannah nods.

"Matt got your car towed," Hannah says, and she holds up a hand when you open your mouth to ask. "To a shop. His buddy works there, and he might not get to it for a few days, but Matt's taking care of it."

Shame fills you, along with an unfamiliar burst of helplessness. "I told him I can't afford—"

"He knows, Will. Matt's taking care of it. We both are. He wouldn't let me put more than a hundred in, but I—but I did that much." Hannah looks at you as if she's seeing you for the first time, and something in her face reflects it back to you. Something vulnerable and afraid. "You don't have to pay us back. Let us help."

"It's so much money," you say.

Hannah opens her mouth and closes it again. You think she was going to say *it's really not*, but realized that was only true for her.

She gets up to leave, but she stops a couple of feet away from you where you're still hovering at the edge of the breakfast bar.

"I'm really sorry," she says again. "I'll be better. You deserve that from me. You may not have told me everything always, but you trusted me with everything that's happened lately, and I messed up. I won't do it again."

Hannah feels closer than she has for the past month. You believe her.

On impulse, you hug her, and after a startled moment, she hugs you back. Hard.

When you pull away, you stand there, wheels in your head turning with an impulse that never would have occurred to you six months ago. It's not the money; it's not that Matt and Hannah conspired to pay for those tires. It's the fact that they helped—and that they've been here all along. Hannah said her mother can be trusted.

All of a sudden, you are recalculating risk.

"You look like you're either about to cry or about to yell." Hannah watches you sideways.

"Maybe both," you say in a wobbly voice. "Do you really think your mom can keep me out of the system?"

It almost doesn't feel like you saying the words, but it is.

Hannah's eyes widen. "Yes, I do. Without a single doubt. I've been researching myself, and most court processes seem to take, well. Longer than the time before your birthday, for one. But Will, Maryland lets minors weigh in on who they live with from age *sixteen*."

"What?" This shouldn't be news to you, but it is. You've been so used to treading water that you stopped looking around for a lifeboat long ago. "How long have you known this?"

Some of the uncertainty returns to Hannah's face, but she plows on anyway. "Only a few days, but I didn't want to seem like I was pushing you to go to the authorities, and then . . ."

Right. Then Ashtongate. You don't actually want to think of it that way, but before you can replace that impulsive name, Hannah continues.

"That's not all," she says. "The courts also have to consider what's in your best interest, and I *know* we could convince them it's not in your best interest to uproot you."

You're about to protest, but she holds up a hand, desperation taking root.

"I'm not just saying that, Will. You have evidence. You have looked after yourself even while Frances was alive. All the bills you paid, how you've handled Frances's death yourself, all of it. No one could argue that you aren't capable."

That, for the first time in a while, makes you feel like Hannah really is trying to understand. Your eyes prickle with a sensation all too close to tears. Blinking, you swallow as if you can make it go away. It's only half successful.

"Okay," you say. "You can—you can tell your mom."

Hannah throws her arms around you again, somehow with an even more crushing grip than before. You hug her back, the world spinning around you, dizzying with the leap of faith.

"We'll make sure you get through this," Hannah says. "I promise."

Chapter Nineteen

Even though you had the foresight to take the horrible air freshener out of Frances's car before you went to bed Friday, when you open Frances's car door Saturday afternoon, a gust of sickly rose-scented cigarette residue blasts you in the face. Hannah wasted zero time after she left your house, and you're going to meet with a lawyer called Joseph Landry—and Dana, Hannah's mom, who got this meeting set up an hour flat after Hannah told her.

After the meeting, you'll update Julian on how it went—you told them last night—and ask about Raz. One thing at a time.

You read the email Dana sent last night again while the car warms up.

Hi Will!

I've cc'd Joseph Landry on this email to introduce the two of you. He will be able to tell you what documents he needs from you to be able to move forward with probate, and we will see you tomorrow. It's okay if you don't have all the documents right away; we can figure it out together. Probate cases can be overwhelming even to people who are prepared to face them.

I hope you're holding up okay. Please don't hesitate to reach out if you need anything.

Dana

It's a nice email, and you really do appreciate this Joseph person offering to help you pro bono. You actually managed to find most of what he asked for—the deeds to the house and cars, bank statements, all things you kept track of for Frances.

In spite of the chill in the air, you drive into town with the windows down so you don't go into this potentially life-altering meeting with a blazing headache. Frances's death certificate sits on the seat next to you along with the rest of the documents you thought might be important. You probably won't need all your pay stubs from the library, but just in case, there they are.

This is really happening. You're really going to meet with lawyers.

You pull up in front of Bright Springs's small strip mall on the east side of town. There's not much there but the Subway and a nail salon, and this lawyer's office. Landry and Smalls, attorneys at law.

The sight of the place is strange and sobering. You don't know how to do any of this, but Dana promised to help. You get out of the car and gather up the documents on the seat.

No one told you what to wear, so you opted for comfort. Black jeans, white T-shirt, your usual jacket.

You wish you had a folder or something to put all this stuff in.

There's a light on inside, and the door opens easily when you pull on it, but no one is at reception. A bell jingles on the door, though. After a moment, a skinny white man in khakis and a blue button-down shirt walks out. He's younger than you expected. Maybe in his thirties? You're terrible at judging ages. He gives you a warm smile.

"Are you Will?" he asks. "I'm Joseph."

"Hi," you say, clumsily shaking his hand around the papers you're holding. "Is Dana already here?"

"She sent me a text to let me know she was running a couple of minutes late. Come on in. Can I get you something to drink? Tea? Cocoa? Coffee?" Joseph leads you past the reception desk to a conference room with a Keurig in the corner.

"Can I put the cocoa in the coffee?" you ask with a sheepish smile.

He gives you a pair of finger guns. "Kid after my own heart. Have a seat. I'll get it going."

You sit at the table, wishing you'd organized your stuff better. There's a burbling in the corner while Joseph makes the Keurig do its thing, and just as he asks you something about creamer, the bell at the door jingles, and Dana comes bustling in.

"Will, honey, sorry I'm late," she says. "I'm truly sorry you're having to go through this."

"I just got here," you tell her, and she smiles gratefully, sitting down in the chair beside you.

The "I'm sorry about your mother" is notably missing, and you're grateful. You don't think Dana is a hugger, and it's a bit of a relief that she doesn't try to hug you. This is a lot without factoring in physical contact.

Dana is in the same sort of lawyer casual as Joseph, but with dark blue slacks and a white blouse. Dana always looks very together.

"May I?" she asks, nodding to the papers beside you.

This could backfire.

What if they want to call social services or something? Your back tightens, the muscle clenching all the way up your spine for a moment until you physically try to relax again.

"Sure," you say.

Joseph puts a steaming mug in front of you, complete with little hard marshmallows.

The lawyer sits down while Dana pages through the stuff you brought. You notice she's sorting into piles—death certificate, deed for the house, car titles, and bills in one pile and your report cards in the other.

Your face is suddenly a bit warm.

"All right, Will," Joseph says. "Right from the start, I want to establish that you aren't going to get put back in foster care, okay?"

This is not what you expected him to lead with. "I'm not?"

"You're almost eighteen, sweetie. Legal proceedings are generally not quick. It's what, six weeks until your birthday?" Dana frowns. "I should know this by now."

"Yeah, it's in November," you say. What Joseph just told you hasn't sunk in. They're really not going to haul you back into the system? "So I'm free?"

It's maybe a silly choice of words, and Dana and Joseph exchange a glance.

"You're almost legally an adult," Joseph says. "The courts generally try to avoid doing things they feel are out of line with the best interests of a child, and if the little Dana has communicated to me is even a fraction of what you've dealt with, you have nothing to worry about."

Well, that just sounds wrong. You always have stuff to worry about. There's the drug thing, which you should probably tell them, but you are stubborn. You don't really know if you can trust them. You trust Raz, and since she should be back any day, you want to wait to find out what she thinks. Her opinion is the only one you particularly care about right now.

To disguise your thoughts, you take a sip of your cocoa-coffee. Mocha. Whatever.

You go through the basics of your history. After that, Joseph starts walking you through the months-long probate process, which is complicated and overwhelming, and you kind of hate every second of it. That said, you're also aware you'd have no idea what to do without his help. He goes through the papers you brought slowly, asking questions that get a little too close to Frances's "self-employment" but you manage to skirt, and you rattle off your financial choices of the last week (with the exception of the PlayStation) as well as write down your monthly budget.

When you're done, both Dana and Joseph are staring at you.

"Is something wrong?" you ask.

"Will," Dana says gently, "you really paid all the bills yourself? While Frances was alive?"

Guess Hannah didn't tell her that part. You have one of those moments. You know the ones, where you are just kind of doing your thing and you realize your thing isn't normal to most people, and it always sends you spinning because all you really know is your normal, so you *forget.*

Even though you know intellectually that Hannah doesn't pay bills herself, you guess you thought you just weren't *that* abnormal. That she was the weird lucky one, maybe, and you were the normal one, that your life is just life. The existential crisis from your conversation with Matt comes back in full force. What if Raz should have been the normal and not everything else? You cannot think about this now. Not yet. Not here.

But when you make yourself meet Dana's eyes and nod, Joseph suddenly clears his throat and looks down at the pile of papers you brought as if seeing them for the first time.

"I know you said that you've never known your father," Joseph says, "but you're sure you don't have any other family?"

You shrug, because you just don't know. "Frances lied a lot. I don't even know if my dad's really dead, I guess. But he probably is. She always said she didn't have any siblings. Her parents died when I was a kid and still in the system, so I never knew them."

In fact, it was her mother's death that Frances cited as the reason she got her shit together to steal you back from Raz. You'd forgotten about that.

"Okay," Joseph says. He breathes out. "Your situation is unusual, Will. I think if I'd found you sooner, I'd be working on an emancipation plea."

You blink at that, and this man you just met an hour ago looks you in the eyes.

"I work with a lot of families, Will," he says. "There are a lot of messes I get called in to help clean up or help fix, and because of that, I see a lot of things most people don't. I'm on your side here. A parent's job is to take care of their child. Providing a stable home and food and paying the bills is the literal bare minimum of that expectation. It's not a bonus. It's supposed to be level-one parenting."

He smiles a little at that, but you can't move.

"Did Frances ever do anything that could be considered abuse?" Joseph asks. The way he asks makes you go even more still.

You hear Matt's words in your mind all over again. *Jacob's dad was abusive like that.*

This is another one of those moments. Most people, even people who met Frances, never brought themselves to ask that question. If they didn't ask, you didn't have to tell. And it's one of those questions that you feel like someone knows the answer to the moment you don't immediately jump in with a no.

So you swallow and reach for your makeshift mocha and take a drink of it, staring at the film of melted marshmallow sugar clinging to the top of it.

"Yeah," you say finally. "She'd get drunk and yell at me pretty often. Up 'til last year sometimes she'd go after me with a belt or her fists if I didn't do something right. Then last year she hit me with a chair pretty hard in the leg. But I got taller than her, and that was the—that was the last time she did. I think she thought I might start hitting her back."

You've never said those words out loud before. You're also pretty certain it's not the worst thing Joseph Landry has ever heard.

Both lawyers let out a slow breath, and Joseph nods. "Thank you for trusting me with that, Will," he says. "While obviously there's nothing we can do to retroactively make this better, knowing should help me with your case, especially since there's no will."

No will. Ha.

"Your former foster mother, Esmeralda?" Dana says. "You say you've been trying to reach her?"

"Yeah." You told them about Raz earlier. "She's been out of town, but she's supposed to be back any day."

You've really got to pee. When you ask where the bathroom is, Joseph points you toward it, and you go, as much for a moment to clear your head as for anything else.

When you come back, you hover at the door because you hear the lawyers speaking in quiet voices.

"I had no idea, Joe," Dana breathes. Her voice sounds a little muffled, like she's got her face in her hands. "I've known Will for years, and I never knew. I don't even think my daughter knew—she would have told me, I think. She said Frances was controlling, but—"

"Dana, the one thing about cases like this that you have to understand is that you're coming from a healthy home and a healthy family, and you can't see clearly what it's like for someone who doesn't," Joseph says. You feel like you should move, make a noise, something, but you can't. "What horrifies you is just their normal. Human beings can adapt to just about anything, which is a blessing and a curse. And Will is doing remarkably well for someone with such upheaval. I've seen it before. We're dealing with someone who has the life experience a lot of adults lack. They probably didn't tell Hannah because on some level, they wanted to protect her."

You swallow. You know that tone in his voice. It echoes with something familiar. Suddenly you think Joseph Landry chose his job because he really knows. The thought fills you with gratitude. Stamps a big old *what you feel is real* on your hand.

You scuff your foot on the carpet, and their voices fall silent. Dana indeed has her face in her hands, but she straightens and smiles at you when you come back in.

The rest of the meeting goes by quickly. Joseph gives you his card with his personal cell phone number written on the back of it.

"Let me know as soon as you hear from Esmer—from Raz, okay?" he says. "In the meantime, I'll get going on everything."

You leave feeling like you've gotten another year older.

Having accomplished something so adult feels like such a triumph that on impulse, you pull in at the local pizza place on the way home. Treat yourself, and all that.

All the papers you brought are on the seat next to you when you park, but the lot is otherwise pretty empty, so it doesn't even cross your mind to move them. You go inside, mouth watering at the scent of tomato sauce and pepperoni in the air, and you order an extra-large loaded with pepperoni, sausage, peppers, olives, and jalapeños. And then you order a medium Hawaiian with triple pineapple and red peppers, because you're going to eat until you have to roll yourself to bed.

But when you walk out the door with your pizza boxes, Levi is leaning against the passenger door of your car.

"Hello, Will," he says.

"Fuck all the way off, Levi." Anger fills you to the eyebrows at the sight of him. "If you touch my car again, I'll—"

"You'll what? Even if I knew what you're talking about, which I don't, you're not going to do shit. You breathe one word to so much as a mall security officer and I'll make sure the cops know you're dealing." He smirks as he says it, and suddenly the coffee in your stomach churns.

"Are you following me or something?" Part of you wants to tell him you just came from a lawyer's office, but you don't think it'll help.

"No, this is just a happy coincidence," he says blandly.

The tanning salon is in that strip mall you were just in, so that's probably where he was. He smells slightly of coconut, which you can smell even over your pizza. You go to the car and open the back door, putting the pizzas in the back seat. If he decides to beat you up, at least you can eat when he's done.

It's a messed-up thought, but you're not particularly afraid of him at this moment. You lived with Frances, and your meeting today just reinforced the Herculean feat of your own survival. Compared to that, Levi's just . . . a bully.

"What do you want?" You shut the door and eye him over the roof of the car.

"I can't seem to get ahold of your mother," he says thoughtfully. "So you're just going to give me my two hundred dollars back, and you can tell your mom she's lost a customer."

As far as Levi goes, that's downright mild.

"Fine. Whatever. Gotta keep you in shining Trump luster, right? Daddy must not give you a high-enough allowance for all that fake 'n' baking," you say, and he actually looks embarrassed.

As chance has it, you were planning to stop by the bank and finally deposit the money Frances had in that box in her closet, so you have enough on you to pay off the high school bully. But you don't want him to see that.

"I need to go to the ATM," you say. It's back where you just were. "You gonna follow me, or should I just come back here?"

"I'll follow," he says. "Wouldn't want you to decide to drive home instead."

The kid knows where you live.

If whoever sent that text really was talking about Levi, he probably already knows where to find you. You swallow, thinking of the gun in the condiment bowl and thankful for your hypothermia-induced hallucination that put it in easier reach than the door.

Jesus, are you really thinking about shooting Levi if he turns up at your house?

It might not be Levi.

That thought makes your mouth go sticky.

Without a word, you jerk a nod in Levi's direction and get in the car. It now smells like roses, cigarettes, and pizza, which is almost an improvement. You drive the short distance back to the strip mall and pull up in front of the ATM. You don't see any cars outside the law office now, so Dana and Joseph are probably gone. Good. They don't need to see you handing money to Levi.

He waits somewhat patiently in his BMW while you block the ATM with your body and check your balance instead of getting any money out, but you still get a receipt.

You walk over to where he sits with the window cracked.

"If I give this to you, I don't want to hear so much as a word out of your mouth to me or Hannah for the rest of the year," you say. You are so sick of his smug, square face that it drives you to let some of your anger at him out in a torrent. "You think you can screw up my life? I've got nothing to lose compared to you, and I've dealt with people much, much scarier than your spray-tanned ass of a face. So leave me the fuck alone."

You crumple the two hundred-dollar bills and shove them through the crack in the window and walk away before he can say anything back.

It's only when you finally make it home that you realize the paper on top of the pile on the seat, right where he was leaning waiting for you, is Frances's death certificate.

Chapter Twenty

You think you might be dying.

Your pizza is sitting on the breakfast bar, probably getting cold, but you don't even care right now.

Maybe Levi didn't notice. He's such a self-centered prick that he very well could have failed to look down and see Frances's death certificate, but you wouldn't place a bet of five bucks on those odds.

The entirety of your body feels like it is going to fly apart at any second. Your heart is beating so quickly you can feel it in your eyeballs, and no matter what you do, full breaths evade you.

You think you just might be having a panic attack.

There's no way you can think rationally right now, but the words you threw at Levi before you stormed away spin through your mind like a hurricane.

How could you be so *reckless*, Will? In spite of what Joseph and Dana said, you don't know what could happen if people find out about Frances. Also there's the whole drugs thing. You could end up in jail. And there's still no sign of Raz.

The corner of the pizza box has just the tiniest sprig of cardboard curling away from it, and you stare at that pointless detail as you clutch the edge of the breakfast bar.

Okay, Will. Breathe. Think. But mostly breathe.

You force yourself to breathe all the way in, counting as you do. You get to seven, which is a weird number, but then you breathe all the way back out. You repeat that.

Slowly, your heart stops pounding. The oxygen helps.

After a few minutes, you put the pizza on the coffee table, go directly to the fridge and pull out two Cokes, and walk back to the sofa. Each movement is a point on a line, and it somehow helps.

Thinking about checking your phone is too much, but you bought this pizza, and you're going to eat it, damn it.

You start with the pineapple, and it is *heaps* of pineapple. Enough that you're actually impressed, and this one silly little thing helps ground you back into reality just a little more.

The pizza is still mostly warm, much to your surprise and gratitude. You manage four pieces before you officially call it, and one-and-a-half cans of soda. You're not sure if you actually feel *better* full of cheese and bread and sugar, but at least you're not hungry.

After the pizza, you feel fortified enough to look at your iPhone. It's still on your dresser where you left it, and there are a heap of messages again, mostly from Julian, but a few from Hannah.

Mom said the meeting went well. Here if you want to talk. Xx. That from Hannah.

Julian wants to know about the meeting, but a solid half of the messages from them are just memes, which you deeply appreciate.

An idea strikes you. It might even be a good one.

Before your brain revisits a place of panic, you respond to Julian.

Hey, are you doing anything tonight? And if I were to say . . . drive to Baltimore, would you want to have a Korra marathon or something? I am stuck in my own head and I don't think even the Dreadwolf could drag me out of it at this point tbh.

You're terrified they'll say no, but almost immediately you get a *Hell yes!!*

Your heart gives a flip-flop, and you feel the first bubble of actual lightness you've encountered all day.

I'm at work, but I'll be off by nine, home a bit after that! A Korra *marathon sounds perfect.*

This is good. This is good, right?

If you leave now, you'll be there right around the time they get home.

You're still not back to a hundred percent with Hannah, and you don't know that you will be by Monday, either, but you can get out of the house for a night. Besides. Maybe Raz will be back by the time you have to drive back to Bright Springs tomorrow.

That thought is almost too much. You shoot Hannah a quick text letting her know you're okay and that you're going to Baltimore for the night but will see her Monday. It probably won't be the thing she most wants to hear from you. For a moment, you feel like a jerk.

Then you remember she stood you up on a day she was literally supposed to be apologizing for another mistake.

Right. She'll live.

Figuring Julian might want some pizza, you load up the car with the rest of your twelve-pack of soda and the pizza boxes, but you take care to put all the documents away in the house. Which means you bury Frances's death certificate at the bottom of the drawer where you keep all the plastic wrap and ziplock bags, because now you're feeling paranoid.

You lock the door and the deadbolt and get in the car.

Three hours to Baltimore.

It occurs to you that you're just running away right now, but you do not care.

Julian answers the door with wet curly hair that sparkles with tiny droplets of water glinting in the porch light, and they're wearing a pair of black flannel pajama pants and a black T-shirt that clings to them in a way that makes your mouth suddenly very dry.

"Hi," you stammer.

"Hi yourself," Julian says with a grin.

They stand back so you can come in, swooping in to grab the pizza boxes so you don't drop the sodas that are dangling precariously between your hand and hip bone.

"Pizza?"

"Fresh from Bright Springs," you say, swallowing. Your throat sticks a little. You cough. "Got it this afternoon, so hopefully the few hours in the car haven't made it into a biological weapon yet."

"You're talking to someone who found a packaged salad on the sidewalk and ate it," Julian tells you, walking into the tiny kitchen where you first sat around their table with Matt and Hannah. They put the pizza down, looking over their shoulder at your probably horrified face. "I mean, the packaging was intact. No holes or anything. I didn't want it to go to waste."

You grin sheepishly. "I'd probably do the same thing."

"Yass," Julian says. They grin back. "Join me on the dark side. We are all just creachers here."

You hear the meme spelling, and your smile gets wider. "Did you just get home?"

"About twenty minutes ago. I may have sneaked out from work a few minutes early just to make sure I wouldn't be greeting you with eau de kitchen grease." When Julian shakes their head, a couple little drops of water splash you.

"I probably just smell like pizza." You're suddenly chagrined for some reason.

"You smell good," Julian says. "Nothing to worry about there."

For a short while, you both make small talk. Still no news from Raz or from the sitter, but now that at least you know Raz isn't *missing*-missing, there's more annoyance at the sitter's incompetence than fear.

Until you remember that Levi probably saw the death certificate.

Julian is midsentence with a half-eaten slice of pizza in their hand when the memory hits you, and it must show on your face, because they immediately stop talking.

You tell them what happened, and they put the slice of pizza on the lid of the box.

"What do you think he'll do with the information if he saw it?" they ask.

"Something rotten, probably. Levi is the kind of person who would barbecue slugs with a magnifying glass in the sun for fun." You hate how dejected your voice sounds, and you stuff almost half a piece of pizza in your mouth in one bite. It sticks going down. "He just—ugh. He doesn't care about people. I'm not even sure he'd choose to save his own father."

"My favorite type of person." Julian leans back, drumming their fingers against the lid of the pizza box. But then they cock their head at you. "Will, whatever happens, we'll deal with it. Okay? Raz will be back soon, and we know she'll have your back."

"I flushed a bunch of drugs down the toilet," you confess. "When we found out what Frances was doing. And then again when I found more in her PO box. And I kept the money."

Julian waves a hand. "Who's going to report that missing? The cops would just pocket it themselves anyway. Like literally. They do that. It's even legal. Better your pocket than theirs."

That's . . . not a bad point.

You both finish your slices of pizza in silence, and when that's done, you remember you were going to have a *Korra* marathon.

"We have a very important decision before us," Julian says very seriously. "Each comes with its own dangers. We need to choose wisely."

You settle yourself on the chair and fold your hands over your knees, playing along. "I'm ready."

Julian lets out a little breathless laugh. Are they *nervous*?

Their dark hair is starting to dry, little wisps of curls fluffing up above their ears.

"Option one: the living room. Easy access to the kitchen for snacks, big TV. Sofa, though. It's cheap and not very comfortable. We risk our butt bones." Julian swallows this time, like it's their mouth that's gone dry.

"Noted," you say lightly, trying to encourage them. Your heart gives a little jump in your chest, like it's a bunny that just got goosed. "Option two?"

"Option two," Julian says, swallowing again, "is my room. Farther from the snacks, and the TV is my laptop. Comfier, because bed, but the nightstand is the drink holder, which can be dangerous. Among other things."

Oh. *Oh.*

Your skin tingles at the words *other things*, and from the way Julian is looking at you, you think the body-wide goose bumps that have just washed over you are probably visible. But they're in short sleeves, and you can see their arms, and *their* arms are pebbly like yours feel.

"No judgment either way, and no . . . pressure," Julian says, almost a squeak. "I mean, whatever you're—"

"Option two." The words come out of your mouth unbidden, and Julian's lips close tight on their little glinting lip ring.

It's suddenly warm in this kitchen, or maybe it's just that you can see a blush creeping up the pale skin of Julian's neck.

"Option two it is," they say, and when they spin to pick up the pizza box and put it in the fridge, you think you see them actually *teeter* a little.

It's . . . adorable.

You follow them on shaky legs to their bedroom, and somehow in just a few minutes, you're propped up against a mountain of cushions on their black comforter, feet stretched out in front of you while Julian settles in beside you with their laptop.

They fumble for just a minute with the cord, pulling it behind the lamp on the cluttered nightstand to plug in the laptop, and your heart feels like it's beating somewhere in the vicinity of your teeth.

There is nothing but the sound of your blood rushing through your body for a moment, thick thuds you're half-afraid Julian will hear when they get too close.

Julian keeps swallowing, and their Adam's apple bobs a bit each time. They cue up the show and say something lighthearted that you respond to without hearing either their words or your own reply.

They're so *close* to you. When they turn to you and giggle nervously, a small dimple appears in their cheek that you somehow haven't noticed before. Or maybe you have? Something about their proximity makes everything feel very, very new.

"All set?" you ask. Your voice cracks on the second word, and Julian gives you a crooked smile.

"Definitely," they say.

There's something needy inside of you, hungry. Like it soaks up every ounce of warmth Julian gives off—which is a *lot*—and it still wants more. Right where Julian's shoulder touches your arm is suddenly alive. More alive than you think that patch of skin has ever been.

You simultaneously feel like you are hooked up to a wall socket to charge and like you're nothing more than a conduit with Julian's energy zooming right through you and out the other side where there is just wall.

It seems like such a small thing. You didn't realize you were so starved for touch. You usually don't want anyone to touch you. Between Korra airbending a bad guy into a wall and her giant polar bear dog galumphing down a street, for the first time in your life, you take hold of the very belated epiphany that being touched by someone you actually want to touch you is the entire difference.

The thought brings pinpricks of tears to your eyes, and you blink, hoping Julian won't notice.

When the episode ends, Julian hits Pause. "Do you want anything for a snack? I'm dying for something to drink."

Your mouth is drier than desert sand at midday, and you nod. When Julian gets up, the loss of contact is immediate and vast.

You take the opportunity to pee, sitting in the bathroom for a heart-thudding moment and wondering how it was only just a couple weeks ago you were here before, with Hannah and Matt in the other room, both uncomfortable for different reasons. You called Raz from this bathroom.

When you come back to the bedroom, Julian has two cans of Sprite on the nightstand, and they're standing there with a crooked smile on their face again. They make a grand gesture.

"After you," they say.

You pause, hovering by the edge of the bed. Mere inches from them. Looking up into Julian's eyes for a moment, you think you see something in their depths. Something yearning and hopeful, and for that moment, you imagine closing that small distance. What would it be like to just be in their arms?

Julian watches you back, and you chicken out. Climbing back onto the bed, you settle back into your spot, wondering if the contact between you is over.

But Julian hands you your Sprite, and when they settle back, their shoulder is back against yours, the contact spot doubled in size so that your entire arms are pressed together, and you start the next episode.

Chapter Twenty-One

When your eyes fill with sand and neither you nor Julian can stop yawning, you finally turn off *Korra*. Your arms are stuck together, and when you look down, there's a pink elliptical shape on your skin and Julian's both.

"You are welcome to sleep in here if you want," Julian says suddenly. "If you want. You can—I'll take the couch if—"

"I'm not kicking you out of your bed," you say.

Your brain isn't quite working properly, but whatever instinct tells your nervous system to send a flash flood of blood to your face is functioning fine. Your cheeks get very hot very quickly.

"I mean," you say. "I'll . . . I can sleep on the couch if you want. Or—"

Your voice practically falls off a cliff. *Or?* Will. What are you doing?

It's a good question, and Julian seems so blindsided by those two little letters that they don't move a single muscle for the space of several heartbeats.

"I wouldn't want to make you uncomfortable," they say. "But if you are okay with it, we could—we could both sleep here."

Neither of you are looking at each other. You're personally staring at your now-empty can of Sprite, at the small glint of lamplight in the dark blue-green aluminum. It's a pretty color.

"Here works for me," you hear yourself say.

This is new. This is very, very new. You're almost eighteen, and you've never been kissed, let alone shared a bed with someone not-Hannah.

"Okay," Julian says.

"Are you okay with that?" you ask. You don't want Julian to feel uncomfortable at all, and the sudden thought that maybe you were too forward, too eager, is cut off by their next words.

"More than okay," they say softly.

It's then you realize that you did not bring pajamas.

When you say so, Julian laughs. "Never fear."

They go to a chest of drawers and pull out a pair of soft cotton pants and an even softer T-shirt.

You're too scared to change in front of them, so you take the proffered pajamas with a small smile that feels like it might slip right off your face and land in a puddle. You go to the bathroom and change quickly, rinsing out your mouth with water.

Julian's pants are super long on you. They drag on the floor and, surprisingly, are droopy in the hips. Julian is quite tall. Apparently broader than you thought, too. When you go back into the room, they're in shorts and the same black T-shirt, and they grin at you.

"Oh my god, those pants are huge on you," they say. "You look adorable."

You're not sure that's a good thing, but you grin anyway. "Thanks for the loan. And the compliment."

You climb back into the bed, wondering if you'll manage to sleep close to the wall. You're used to being able to roll right off either side of the bed, but you think that maybe being between Julian and a wall might not be such a bad thing. When they follow you in and settle beside you, neither of you is touching now. You can see their pulse fluttering in the hollow of their throat.

"I've never done this before," you blurt out. The moment the words escape, you feel utterly ridiculous.

"Shared a bed?" Julian asks.

"Well. Not really. Only with Hannah at her place." That makes it worse. You've just very clearly delineated Hannah-bed-sharing from Julian-bed-sharing, which is . . . dangerous. "She snores."

Julian gives you a shy smile. "I don't think I snore."

"Me neither." Bodies. What even are bodies? Yours seems to have become an adrenaline factory in the past thirty seconds.

"Will," Julian says. "You're safe here, okay? If you're not comfortable—"

"I know," you say. Your face gets hotter. "Sorry. I don't mean to keep interrupting you. It's—I'm nervous. But not in a—ugh. I mean—"

"I think I get it," Julian says with a shaky laugh. "Would you—would you like to cuddle?"

You're nodding before your words can form, and suddenly you are in Julian's arms and them in yours. Is this even happening? How did this happen? They just said it and then it did, and now you're here.

You can hear their heartbeat now, beating fast and tight in their chest. It's miraculous, warm, alive. When you look up, they're looking down at you with something like wonder.

You must be staring, because Julian looks at you curiously after a moment. "What is it?"

Answering that is terrifying, but somehow you do anyway. "I've never felt this before."

Their face changes, their eyes suddenly a thousand times the depth they were even moments ago, and you are suspended in them, floating. You think you could stay here forever, Julian's eyes supporting you on all sides with something that feels like surface tension and you inside the bubble.

"Can I—" You swallow. You are not even a little bit sure what you are asking, but then Julian's face is closer, and you see the glint of the lamp-light on their lip ring, and you know. "Can I kiss you?"

You've never kissed anyone before. You might be totally terrible at it.

Julian nods without saying another word, and you feel every single moment as your bodies adjust to give your lips space enough to touch.

When they do, a jolt goes through you.

Julian's lips are soft, the small ring of metal in their bottom lip warmed from their body heat, and—Dog above—they actually tremble against you.

Or maybe that's you. You might both be trembling, quaking on the fault line that your bodies make together.

All you can do is just feel. The slowness of it, the nervousness of it. It is relief and tension at the same time, and all the emotions you've been bottling up spill into it.

You're not sure which of you finally breaks it, just as the intensity of it is getting to lean toward Too Much, and when you lie back on the pillow to look at Julian, they're looking back at you with just as bewildered an expression as you probably have plastered on your face.

Part of you wants to apologize in case it was terrible, but something in Julian's eyes tells you that'd ruin the moment.

Julian reaches out a hand and gently touches the bridge of your cheek. "Beautiful."

You don't know if they mean you or the kiss, but your skin flushes anyway, and you stammer out a "Look who's talking."

"Can I ask you something?" they ask. "You don't have to answer if you don't want to."

"Ask anything," you say, and for the first time in your life, you think you mean it.

"Was that your first kiss?"

"Yes." You could have lied, you realize belatedly, but you don't want to lie to Julian. "Was it yours?"

Julian shakes their head just a tiny bit, and their eyes cloud a little. You want to chase the clouds away.

There is quiet here for a moment, floating between you.

"I hope it was a good first kiss, then," they say after a moment.

"It was perfect." You are maybe a little too vehement, but they smile, and the clouds do clear from their eyes. "I—no one ever *wanted* to kiss me before."

"I can't imagine why they wouldn't," Julian says.

This is a lie, and you both know it, but it's not the kind of lie that hurts. You are both nonbinary people in a world that doesn't want to understand you, let alone romance you. You know this. Julian knows this. In some small way, you feel a surge of defiance. Triumph. Because here, in this cocoon of warmth and *Korra* and empty Sprite cans, on Julian's black sheets with their silver pillows strewn around you, you and Julian got to share the kind of moment that your world doesn't want you to know can be yours.

And it is yours.

Tonight it's yours.

When Julian turns off the light, glow-in-the-dark stars light the sky above your tiny world, and you keep talking in increasingly nonsensical murmurs, snuggling against each other's shoulders until you lull yourselves to sleep.

Part of you is surprised the next morning when you wake up in Julian's arms. You're tangled around each other, a little sweaty from the unfamiliar sensation of sharing a bed with another warm body, and you think this is the first time in your life that you've woken up blushing.

Julian stirs when you move, opening one eye first. "Mrm."

"Yes," you agree.

You both fumble yourselves to wakefulness, kicking off the covers that were only half acting as such anyway.

The elation of getting to be here, of getting to see Julian tousled and fuzzy-curled and half-asleep? Magical.

The smile that tugs at your lips won't seem to leave as you get up and check the time. Eleven.

"Ugh. I wish I didn't have school tomorrow," you say as you shuffle into the kitchen. "Or just that I had a teleporter to skip the drive back."

"Someone really needs to get on the teleportation thing," Julian says, stifling a yawn.

There's a smile dancing around their lips, too.

They start making coffee, producing a box of blueberry freezer waffles and a veritable vat of butter-flavored syrup.

For a while, you just eat and drink and wake up, the sweetness of the waffles matching the sweetness of . . . whatever this is.

You're afraid to ask.

You're just putting your dishes in the dishwasher when the sound of a car makes your heart jump high enough you're afraid it'll bounce off the roof of your mouth. *Raz.*

Julian is clearly on the same wavelength. Together, you make for the window, tugging open the blinds.

No Raz, though. The car is a little white Volkswagen bug, and Julian makes an exasperated sound.

"That's the pet sitter. Want to come with me?" Without waiting, they throw on a pair of flip-flops in spite of the cold and open the door.

The pet sitter is a short, blonde white woman who doesn't look much older than you yourself.

"Oh, it's you!" she says, then she cringes. "I totally forgot to ask Raz if I could give you the landline number. I'm so sorry—she's flying back tonight, though!"

Your stomach turns on the waffles. "Tonight?"

The pet sitter looks past Julian at you, then back at Julian. "Is this—"

"Raz's foster kid, yeah." Julian's good mood is gone. "It's really important that we talk to her. Will's been trying to get in touch with her for ages."

"I already told you that it's a confidentiality thing," the woman says, frowning.

"My mom died," you say sharply. "Raz would want to know. Like immediately."

You're surprised at your own anger at this woman who completely spaced out on following through with an urgent request but also lost Raz's cat.

"I'm sorry about your mom," she says. "I'll try to call her right now, okay? She might already be back in service range."

"Please do," Julian says.

Their voice is cold and almost distant in a way you recognize all too well. It's that *I'm more responsible than this adult* voice. The *I can't believe I'm having to babysit this person* voice. The *why can't you clean up your own mess* voice. The exhaustion behind it is palpable. You feel it in your mitochondria.

The young woman pulls out a brand-new phone and starts scrolling through contacts. She gives you a tight-lipped smile. "It's ringing."

The seconds that pass are relentless. Excruciating. You're still in pajamas, and it's not warm out, but your nervous anger is keeping the chill off for now.

"Voice mail," she says apologetically, and she moves to hang up.

"Wait!" You close the distance between you and almost snatch the phone from her hand.

"Hey!" She looks like she wants to take it back, but she clearly doesn't want to risk dropping the shiny phone onto the asphalt of Raz's driveway.

A voice is just finishing the greeting, and you hear the beep.

"Raz, it's Will. Your pet sitter was kind enough to let me leave this message, since she wasn't allowed to give out the number. Frances is dead. I thought you'd want to know. Please call me. I'd really—I'd really love to see you." You rattle off your number, then hang up. Your fingers are numb on the phone, and you pass it back to its owner.

Julian looks pleased, but the pet sitter does not.

"Rude," she says.

"Ask Raz when you talk to her how she feels about you keeping Will from contacting her, and then we can discuss rude," Julian says. "And don't let the cat outside again."

With that, Julian turns and heads back inside, and you hesitate for a moment before meeting the still-fuming woman's eyes.

"Know that room upstairs?" you ask her quietly. She doesn't answer, but you know she knows. "Yeah. That room was meant for me."

Then you follow Julian. Fuck that pet sitter.

Chapter Twenty-Two

You somehow pry yourself away from Baltimore in time to get back to Bright Springs at a relatively reasonable hour. Julian kisses you shyly on the lips in farewell, and you blush all the way to Frederick.

Once you get home, you answer a few texts from Hannah and collapse into bed. She's dying to know what happened at the sleepover with Julian, but you don't feel like gushing. Now that you're back at home, your stomach is all tied up in knots. Is this what it's always like with crushes? You text Julian to let them know you got home safe, and they send back a selfie of them giving you the sweetest smile, a curl falling across their forehead.

You send them one back, and they reply with the heart eyes emoji and a simple *Omg, are you actually James Dean because . . .*

That's a compliment you will hoard forever.

Sleep is welcome. You miss the warmth of Julian next to you already.

When morning comes, you stumble through your school routine and arrive to a hushed parking lot a little early. No Hannah, no coffee, which makes you feel off. You miss the way things were, and the pang that comes from realizing Hannah might be stopping for coffee with Ashton now instead of you is surprisingly fierce. You forgot to charge your iPhone again—which makes you think of the seemingly self-charging Galaxy you're pointedly ignoring in the kitchen—but you can maybe borrow Hannah's portable charger when you see her. If you see her.

You're just heading into your first period class when the teacher looks up.

"Will," Mr. Perez says. "The counselor would like to see you in her office right away."

You're the first person in the classroom, but your face reddens anyway. "Did she say why?"

He shakes his head. "Just that it was urgent."

You make your way to the office as fast as you dare. The halls are starting to fill with a trickle of other early-comers, and you avoid their eyes without knowing why.

Maybe it's Raz. Maybe she got the message and came straight here—the terrible pet sitter said she was flying back last night. She could have gotten to Bright Springs, right?

But when you walk through the door into the office, a white woman with blonde hair in a severe bun at the nape of her neck is talking to Suzie.

You don't have to ask. You know that look, that entire look. There's a badge hanging from the woman's lapel, and you don't have to read it. Is this what Suzie was wanting to talk to you about? She *promised* it wasn't bad.

Suzie sees you before you can flee.

"Will," she says. Her eyes are dark and pitying. "Please come in."

For a moment, you consider turning and running. But where would you go? Your heart is beating harder with every shallow breath you pull past your teeth.

You have no choice. You follow.

The door shuts behind you with that hollow thud all school doors seem to make, like they're sturdier than they should be.

"Will," the stranger says, extending her hand. "My name is Elizabeth Bryce. I'm with the Department of Child Protective Services."

You shake the hand without meeting her eyes. "I know."

"Will, everything's going to be okay." Suzie looks like she wants to put her arms around you and hug you but knows it wouldn't be appropriate. "You're safe here."

"False," you say.

Your voice sounds like it's far, far away. You're a monster again, inhabiting a human body.

"Please, sit." Elizabeth Bryce motions at one of the chairs in front of Suzie's desk, but you shake your head, moving farther away from her.

If she's here, they know. Levi. It had to be Levi.

"We found out this weekend that your mother passed away just before the beginning of school," Suzie says gently.

You hardly hear her. You pluck at the hem of your shirt. You don't really remember putting it on. It's a navy-blue T-shirt, and you got it at Target because it was on sale and you liked the neckline. You wish you'd put your binder on today.

"I tried to call you this morning," Suzie says. "I'm glad you got here early."

Her voice is gentle. You do actually like Suzie the Counselor. She's just not used to dealing with monsters.

"Phone's dead," you say.

Suzie rummages in her desk and puts out her hand. "Here. iPhone? I'll get that charging for you. I know this is hard, Will, but we need to talk about next steps."

You hand her the phone. Your fingers are really cold. "I already got her cremated and paid all the bills. And I have a lawyer who's helping me with the probate process. You don't have to do anything."

"Will, that's good that you have someone helping you. But you are still a minor—" Elizabeth Bryce stops midsentence when you slam your hand against the wall.

Suzie jumps and almost drops your phone.

You didn't realize you were so close to the wall.

"I'm not going back into the system. I'm almost eighteen, and I'm *not*. I've been looking for my foster mother, but she's been gone, and her stupid pet sitter wouldn't give her the message or give me her phone number, but she wants me, and I won't go with anyone who's not Raz." You are almost yelling by the end, and it feels good to yell, to be loud, to take up space. "It's just like you people. You turn up and bad things happen. You took me away from her! You gave me to *Frances* instead of Raz!"

Once again, your words sound like a child's words, and that makes the anger all the stronger until you're just slamming the heel of your hand into the wall behind you over and over and over and over and over again. The pain is a focus; you have a wild impulse to do it with your head like you used to as a kid. The memory feels so distant that you're not even sure it's real, but hitting the wall with your hand seems to have jolted it loose.

Back before you poured every feeling inward instead of letting it explode out.

The thought unmoors you enough that you stop hitting the wall.

The office is silent except for the ragged sound of your breathing. You think if you open your mouth again you might bellow.

"Will," Suzie says softly. "Nobody here wants to hurt you."

"Too late," you say, and she flinches. It's a small confirmation of your monstrosity. "Where were you when Frances hit me with a chair? Where were you when my foster dad punched my foster brother? Where were you when I actually fucking needed you? You showed up when I was happy. When Raz was about to adopt me. You took me from her and gave me back to Frances, who made me pay for everything while she—"

You bite off the *sold drugs* because that's the last thing you need to spill right now. The absolute last thing.

"And you show up now? I'm going to be eighteen in six weeks. I'm already an adult. I make sure the trash is out on the right day and the electricity gets paid. I paid for Frances's phone and pay my phone bill." You jerk your chin at the phone charging on Suzie's desk, and she blinks at it as if seeing it for the first time. "I take care of me. You don't know the first thing about taking care of me."

You're all the way flat against the wall now, your back pressed up against it. You didn't realize you started crying until now. The tip of your nose is cold like your fingers in contrast to the buzzing burning of your palm where it struck the wall, and you fight the urge to just scream as loud as you can.

"You're right," Elizabeth Bryce says softly.

That snaps you out of it a little.

"What?" Suzie says what you're thinking.

Elizabeth Bryce glances at her, then perches on the edge of Suzie's desk. "I read your file, Will. But that doesn't mean I know what your life has been like, and I'm so sorry that we've failed you."

Her voice is . . . gentle. She looks like she means it, or at least you think she does. Her eyes don't hold pity, only regret. There's a small crease slightly off center on her forehead. Despite your violent outburst, no one is moving to restrain you.

When you don't say anything, she goes on.

"Raz—is that Esmeralda Olmos-Adams?" Elizabeth Bryce asks the question as if she already knows the answer.

"Yes," you manage. "She was going to adopt me."

"Is she the one who sent you that letter?" Suzie asks cautiously.

"Yes." You slump against the wall. Part of you still wants to dissolve into the floor. Anything to escape.

"Will, are you aware who Esmeralda Olmos-Adams is?" Elizabeth Bryce asks.

You stare at her blankly. "She's a good person, and she wanted to be my mom."

Suzie's face crumples for a second, but her counselor mask is back immediately.

This is another one of those moments.

Breathe, Will.

"Will," Elizabeth Bryce says. "Esmeralda—Raz—is your biological aunt."

Chapter Twenty-Three

You don't remember to breathe.

You're dimly aware of the wall against your back, of two pairs of eyes watching you like you're a rabid dog, but all you can hear is the same sentence over and over again.

Raz is your biological aunt.

Raz is your biological aunt.

You must have made some sort of noise, because Elizabeth Bryce is going on.

"Your father's sister," she says. "That's how she got you to foster."

"No one told me," you say.

The world seems very far away all of a sudden. Like if you move, you'll fall into space and never come back.

"I don't know the whole story, but I am certain she will tell you everything you want to know," says Elizabeth Bryce.

Raz is your dad's sister.

"Where's my dad?" You ask the question, hearing it in the air and immediately wanting to take it back. "Don't tell me. I don't want to hear it right now."

"You can ask again when you're ready," Suzie says. "It's good that you are taking care of yourself."

It's such a Suzie thing to say. She taught you about self-care, for all the good it did you. But you think you just set a boundary, so maybe something sank in.

"You're not going to put me back into the system," you say again, with less venom.

"No," Elizabeth Bryce says. "As you said, you're almost eighteen. I'm just here today to help you make plans, whatever you need to transition."

You almost laugh at the word, because *transition* is basically your entire theme song, because you're trans, because you no way could afford to medically transition, because there is nothing in your life that doesn't live under that word.

"I want Raz," you say.

"Then we'll make sure we find her. I am certain that she will come here immediately. I wanted to speak to you before I contacted anyone in your file."

This Elizabeth Bryce is . . . different. You feel a bit stupid thinking of her as her full name every time she crosses your mind, but also you don't know what to call her.

"You can call Raz." You wave your hand like you're giving a blessing or trying to do magic or something.

Almost on cue, your dead phone buzzes to indicate it's charged enough to turn back on.

Suzie glances down at it. Smiles.

"I think she might have already called you," she says.

You freeze.

Raz called you?

You feel skittish walking toward the two women at Suzie's desk, but you do it anyway, because Suzie just said the one thing that could have made you do it. You pick up the phone, which is charging at Suzie's portable charger (you should maybe get one of those), and sure enough.

There's Raz's name because you saved the contact. It says you have a voice mail.

Maybe the better thing to do would just be to call right back, but faced with that prospect, your belly gives a literal gurgle of nervousness, and you hit the Voice mail button instead.

The sound of Raz's voice after the AI voice gives your whole body a jolt.

"Will," she says, sounding breathless. "I am so sorry it's taken me so long to call you back. I've been out of service area, and Lena said nothing about this when I spoke to her."

There is an unmistakable tinge of anger in her voice, which makes you feel warmer.

"I'm back in Baltimore now, but I'll be in Bright Springs as soon as I can. Tuesday morning, okay? I love you, Will. It's going to be okay."

You put the phone down. Your entire body feels like it's hooked up to the charger instead of the phone.

"She's coming tomorrow," you say. Raz. Here. Tomorrow.

"That's excellent, Will," says Elizabeth Bryce.

Suzie looks relieved.

For the next hour, you listen as this woman from CPS—she insists you call her Elizabeth, so you do—goes over what happens next, and it almost feels okay. Like things could be okay.

Raz is coming. Here. Tomorrow.

Suzie excuses you from school for the rest of the day. You drive to the gas station, because the trip to Baltimore and back almost drained your tank, and you're absently filling up when you see the car.

You don't know the car, not in the way you know Hannah's car or Matt's, but you've seen it before. It's the same beat-up red sedan full of men, all of them white with the same sandy blond hair that makes them look strangely cohesive even though they don't really look anything alike beyond those two traits.

You trust your guts, and the moment you see them, something sinks into the pit of your stomach, slimy and heavy.

It feels like they're looking at you, even though none of them are facing you—the car is parked between you and the convenience store. But none of them are getting out. They're just sitting there. Unlike the last time, though, this time they don't lose interest in you.

You finish pumping gas and put the nozzle back. Every movement you make feels so clear. You've never really felt this hunted-feeling here before.

You're about to get back in the car when you hear their doors open. All of them at once.

"Where's Frances?" one of them says just as another goes, "Where the fuck is Frances?"

You freeze because they're all looking right at you now. "I don't know what you're talking about."

"The kid's a liar. That's Frances's car, and she's late." This one seems calm. He's tall, as tall as some of the basketball players at school. Big feet in Timberlands. *Footprints in snow.* "So where is she?"

"Frances is dead," you say, because you don't know what else to say. If Levi is involved with these assholes, you guess he didn't get the chance to tell them that himself.

One of the others laughs. "I doubt you could kill Frances with an AR15. She's made of nails and leather."

"Heart attack," you say. "You can probably ask the morgue."

"Nah, so that doesn't add up, because somebody"—the tall, calm one is looking at you, assessing you—"somebody collected for her in the last few weeks, so either her ghost is running around, or you're protecting her or—"

You're at the door to your car, but they're all coming closer, and they're spreading out in a way that tells you they're going to try and surround you.

He takes another step toward you, and your fingers tighten on the door handle.

"Or you took the stuff yourself."

You don't know what they're going to do to you. There's no one around—you can't even see the clerk inside the store.

That's when you remember. You're at a gas station. There are cameras right above you.

"What's that?" you say, looking up, and they all glance up in the direction you are.

"There's nothing there," one of the shorter guys says, but the tall one gives you a knowing look.

You meet his eyes with as much defiance as you can. "Leave me the fuck alone."

With that, you open the door to your car, and even though the pair of shorter guys makes a move to stop you, the tall one shakes his head, and they back off.

The threat in the tall one's face is almost audible through the windshield when he stands staring at you.

You fumble the key in the ignition, but the moment the car starts, you reverse so quickly you're afraid you're going to hit something. You turn back toward the school. They could follow you home, and that would not be good, even if you're certain they already know where that is.

But for now, for a moment, you're safe.

You drive aimlessly for a half hour, wishing you'd had the presence of mind to get the license plate number of the car they were in. You remember the car itself well enough.

Hannah's at school, so you pull over and text Matt and tell him what happened.

Shit, he says. *You're not home alone, are you?*

Nah, you text back. *But I need to go home. I can't just drive all day.*

I'll meet you there. Keep the car running until I get there.

K.

You do exactly that, but no one so much as drives by the house in the five minutes it takes for Matt to get there.

"Do you have to work today?" you ask him as you unlock the door and go inside.

"Nope. I'm four on, three off this week, so I've got a shift tomorrow afternoon." Matt locks the door behind you when you kick off your shoes. "Fill me in."

It doesn't take long for you to tell him what happened in more detail.

"It had to be Levi," you say. "That told the school."

"I wouldn't put it past him," Matt agrees. "Piece of toe jam."

You put the coffee maker on and throw some Tater Tots in the oven along with a pair of frozen burritos because you don't really know what else to do.

But you tell Matt about Raz, and he listens.

"If she'll be here tomorrow, are you going to tell her about what happened today?" Matt asks you.

You don't even hesitate. "I'm going to tell her everything."

Now that you're home, you want to call her back. But you don't want to be interrupted by the food, so you and Matt talk about other things—like whether the Caps will make it to the Stanley Cup this year—you think he's trying to distract you, and you're thankful for it.

When you're done eating, though, Matt goes into the living room and turns on the TV, and you go into your bedroom with your iPhone.

This is it. It takes three tries to get your fingers to press that green Call button, and you almost hang up again immediately. How many times have you wished you could talk to Raz?

The phone rings maybe once, and you hear her voice, full of love and relief. "Will."

"Raz?" Suddenly you're eleven years old again, and she's made you blueberry pancakes. You sound ages younger than you are with that one syllable.

"Oh, honey. Oh, Will. I'm so glad you called. Honey, I'm so, so sorry."

Some part of you recoils in shame that she would apologize to you, because you're the monster here. She's the one who's done everything right.

"I'm just glad you're here," you say. It sounds stupid. She's not actually here, but from the small sound you hear over the line, Raz gets it.

"Me too, honey. Me too. I'm going to have a chat with Lena when I see her. She should have given you my number immediately or called me immediately. We were way in the backcountry, but we had a satellite phone in case of emergencies that she could have called. I was with—" Raz stops midsentence. "Did your mother ever tell you who I am, Will? She made me swear not to tell you because she wanted to—"

You don't hear the end of that sentence because your brain flashes bright red so incandescent it leaves you seeing spots.

"Frances never told me you're my aunt," you say. "I found out from CPS today at school."

"Oh, Christ on a cracker."

You can't help it. You laugh. You laugh, and you laugh, and you laugh, because it's such a *Raz* reaction, and you're talking to Raz on the phone, and she's actually your aunt and you're related, and she is your real mom, and here she is, being a mom. You're talking to Raz.

And then she's laughing too, helplessly and a little confused, and you start talking. You tell her about Frances and the years since she stole you back. You tell her about Frances burning the paper with her phone number on it—which prompts an expletive—and you tell her you only just found the letters she wrote because Frances kept them locked in a box in the bottom of her closet. You tell her about the PO box and flushing all the drugs and keeping the money. You tell her about Hannah, your best friend, and about how it's been the last few weeks.

And you tell her about Julian because you can't not. She makes another little Raz noise at that, and when you pause, you can almost hear the smile.

"I knew you and Julian would get along, but I didn't quite think you'd get along that well." She laughs a bright, Raz laugh. "Oh, that is perfect."

Perfect.

You suppose it is.

For an hour, you talk. She listens. You tell her everything about Matt, how he's here with you right now, and awkwardly, how he's fixed your car for you. You tell her about the men, how they probably know where you live. When you finally wrap up the conversation, Raz tells you she's getting in her car and driving straight to you, because fuck waiting, because you've both waited long enough, and she doesn't want you to have to worry for another second.

"Will," she says just before she hangs up. "I'll see you soon. I love you."

You don't know the last time you heard someone say those words who wasn't Hannah. You think she might have been the last person to say them to you. You don't know.

"I love you," you say, batting at a tear on your cheek.

Chapter Twenty-Four

The next three and a half hours are the longest of your life, with the possible exception of the first three and a half with Frances when she stole you back.

Matt puts up with your relentless pacing. He hovers near the peninsula of the kitchen counter and clearly doesn't feel comfortable leaving you alone while you're waiting for Raz, but he also clearly doesn't feel comfortable invading this reunion. By the time you get a text that Raz sends from the nearby Wawa, he looks like his insides are about to tear in half.

"It's okay," you tell him. "You're not going to ruin anything, but if you want to run, it's okay too. I doubt anybody's going to turn up in the next five minutes before she can get here."

Matt's feet are planted to the floor with indecision for a few seconds, but then he grabs his keys, glancing at the bowl of condiments and Colt .45 without appearing to see it. "I can't wait to meet her, but you deserve to be alone for this. I mean—"

You snort a laugh. "I know what you mean."

He wraps you into one of those big brother bear hugs before he moves toward the door. "You okay if I tell Hannah about this when I see her?"

Shit. Hannah. You didn't text her or anything. She was in school all day—at least you assume she was—but still.

"Yeah, tell her I'm sorry I didn't let her know sooner."

"She'll understand," Matt says in this grim voice that you're starting to recognize as his exasperated big brother voice.

"Thank you," you tell him. "For everything."

"Yeah, well," he says. He scuffs his hand through his hair, his back to the door. Suddenly, his gaze zooms back to the bowl of ketchup packets and hot sauce. "Is that a fucking *gun*?"

"Uh, yeah," you tell him sheepishly. "It was Frances's and I got scared the other night."

He points at it, looking every inch the stern big brother. "The second Raz gets here, you give her that thing."

"I will. I promise."

Matt seems mollified by that, but the frown seems etched into his forehead as he scrubs a hand through his hair.

You don't know what else to say, so you hug him again, and he leaves.

In the past few years, you never thought you'd see Raz again, let alone like this.

The sound of tires in the drive chases away every thought you have. For a moment you're afraid it's the *Brady Bunch* dealers again, but the car is a Subaru, and then Raz is getting out of it. Her hair has a streak of white at the front that wasn't there before, but she still looks the same. And she is running up the driveway to you, and you're running down the stairs, and you don't care for half a second that it's cold, because it's *Raz*.

She throws her arms around you.

Her hair smells like raspberries—she always used to buy the same body spray at the Body Shop—and she grasps you so tight you think she might never let go. And that would be just fine.

You cling to her, and she clings right back, murmuring at you how much she loves you, how much she missed you.

When Raz finally pulls back, she looks into your face, her hand gently patting your hair, your cheek, and her warm brown eyes locked on you in something that looks like awe.

"Look at you," she says. Her eyes are leaking. She blinks a few times quickly.

"I'm so glad you're here," you say.

It's not adequate. You don't think there are any adequate words for how this feels. It's like the first night in her house where you didn't know her yet, but you went into your room and there was a lock on the door, and you locked it, locking her out, and she just said gently, "It's your room. I'll never go in without your permission."

And you believed her. And she never did without asking, even when you stole an entire carton of ice cream and ate it, and the next day you got really sick, and she just held your hair back while you barfed.

So you go inside.

You show Raz around the house where you've lived with Frances for years, the rooms you've cleaned, the carpets you've scrubbed within an inch of their lives. You tell her about Levi and the red sedan full of men. You show her the gun and tell her about the footprints and why you had it in the fruit bowl in the first place. To your surprise, she checks it with even more expert efficiency than Hannah did when she first found it. Raz empties it of bullets completely, double and triple checking it before carefully putting the bullets in a plastic bag and the gun itself in her purse.

"It's likely a stretch to think Frances had a permit for this," Raz says in explanation, "but I'm not leaving a loaded gun around the house for any reason."

This—this is what a mom is supposed to be like.

Before your brain can explode, you continue showing Raz around the house.

Raz's presence chases the lingering smoke smell away a little more with every step she takes into the house. You don't want her to have to sleep in Frances's bed even with the clean sheets and everything, but Raz just shushes you and says she's slept in worse places than a bed that used to belong to a terrible individual.

For hours you just talk. She laughs and shakes her head when evening rolls around and all you've got is frozen dinners, and then she drives you to the store, and you both go shopping, and when you get home, she shoos you out of the kitchen and cooks a meal that would feed four people.

When you eat, you sit next to each other on the sofa.

It takes a while for you to get the words out of your mouth. "You're my dad's sister?"

Raz gives you a soft smile. "Yeah," she says. "I was with his kids the past couple of weekends, actually."

Your head snaps up. "Kids?"

Holy shit. You have siblings?

Raz closes her eyes for a moment, nodding her head and breathing out. "Your mother should have told you, but I'm not surprised she didn't."

"Will you tell me?" Your voice comes out small, so small. You forget about the chicken leg on your plate even though the food is delicious.

"Of course, Will," Raz says, opening her eyes again and watching you sadly. "Your dad, Jaime, had two kids with Mara before he met your mother. He was in a bad place at the time, and he and Mara were always on and off. But he loved those babies."

There's pain in her face, and even though you were always pretty sure your dad was dead, it's something else entirely to hear him talked about in the past tense.

"He'd served in Iraq, Jaime," Raz says softly. "Got caught in an IED explosion and had a lot of internal bleeding. He never really was the same after that. Then he met Frances. She got pregnant almost right away with you, and Mara—well. She didn't want Frances anywhere near her kids. Mara moved off-grid in Pennsylvania. She's practically raised those kids to be frontierspeople, I swear. Made one of me, too. My brother'd laugh himself sick if he knew I'd willingly gone on a two-week hiking trip carrying my own sixty-pound pack along with his kids and Mara." Raz's voice grows wistful. "Jaime died of an aneurysm while Frances was pregnant with you. It happens sometimes with traumatic brain injuries like he'd had, even years later, but it's rare."

The news hits like a sack of lead to the stomach.

Raz takes your hand and squeezes it. "If this is too much—"

"I need to know," you say.

Everything is spinning. Your whole life is not what you thought it was, carved out of Frances's lies and all of this—all of this is too much. It is. But you need to know.

Raz nods. "Mara is a good woman. Your older brother and sister are both at Temple University in Philly, and Mara has a pair of younger kids as well. José and Isabel are the oldest—José's just twenty-one, and Isabel's nineteen."

They're so close to your age. You have . . . siblings.

"They've always wanted to meet you, Will," Raz says softly. "If you want, I'll take you up to Philly any time."

"I—yeah. Yeah, I want that." You don't think you've ever felt this before. This *big* feeling. A sense of largeness that encompasses you, your world expanding with it.

You're afraid to ask the other big question, the one you haven't asked since you were about eight years old and found out that your memories of being cold in a big metal box were real.

"How did I—how did I end up in the system?" You don't know if you really want the answer, only that you need it.

"I wish I could tell you more, Will. I only know what your file said, that you were found in a dumpster in Hagerstown. Frances had disappeared with you after Jaime died, and neither myself nor Mara could manage to track you down. We weren't even sure you were alive until you were about nine." Raz's face contorts with anger. "After that, I spent the next two years trying to get you myself, but it was a lot harder than expected. I was young, barely an adult myself, and I was terrified of tipping off Frances that I was looking for you. She always hated my guts, blamed me for Jaime dying."

You didn't know that. You didn't know Frances was fighting with Raz before that day she showed up in person to steal you back. But that last part? The part about her blaming *Raz* for your dad's death?

This is your fault.

Suddenly, you don't think you're the only one Frances ever said those words to.

"Frances was—" You stop. Your mouth is so dry, so dry.

You don't think chicken will help, but you shove a bite in there anyway, more for something to do than anything else.

"Will, it's my fault she found you," Raz says, and the pain in her voice makes the chicken turn to ash in your mouth.

"It's *not* your fault," you say with a ferocity that is dampened slightly by half-chewed chicken spilling over your lip with the force of your words. You manage to swallow and clear your throat. "Frances ruined everything, always."

Something sags in Raz's face, or maybe relaxes. Even as you think it, you adjust—that's a Raz look you know. That's relief.

"She only found me because you were adopting me, right?" you say, your voice surprisingly calm. "I remember what you said in the letters I found."

"Legally, she had to be notified. I won't get into the process, but it was . . . well. Trying." Raz's relief is gone as soon as it came with the remembered stress. But then she looks at you, and that stress vanishes too, leaving only love. "She tried to prove to the department that she could take care of you. They didn't actually have proof that she'd abandoned you. She claimed someone kidnapped you."

"Of course she did," you say faintly, around a new mouthful of chicken, this one better considered than the first.

"I *was* going to adopt you, Will. I wish I'd fought harder. I couldn't afford a better lawyer at the time, and there is nothing I've regretted more in my life. I should have—" Raz breaks off, swallowing hard. Her eyes are glassy. "I should have gotten a loan. Anything to afford it, to keep you."

You could be mad at her, you suppose. But you're not. "You didn't do anything wrong. Frances did. And now she's gone, and we're both here."

The words come out without you even thinking about how that might sound in the open. But instead of recoiling from you basically confessing you're glad Frances is dead, Raz just puts her arms around you again and pulls you close.

"I'm not going anywhere ever again," she says into your hair.

"Please don't," you say.

And then you're crying.

You, Will. You're crying. Big, hiccupping sobs that taste like chicken and roasted potatoes. And Raz is shaking softly, but she holds you so tight, so tight to her chest, and she just lets you cry.

All the years. All the nights you lay there in bed thinking the year you spent with Raz was just a glimpse of a dream to fuel your torment. All the exhaustion from going to school and then work and then back and doing it all over again. All the chores and the bills and the everything. The bruises and the heavy footsteps outside your locked bedroom door. The stench of alcohol and smoke. The fear that the person Frances brought home would hurt you. The relief every time she left.

You're probably getting snot in Raz's hair, but you know she doesn't care, and she just strokes the back of your head the way she did when you were young.

You almost don't believe this is real.

But she's here. She's really here.

Chapter Twenty-Five

Is that . . . bacon you smell when you wake up?

It's definitely bacon.

You don't think you've woken up to the smell of bacon in this house ever. There's coffee smell too.

There's not so much as a whiff of tobacco, and your nose is so trained to it, you think you could smell someone smoking in the next county.

When you stumble out of your room, there's Raz, awake and still pajama'd, making breakfast. And she beams at you.

You almost turn right back around and go into your room to come back out again just to make sure you actually did wake up.

"Morning!" Raz says.

"Morning!" Have you ever heard that chirpy note in your voice before? Are you actually *smiling* before ten in the morning?

You can't believe how normal this feels. Sitting down (at the table this time) and eating breakfast with Raz, telling her about how school has been—it just feels like this is how it's always been.

Raz asked to meet your lawyers. She wants to establish a plan on how to handle Frances's dealing and the PO box you discovered. Last night you called Dana before bed to ask her if she and Joseph could meet with Raz today, so while you're at school, Raz is going to go talk with the lawyers. You're supposed to work at the library after school, but you call out for the first time in your life. You think Mary will forgive you.

Euphoria is a word you've always looked at sideways, but driving to school you're pretty sure that's what you're feeling. It sucked to say good-bye to Raz, yeah, but she's going to be there when you're done.

She's here. In Bright Springs. With you.

Naturally, the first person you see at school is Levi. He's in a puffy blue coat and has just gotten a haircut from the precision of the fade, but his tan looks practically painted on. It's like it hovers in a sickly layer above his skin, and he flashes a friend a wild, almost frenzied grin before he sees you. His eyes fall on you then, and you miss a step.

He gives you a winsome smirk as he closes the distance to you. Before you can get away, his hand grabs your upper arm. His grip is not light, and he smells like tinny sweat and something else that reminds you all too much of Frances. "You should have taken your shit car and gotten out of town."

Bracing yourself for more, your entire body goes rigid, but to your shock, Levi's hand's pressure vanishes from your arm, and he spins away laughing like he's told the best joke in the world.

You should worry more about it. However, the moment you walk inside, a ginger-haired bowling ball almost knocks you over.

"Will! Oh my god, was Matt telling the truth? Is Raz here?" It's Hannah, of course, and she's babbling. "He came home and said something happened and then that Raz was there but he didn't meet her? This is insane. I'm so glad she's here!"

"She's really here," you say. The lump in your throat dislodges a little. You missed this Hannah. "She made me breakfast."

Hannah's face softens in that way that tells you you just said something a little weird—but she beams at you.

"Tell me everything," she says.

The two of you find a quiet corner in the library, and you run through the events of the past few days, since you haven't even told her about Julian yet. *Julian*. You need to text them as soon as possible. You exchanged a couple of hurried texts last night, but they were at work, and you were in Raz-Mode, and all you know is that they are thrilled that Raz is here.

"So the school knows about Frances," Hannah says, exhaling loudly when you're done. "And they aren't taking you away?"

"No," you say. "I mean, yeah. They know, and no, they're not taking me away."

You feel like Hannah kind of wants to say *I told you so*, but thankfully, she seems to think the better of it.

"Can I—" Hannah breaks off, looking suddenly shy. "Can I meet Raz?"

You stare at her. "Of course you can meet Raz. She's meeting with your mom and Joseph today, and then maybe tonight we can all have dinner or something?"

What a bizarre thing this is. Family . . . dinner? With you and Raz and Dana and Hannah? Not Matt, since he said he's working tonight, but still.

Hannah beams at you. She opens her mouth again, then shuts it with a slight shake of her head. You think you know what she was going to say. Or rather, going to ask. You are thankful that she doesn't actually ask if Ashton could come too. Not tonight. Not to this, at least not yet.

The school day actually speeds by. The only weird thing is Levi, who just keeps smirking at you now and then. He's still giving off waves of jittery, metallic wildness that make you want to recoil. Ugh.

Right before the end of the day, you get called to Suzie's office again.

No Elizabeth this time, so when you go in and shut the door, you wonder what's going on.

"Thanks for coming," Suzie says with a small smile. "Sorry to page you right before the bell, but—"

The bell itself punctuates her sentence as if to prove a point. You sit in your usual chair, and she perches on her own. Her hair is in a messy bun on top of her head today. Her curls are excellent.

"It's okay," you say.

It is, you think. What a weird feeling.

"Will, I wanted to apologize to you," Suzie says gently. "You clearly didn't feel safe telling me what was going on with you, and I should have—"

You interrupt her. "You couldn't have done anything to help."

"I don't believe that's true, but I am sad that you do. I also understand why you do."

"Do you?" Her statement surprises you.

Suzie gives you a wry smile. "Will, I've done this job for fifteen years."

Oh.

You talk to her for a while, first tentatively and then more comfortably. She seems so genuinely happy for you and Raz that your opinion of her gets even better.

Just before you leave, she says, "I just want you to know that none of this is your fault. You deserve family who cares for you. I won't give you platitudes telling you how brave and strong you are, because even though you are brave and strong, your normal is your own normal. But I do want you to know that you can talk to me. I also want you to know that Elizabeth's visit had nothing to do with the thing I had mentioned before—that was something else entirely, and we can talk about it another time if you want."

"Thank you," you say, and you mean it. Whatever it is can wait. But her bringing it up to reassure you that she hadn't ambushed you or lied does help.

You leave the office feeling like your feet carry you better, making your way out to the now-empty parking lot. You didn't realize you were talking quite that long.

You parked in your usual spot, at the far back side of the lot since you don't really mind walking that far, and besides, it gets you out of range of the people who crowd around the school entrances.

Something's wrong when you approach the car. It sags in its spot, strangely uneven despite the level ground.

It only takes you a second to spot it, and for the first time in your life, you think you're too angry to curse.

The tires have been slashed *again.*

A sound is coming from your throat that sounds almost like a growl.

Working up the mental capacity to make a phone call takes longer than you think it should, but you're just so angry.

It had to be Levi. Him with that smirk all day. You feel the ghost of his hand wrapped around your arm.

Matt just spent a thousand dollars to fix *your* car, and now Levi's slashed the tires on Frances's too. It's not like you even need the car. You could sell it. But with four slashed tires, you're going to get a whole lot less for it.

Aren't you allowed to have one good fucking thing? Of course not. Because you're a monster, and every good thing that happens to you has to be balanced out by at least one really bad one.

You finally pick up the phone and try calling Raz—you don't know much right now, but you do know she would want you to. It goes directly to voice mail.

"Raz, it's me. I'm at the school, and Levi slashed the tires on Frances's car. I just—ugh. He's the superintendent's son, so he's probably going to just get away with it, but it had to be him."

There is a text from her that you didn't see, time-stamped thirty minutes ago. *Meeting with the lawyers 'til five. Don't you dare cook dinner!*

It's just about four now, but you're not hungry.

You decide to call Hannah, thinking she'd appreciate being able to help.

She answers on the third ring. "What's up?"

"Levi slashed the tires again."

"What. The. Fuck."

"I know." You kick one of them, which doesn't make you feel better and does make your toe throb a little. "Can you come get me? It's not snowing, but I don't want to like . . . walk. Not with all the other stuff."

You can almost hear her eyes widen. "Yeah, of course. I just got to Hagerstown, though, so it'll be about twenty-five? I'll turn right around."

"Thank you," you say.

"I seriously owe you one. I'm going to drive now, okay? I'll see you soon."

She hangs up, and you take a breath. Okay. Okay. Not the worst thing, this.

Relief pools like hot cocoa in your stomach.

At least you can wait in the car with the ignition on and the heater running, which you decide is the smartest idea. You wish you were a mage and could just summon a fire glyph or whatever, but the technology to make a box of warm on a cold day is acceptable.

You send a text to Julian. *Levi the loser slashed the tires again.*

Your phone buzzes immediately.

Omg he didn't.

Hannah's coming to get me, but basically, yeah. He did. Raz is meeting with the lawyers right now.

I'm just so glad Raz is with you, Julian says. *You deserve this, Will.*

You don't know what it means to deserve anything, but seeing Julian say that makes your heart give a little extra oomph of a thud.

Sitting there in the car with the heat blasting, you can't quite believe what's happening. Any of it. That someone like Julian is even interested in someone like you—well. You never thought anyone would be interested in you. Hell. You never thought you'd really be interested in anyone that wasn't an ancient elven demigod.

With the heat on full blast, you don't hear the sound of the car pulling up beside you at first, and when you do, you assume it's Hannah, and you finish your text to Julian before you look up.

But it's not Hannah. It's a Ford sedan with chipping maroon paint.

Your phone drops into the cup holder.

Chapter Twenty-Six

You grab the phone again, hit Hannah's number as fast as you can. She's driving, and she doesn't answer. You've never prayed for voice mail as hard as you are just now.

"Hannah, it's me. The guys from the gas station are here, and I'm alone. Don't come. Get Raz."

Hanging up, you drop the phone between the cup holder and the seat, where it'll be a pain in the ass for you to get out, but less likely for them to steal, even if that would surely be at the bottom of anyone's list of priorities.

A small, insignificant action to protect what is yours.

You hear their doors open. The sound is unwelcome, hostile. You could try and drive away, but on four flats, you're not going to get far.

Levi planned this. It had to be him.

You've always known Levi was an asshole, but you never thought he'd stoop to . . . anything like this. All those sly looks he's been giving you, like he had X-ray vision and could see through your shirt, your skin, all the way into your guts to know everything you don't even know about yourself. The tires, so you couldn't leave.

And the goddamn *car*—the maroon sedan. These guys have been on school property before. Right fucking here, when Levi shoved that first-year into it right in front of you.

It's not even a surprise when he's the one who wrenches open the door to Frances's car.

"Hi, Will," he says. He smiles like an anglerfish, all teeth and death.

"Hi, Trump's understudy," you say.

"Get out of the car." Levi moves aside so you can, expecting that you'll just obey.

When you don't move, Levi leans both arms on the top of the door and peers over it at you. It strikes you that he's not even a little bit worried about being caught.

"Let's be clear. You can get out of the car nice and easy, or they can drag you out." Levi motions at the quartet of sandy-blond stooges. "Don't be stupid."

You are a lot of things. Frances used to call you the stupidest smart kid on Earth because you could get decent grades but not read her mind. You might not be that smart. But you do know the outline of the gun under the tall stooge's T-shirt.

The Colt .45, the one gun you know Frances had, is in Raz's purse now, far away.

Even if it were here, you're definitely smart enough to know that pulling it out would make this situation much, much worse.

You really hope Hannah isn't coming. You hope she got your message.

You get out of the car.

"There you go," Levi drawls. He moves around the door when you're out, turning off the engine and pocketing the keys. At your look, he rolls his eyes. "You'll get them back if you're good."

You hate him. You actually hate him.

"Will, is it?" The tall guy saunters over.

You just look at him. He's not in any kind of hurry.

"So Frances is really dead," he says. "Huh. I thought she'd outlive just about everyone for sheer spite."

"Yeah, well, her spite probably gave her the heart attack," you mutter.

"Always said her kid was an ungrateful freak," the guy says to you.

You can't help it. You laugh. "You're not creative enough to call me anything she hasn't already, my dude."

"You're going to tell me what you did with the stuff she had at the post office." He stops when you make a noise of protest, shaking his head. "Nah. I know you took it. Talked to my guy there. He saw you. Don't even bother."

The impulse to tell the truth is probably the stupidest one you've had. Way beyond the phone thing.

"I took the money as repayment for me paying her goddamn bills since I was fourteen, and I flushed the fucking oxy down the toilet with the rest of the sewage."

Levi is watching you with detached curiosity, which you return blandly.

"So what are you going to do?" You're still looking at Levi when you say it. "Beat me up to teach me a lesson? Wouldn't be the first time you were too much of an incompetent prick to use words like a big kid. Or use that Glock you've got in your pants. I'm sure whipping that out on school property won't even be noticed in this county anyway."

The guy laughs. He moves his shirt enough that the flash of metal is unmistakable. The other three guys have moved to perch on the back of the Ford and lean against the back of Frances's car. You're trapped.

Do you have a death wish, Will?

You're not reckless, but you are tired. You're tired of cleaning up Frances's mess. You're tired of Levi and his privilege and his smirks and his free pass to do whatever the hell he wants because of who his dad is. You think if you were your character from *Dragon Age*, you'd chuck every single one of their sorry asses through a rift and right into the Fade where they could meet the reflections of your rage and pride and despair and it would eat them all alive.

A car pulls into the parking lot.

Not just any car.

A bright red Jeep Wrangler. Hannah.

You can't move. Your bravado vanishes in one heartbeat, and she's parked beside you and jumping out of the Jeep and then she's almost *throwing* Levi to the side.

"We're leaving, Will," she says.

You've never seen her like this. Fury pours off her.

"We weren't done talking," the tall stooge says to her.

And Hannah just hauls off and clocks the guy in the jaw. She hasn't seen the gun in his waistband or realized the others probably have guns too.

He takes it like someone used to getting punched. He probably is.

His fist connects with her face, and Hannah goes down, out cold.

He reaches for the gun and it's there, in his hand. He flicks the safety off. Then it's more than just a threat.

"Move, and I'll shoot her," he says to you.

You don't move.

Levi is standing stock still, staring at Hannah's prone body as if he wasn't expecting that. It might be the first thing you and Levi have in common.

There's no such thing as safety when there's a monster in your midst.

This is your fault.

"Now," the guy says conversationally. "You seem like a good kid, Will. Heart in the right place, and all that. Don't you think so?"

He waits until the stooges behind you grunt an assent that sounds a bit closer to derision, but you really couldn't care less.

"See, they agree. Bad situation. Real stupid friend. But a good kid. Will's even a good name."

They're wrong about that, though.

Your name is Will because that's what it takes to live among people who hate you for no other reason than that you exist. Just like they're wrong about you not being a monster.

So. Will. Will the Monster, here we are, and here you are in the center of a ring of eyes that feel hot upon you, your best friend unmoving at your feet.

This is your fault. That's all you can think. It's your fault. You froze. You couldn't warn her about the gun, anything.

Hannah's hurt, and she could die here. You think you see blood dripping from her nose onto the asphalt. It's cold, and she's not wearing her jacket.

You did this to her. You fucked up again, Will.

Something punches you in the leg, and you realize it's your own fist, and you do it again and again, and Levi and the stooges just watch you without moving, watch you freak out. What are they going to do, anyway? Stop you? Laugh at you? They do neither of those things.

"Levi!" The voice bellows out across the parking lot. It sounds vaguely familiar.

The man striding with long, purposeful steps is in a pristine charcoal-gray suit.

It's Levi's *dad*. Superintendent Strand.

His phone is in his hand, and his eyes are locked on his son's with rage mottling his face. Levi's mouth falls open; no sound comes out.

Another car enters the parking lot. A Subaru. Raz.

The superintendent doesn't know these men are armed.

"They've got guns!" you yell, and you kick the tall blond man in the nuts as hard as you possibly can.

He keels over with an explosive yelp of pain. "Shit—fucking—freak!"

There's a screech of tires, then another, and Raz is running toward you, and the stooges scatter, swearing and ignoring their downed buddy, and at first you think it's the force of Raz's arrival alone that sent them running until you realize that the screech of tires was too recent to be hers. The Colt .45 is in her hand, and you have the feeling it's no longer empty of ammunition.

A flash of blue light illuminates the afternoon.

The cops.

The gun in Raz's hand disappears into her purse so quickly, you wonder if you might have imagined it. Raz, running at you with a gun when the police are here, their cars screeching into the parking lot. They could *shoot* her if they were to see it. Terror grips you at the thought, but the cop cars come to skidding halts, and when the officers pile out, they are not even looking at Raz.

Raz, though? She seems to see no one but you. Without a single moment of hesitation, Raz is between you and them.

The stooges practically trip over each other to kneel on the asphalt, their hands over their heads. You can't see anything that's happening. Nothing makes any sense. How are the police here? Did Raz call them? Why would she think to do that?

Raz's arms are around you then, holding you tight against her. "Will, are you okay? Did they hurt you?"

"Hannah—" you gasp out, but the superintendent is already there.

He's turned her onto her back and is checking her breathing, her pulse. Blood trickles from her nose, and she's still unconscious.

There are *several* cop cars here. Three. The officers are already disarming and handcuffing the stooges, including the tall one who's still sweating and shaking with pain from your kick. Good.

One of the officers grabs a first-aid kit and a shock blanket and jogs up to the superintendent and Hannah, and you don't see his partner until Levi is pressed up against Frances's car, getting handcuffed.

Holy shit.

His dad's not even looking at him. He's speaking in a low voice to the police officer who's covering Hannah with the blanket, and the bitterness that you feel at that sight almost knocks you off your feet. Nothing's going to happen to Levi.

"My car keys," you say suddenly, and several sets of eyes turn on you. "They're in Levi's pocket."

Levi's cuffed, so the officer looks at his dad, who slowly gets to his feet, closes the distance between Hannah and his son, and reaches into Levi's pocket with a perfunctory jerk, pulling out the set of keys and a baggie. He places the keys on the roof of Frances's car, then looks at the baggie with an unidentifiable emotion.

Whatever's in the bag is not weed; that's for certain. Looks like coke, from the powdery whiteness of it.

The superintendent's lips halve in size, and the officer starts reading Levi his rights as one of the others tells the superintendent to drop the evidence.

Raz's arm is still around you, and you're thankful for it. Your body seems to hum with adrenaline. You feel like tinfoil about to crumple.

"We'll meet you at the station," the officer says to the superintendent. "I presume you'll want to call your lawyer."

The superintendent nods sharply, and you watch as the officer holding Levi tells him to move and escorts him not-very-gracefully to the waiting cruiser. The other officer moves a little distance away, speaking into his radio. You don't know if—oh, god, *Matt*.

"Hannah's brother's an EMT," you blurt out. "He's working today. Somebody warn him that his sister's hurt so he—so he doesn't turn up and find out that way."

The officer looks startled by your outburst but gives you a sharp nod. "Thanks. I'll need a statement from you in a minute."

"Okay." You don't know what they're going to want to know, but you'll deal with that when you find out, you guess.

"Harold," Raz says, and you jump when you see Levi's dad—the superintendent—look over at her with a sigh.

"Yes, you were quite right, Esmeralda. What a disappointing mess," the superintendent says.

Anger fills you. "Excuse you?"

To your utter surprise, he winces. "Forgive me. That was insensitive of me."

At that moment, Hannah stirs. You fly out from under Raz's arm and land hard on your knees beside your friend. She's blinking, a little bleary and with the left side of her face blossoming into a swollen, bruised mess. Flecks of blood show through where the force of the man's punch broke the skin. You wish you'd kicked him even harder.

"Will," Hannah says. She swallows, blinking.

"Hannah, I'm so sorry. I tried to warn you. The guy had a gun, and—"

"I got your message," she says.

"What?"

She looks like she wants to try and sit up, but you shake your head at her, and she leans back down against the balled-up jacket someone put there. Charcoal fabric. You only just now realized that the superintendent took off his suit jacket to make Hannah a pillow.

"I got your message. I called Mom and she called the police. Levi's dad was with her and Raz at the meeting, so he heard everything. I'm so sorry. I know you don't trust cops, but—"

"It's okay this time," you say, shaking your head. You almost want to cry and you're not sure if it's with bitterness or joy. The clout of Dana Straczynski combined with the superintendent probably was enough to make sure nobody ended up dead. "They got the guys. They arrested Levi, too."

"Good," she mutters, and then she closes her eyes again. Her throat is still moving like she's trying to swallow.

When the ambulance arrives a minute later, it is indeed Matt driving it, and he comes running with his partner and the stretcher for Hannah. He reaches her with a small bursting noise of rage.

"I'm sorry," you blurt out to him. "I'm so sorry."

Matt mutters something to his partner, who nods and starts talking to Hannah, and Matt, after giving his sister a kiss on the forehead, comes over to you and wraps you in a hug.

"Will," he says. "You did not do this. This is not on you."

He kisses *your* forehead and turns back to Hannah. With a glance toward the younger cop who told you he needed your statement, Matt gives a muttered "Oh, thank god it's you, Kerrigan." Kerrigan gives Matt a curt nod.

Someone puts one of those shock blankets over your shoulders. You didn't even realize you were shaking.

As Matt and his partner get Hannah loaded into the ambulance, you tell Officer Kerrigan your story. As you're talking, Hannah's mother shows up, and she introduces herself as your lawyer. Raz is there the whole time, holding your hand in both of hers. So you talk, looking at Dana every now and then for confirmation, and when she gives you the okay, you even tell him that you found the drugs, give him the key from the key ring for the PO box and tell him what number it is and that they've got someone working for the post office who is helping them run narcotics.

"Am I in trouble?" you ask when you're done.

Out of the corner of your eye, you see Raz's face harden as if to say *I dare you* to the cop.

Officer Kerrigan exchanges a long, level look with Dana.

"It's up to the district attorney ultimately, but I'll vouch for you. I can't see any reason to press any charges against you." Kerrigan glances at Harold. "Your son's another story, though, superintendent. He's going to be looking at possession, accessory to assault with a deadly weapon, destruction of property—"

"I know," the superintendent says curtly.

And to your surprise—again—the man sighs. He must be cold without his coat, which is still balled up on the ground where Matt and the other EMT now have Hannah on the stretcher-gurney thing.

"I will not blame you if you would like to press charges yourselves based on this incident."

That's the last thing you expected to hear out of Levi's father's mouth. But he looks like he means it. He looks . . . tired. Then again, you're pretty sure at least one of those charges is a felony.

"I think perhaps we can discuss an alternate route on our end," Raz says dryly. "But I imagine the district attorney will be less forgiving."

Officer Kerrigan's mask of neutrality slips just enough to imply that he agrees.

When the police finally go and Dana goes off in the ambulance with Matt and Hannah—you'll have to go in and do more paperwork later, but not today—Superintendent Strand and Raz and you are all who's left.

"Will, is it?" the superintendent says to you. He holds out his hand. "I am truly sorry. How long has Levi been behaving this way toward you?"

Your eyebrow hikes up. "Honestly? He's been an asshole to me since the day I met him. He sexually harasses Hannah. He bullies anyone he perceives as weaker. And I'm pretty sure he's the one who told the school my mother died so he could set me up to get jumped by his dealer buddies. I dread seeing him, and he gets away with everything because he's your son."

Superintendent Strand winces again. "Well. Things changed over the summer when I caught him stealing my Valium. I've been trying to . . . redirect my parenting approach." This, he seems to direct at Raz, who gives him a tight-lipped smile that doesn't reach her eyes. Superintendent Strand actually grimaces. "Believe me when I say Levi will *not* get away with this."

After a moment, he walks over and picks up the bloody, balled-up jacket, shaking it out a little. He pulls a checkbook from the breast pocket.

"This won't begin to make reparations for what you've just told me—or what my son did here today—but at least the car I can take care of. Cars," he corrects himself. Anger is written across his face in bold lines again. "I am truly sorry for my son's behavior. There is no excusing it."

You watch as he writes a check for twenty-five hundred dollars like it's nothing.

He makes it out to you.

Chapter Twenty-Seven

You were assuming there would be no dinner with Hannah and the family tonight, but no sooner do you and Raz get home than do you get a phone call from her.

"Look, my face hurts like hell, and I probably can't eat anything but a mashed potato smoothie, but can you and Raz come over anyway?" It's the first thing she says, and there's no way you're saying no to that.

"On one condition," you tell her.

"What's that?"

"Invite Ashton."

"Jesus, you're mean. You want her to see me like this?" But her voice is softer. She knows why you said it, really.

"She'll want to know you're okay." You hang up a minute later, looking at Raz. "Is that okay? I didn't—I didn't ask you if you wanted to go have dinner with them."

Raz reaches out and brushes your hair back from your face. "Sweetie, I'm just happy to be here with you and that you're okay. I could punch that Levi myself."

You give her a crooked smile.

And you both go to Hannah's house.

It's bizarre walking in there with Raz. Ashton's already there—the girl must have broken land speed records to beat you—and she keeps dancing little kisses on Hannah's cheek, which makes Hannah wince and blush at the same time.

Dana wraps you in a huge hug and then does the same to Raz. You still kind of can't believe it? But Hannah's there, and Matt too (he says someone covered the rest of his shift), and Dana's ordered a whole mess of sushi, and pretty soon all six of you are seated around the big, fancy dining room table that you've never eaten at before when you've been here.

You've got chopsticks full of seaweed salad when the doorbell rings.

"I'll get it!" Hannah chirps just as Matt almost scurries from his seat to beat her.

"Sit your butt down, sis," he says. "You may have more street cred than me now, but I'm getting the door."

You don't know who would be ringing the doorbell at this time of night, but it's probably a family friend who heard what happened or something. (News travels fast in Bright Springs since no one has anything better to do but speed it along.)

But it's not a family friend. Or at least—not 'til now.

It's Julian.

Matt leads them around the corner into the dining room, and you almost fall out of your chair.

"How did you—" You gape at them, a dopey smile made dopier by the fact that your mouth won't stay closed.

"I invited them," Hannah says quietly. "This morning."

You feel a flash of shame. You hadn't wanted Ashton here this morning when you were talking to Hannah, but she invited Julian. You're going to need to work on that one.

You look at Julian. "But I was texting you right before—"

"I was in Frederick," Julian tells you. "Stopped to get gas. My god, Hannah. You told me, but—yikes, my dear."

Hannah cringes, and Dana gets up from the table just as Matt sits back down.

"You must be Julian," Dana says, putting out her arms to invite them for a hug, which Julian gives her. "I'm Hannah and Matt's mom. You can call me Dana."

"Thank you for inviting me," Julian says, and when they see Raz, their eyes light up.

Raz is the next one to hug them, and she plants a kiss on their cheek, too. You can't seem to stop smiling.

Dana pulls a chair in next to yours, and Julian sits while Hannah introduces Ashton as her girlfriend, and every time she smiles, she twitches a little from the bruise.

Your heart might actually explode.

Julian gives you a soft kiss on the cheek when everyone starts eating, and you return it. For the second time tonight, you tell the story of what happened, and even though the mood is light, you see both Raz and Dana tense throughout it. Matt, too. Ashton seems bowled over by Hannah's heroism.

The time sneaks by so fast that before you know it, the food and plates are cleared away, and it's almost ten o'clock.

"I think Will and Hannah should probably be excused from school tomorrow," Raz says dryly. "Maybe the rest of this week."

"I agree," Dana tells her. "There have been enough adventures for one school week."

You get ready to go home, and when everyone's hugging goodbye, you take Matt aside.

"The superintendent gave me a check to pay for the damage Levi did to the cars," you say. "I'll transfer you whatever you need to cover mine."

"Will," Matt says, "I'm not going to take it."

"What?" You say it too loudly and look around to see if anybody noticed, which it doesn't seem they did. "You have to."

"No, I do not. I paid for your car to get fixed because I wanted to." When you start to protest, Matt cuts you off. "Will, I have over thirty grand in savings. I'll be fine. Use it for whatever you need or want. You don't owe me anything."

"But—"

"No buts, dude. You're family."

That stops you short, and even if it didn't, you'd have to turn away, because your eyes are prickling and your nose feels like you have to sneeze.

"Thank you," you say instead.

"We love you," Matt says simply. "You know that, right?"

You guess you do.

Walking into your house with Julian and Raz is surreal. They're chattering happily and for a moment you have to stop and just stand there in the kitchen wondering if this is your life.

There have been plenty of moments over the years where you wondered that, but never in a good way.

But now here you are.

Together, you all go out to the shed with the security light blazing and a flashlight apiece. The silver keys from Frances's key ring open the padlocks, just like you thought.

What *isn't* just like you thought, however, is the shed.

There is plenty in there that isn't visible through the dingy window on the door. Not only is it chock-full of booze—that fact is almost amusing, since it implies Frances thought you would steal it—but you find a box with even more drugs.

You do find one more thing, though. Something you never, ever would have expected.

Covered in dust and moisture damaged on the outside, at first you think it's a long-lost Frances family photo album, but the second Raz sees it, she makes a guttural sound and flies to it, opening the yellowed pages reverently.

Immediately, you know the man staring back at you from the first page is your father.

He's got your nose, your brow ridge. Hazel eyes. His hair is deep brown, his skin a tanned bronze you definitely didn't inherit, and he's got a cigar in his mouth.

"Jaime," Raz says, touching the page with a finger.

Frances did hide a treasure in here. You and Julian take it into the house and carefully clean off the dust while Raz looks on, her face a storm of emotions.

Raz has to call the police for the drugs. Julian hovers beside you and Raz the whole time the police are there, their hand clammy in yours.

When Raz notices that Julian is practically trembling, she sends you both inside with strict orders to make hot cocoa, and she stays out there with the cops until they're done.

Once they've finally gone yet again, there's one more thing you need to do.

Tomorrow's trash day.

With the chalky dregs of instant cocoa on your tongue, you ask Raz and Julian to follow you outside, where you get Frances's ashes from her car.

Julian seems to realize what you're doing before Raz does, and their blue eyes look almost black in the long-cast shadows from the porch light on the driveway as you wrestle the big, wheeled trash can around from the side of the house.

You know that letting them see you do this could make them truly think you're a monster.

After all, you're about to throw your mother's remains in the garbage.

The thing is, she did that to you when you were still alive.

Raz just says, "Oh, Will, honey. You do what you need to do."

So you do.

Frances goes in the bin. The bin goes out to the road, wheels rattling along over the gravelly driveway like the world's most pathetic funeral procession.

That's it. In the morning, she'll be gone. Really gone. Forever.

You put one hand in Raz's and one in Julian's, and you walk back into the house that is now yours and smells of Raz and Julian's berry body mist. Huh. Maybe that's why Julian uses it—the way they seem to need Raz as much as you do, it isn't really surprising to think they chose her body spray for comfort.

The three of you stay up late, all a bit jittery from the emotion of the day, and you talk about what comes next. You tell Raz you want to move to Baltimore when school's done, and she is so thrilled she actually kicks her feet in these little tiny kicks you remember from way back. Thanksgiving is coming up right after your birthday. You'll get to drive to Baltimore and spend it with her. And Julian.

Eventually you all go to bed, and Raz doesn't even blink when you ask if it's okay if Julian sleeps in your room.

"Tonight isn't the night to make any major choices," she says carefully, looking you in the eye and then Julian.

You can't help the bark of a laugh that escapes you. "We're just going to sleep, Raz."

"Just sleep," Julian echoes, looking more vulnerable than you've ever seen them. There's a yearning in Julian's blue eyes, but it has nothing to do with sharing a bed and everything to do with, well. Raz.

They really do need Raz as much as you do, you think.

Raz, as always, knows just what to do.

"I know, my dears," she says. And then she hugs you both, kisses you each on the cheek, tells you both she loves you, and goes off to her room.

Her room. Frances has been chased out of this house.

So you and Julian go into your room.

They actually brought their own pajamas, and together you crawl into bed. Your bed's not as cozy as theirs, and for a while you just lie there talking in sleepy murmurs. And then for a while, you kiss each other, gentle kisses, soft kisses. You listen to their heartbeat, and they listen to yours.

You wonder what it'll be like to keep exploring Julian. You meant what you said—you really are just going to sleep. You're not ready for anything else yet, and you don't think Julian is either, but just being with them is nice.

It's nice.

Just before you both fall silent, Julian murmurs sleepily, "It feels different in the house now. Good different."

They drift off before you can ask what they mean, and you lie awake listening to the sound of both of your breathing.

When you wake the next morning, you let Julian sleep, and you go into the kitchen where Raz is awake and making breakfast again, and you help her the way you used to when you were younger, and she grins at you.

Once, you glance over to the fruit bowl, which now has fruit in it for the first time. Oranges and nectarines and bananas. Frances's phone is sitting next to it, and when you poke the screen with one tentative finger, it doesn't turn on.

It's dead. Somehow, you know it'll never inexplicably charge itself again.

Raz gives you a quizzical look, but because she's Raz, she doesn't pry. Maybe you'll tell her about the haunted phone one day. If anyone'd believe you, she would.

To your surprise, she nudges with an elbow in the direction of the fruit bowl. "That was full of mail. One thing in particular was important—from the school."

"From the school?" You squint at the nectarines as if they'll tell you what previously occupied their new home.

Raz nods, chopping an onion so quickly the knife is a blur. "It's on the table if you want to read it. You don't have to—it's from the counselor, and it is something that could change things for you even more."

The thing Suzie wanted to talk about. It's been in the fucking *fruit bowl* all along. She must have sent it just before school started.

You look at Raz. "What should I do?"

Raz gives you a small smile, setting down the knife and blinking away onion tears. You think they're onion tears, anyway. "It's up to you, but it might help you understand yourself better."

That's plenty for you. You skid over to the table and snatch up the folded piece of paper, seeing school letterhead on it. It doesn't take long to read, and you stubbornly skim over Frances's name in the salutation.

I'm writing because I have observed some behaviors in Will in the time I've known them that lead me to suspect they are on the autism spectrum, and I would like to ask for permission to have them assessed.

You hold your breath, reading through some of the behaviors in question. Physical stims (apparently, poking yourself with that bit of plastic on the chair in her office is a stim). Literal interpretations. Intense focus but reactivity with interruption. Difficulty understanding social cues and a very limited social circle—you snort at that. One person is hardly a circle.

Repetitive behaviors. Engagement with studies heavily tied to level of interest. Highly *specialized* interests.

Face warming as your gaze involuntarily goes to the *Dragon Age* posters on the wall, you thank the Dreadwolf that Frances did not open that letter herself.

Raz watches you surreptitiously, waiting for you to speak with one hand on a package of ham.

"That would—explain a lot, actually," you manage to say, almost a gasp.

"Just one more facet of my Will to love. And for the record," Raz says, "let's just say it runs in the family. My brother and I had very little in common on the surface, but our brains most definitely worked in the same ways."

You suddenly remember again all the shows Raz and you absolutely marathoned over the year you were with her. How she recalled the tiniest bits of trivia from her favorites. Her tiny kicks when she's happy.

How hard she fought for you for *years* to right what she saw as a wrong.

It's several minutes before you get back to making breakfast, because you are again trying not to cry—and *not* because of the onions. You hear your shower turn on. Julian's up. That fills you with more warmth.

It takes you a little while to ask what Raz met with the lawyers about, but when you do, she stops whisking the eggs in the bowl and cocks her head at you.

"I wanted to inform Superintendent Strand about his son's behavior in the presence of legal counsel, for one, but mostly I wanted to see what it would take to formally adopt you before you turn eighteen," she tells you. "That is, if you would want to. Whatever you decide, I'm here for you."

"*Yes,*" you say, and you throw your arms around her.

This time it's Raz who starts crying. It's you who holds her, because she is your Raz, your real mom, the one who has waited for you all this time after you were stolen from her, but now you're back where you belong.

Just like you always knew in the deepest parts of your core. You belong with Raz.

With family. With someone *like you.*

Welcome home, Will.

I know you're probably thinking about it, how we started this journey. Positive self-talk is important, and I started by calling you a monster.

I'm sorry.

You hear that, Will? I'm sorry. Which means you're sorry, for calling yourself a monster and believing it for so, so long. You are, after all, me. And I am you.

You're not a monster, Will. You're not a monster.

You are not a monster.

Sometimes the only way we can unravel the tangled mess of lies others have told us about ourselves is to step outside it, just for a little while. To look at ourselves from a distance and consider how we would feel about watching our lives play out through the eyes of someone who loves us.

Sometimes that's the only way we can catch even the barest flickering glimmer that tells us we are allowed to love ourselves.

You're not a monster, Will.

Frances certainly didn't die because of you.

Hannah didn't get hurt because of you.

And all the things that brought you to this moment, all the things that picked you up by the ankles and bashed you back and forth against the floor like a ragdoll Loki in the hand of the Hulk—all those things didn't happen to you because you deserved them.

(Loki might have deserved it a little, but you didn't. Plus he's literally a god, and he'll deal.)

You didn't deserve that.

You didn't deserve to be taught that your mother giving you a roof over your head was something outstanding or remarkable—it's the bare fucking minimum a parent owes their child.

You didn't deserve to have to put up with the earthquake that was Frances or the aftershocks after she died.

You deserve to be here, Will. You deserve to know what it's like to have family that loves you unconditionally and simply accepts you for who you are without a thought.

You're not a monster, Will.

You're a human being.

You're a good one, at that. You turned out pretty okay, which, considering your life, is pretty goddamn miraculous. You see yourself a little more clearly now, reflected in the eyes of people—plural!—who think you are extraordinary.

You know what? I love you. I do. I'm so proud of you. You got us here, to this point, to this day. You made it home.

So take a moment.

Close your eyes.

Take a breath.
Good. That's good.
Open your eyes.
Here's the part where you decide what happens next.

Hello.

When I first started writing this book, I had one real thought in my mind: this will be the book I wish I had had, the book I wish someone else had written for me.

It came to me, as many of my stories do, with the first few lines fully formed. It sat like that for a time, steeping quietly in life until I was ready to write the rest. This is also normal for me. What wasn't normal was that I knew this book had to be in second person. I'd never written a book in second person before, though I certainly read my fill of choose-your-own-adventure stories as a child. In a way, this book felt like that as I wrote it, albeit without the "turn to page 57 to kiss Julian" bit.

Many impoverished parents do their utmost to make sure their kids are safe and provided for; I know mine did. Anything in here about Frances doesn't apply to those parents. To those parents, you are so needed and all your work is worth it. Whether you have a roof over your family's head or not, whether you move from roof to roof or depend on shelters, you're not Frances. Your kids won't see you as Frances.

Strange things happened whilst I wrote this book. I stopped for a bit after chapter three, which ends on a very specific chord, the type of chord you hear and know everything is about to change in the melody you are listening to, and I wrote that chapter, and then in my own life I lived that chapter. Will already shared much in common with me, but even as I found out someone had indeed been waiting all my life for me, Will was waiting to learn the same. When I went back to continue, I had forgotten where I'd stopped. It took me a bit to collect myself. To figure out what came next.

Queer kids are used to rejection. We are used to being told that we are, well, *queer.* Queer in the sense of weird and in the sense of not belonging. Unwanted and fundamentally unwantable. We are disproportionately likely to be abused, and while we need stories that don't lean on queer pain, sometimes we also need stories to acknowledge it. I spent formative years in a small town in Montana, one state away from where Matthew Shepard was brutally murdered, attending a school where we literally played a game in PE called "Smear the Queer." No adults batted an eye—the words came from their own mouths. We are used to that type of angle on our pain, the kind that doesn't bother to ask us or even admit we might feel it.

But then there is the moment where we realize that we are not alone. The moment someone else accepts us and shows us that we are acceptable, that we are more than that, that we contain multitudes, that our pain can *heal.* That we are not monsters.

My mother is queer. I grew up while the AIDS crisis ravaged our community. It was the first place I met death. And as I grew older, and as my friends weren't allowed to come to my house lest they be exposed to my family, and as I lost friends over it, I took so much of that into myself. I didn't come out until I was almost thirty. I buried my sexuality and my gender identity so deeply that I was a decade into adulthood before I let it come out, before I let me come out.

I know kids like Will and Hannah and Julian now. They are my friends' kids; they are my own friends. At the launch of my epic fantasy novel *Hearthfire* (written as Emmie Mears), a nonbinary young adult just happened by and saw my pronoun badges, and they came up to me and told me how much it meant for them to see someone like *them* writing stories about people like us. I didn't have that. The only book I remember about families like mine was *Heather Has Two Mommies,* and it was notorious because it was banned in my school.

I wrote *The Evolving Truth of Ever-Stronger Will* because I wish I'd had it. I wish I'd gotten to see Will's journey for myself, because it *does* get better for us, and so often that happens because we find the people we need to find, the stories we need to see someone else living, a path that we can follow, and the knowledge that we—just like everyone else—deserve to be here too.

With respect and wolf onesies,
Maya

If you are experiencing queerphobic or transphobic bullying, here are some groups who exist to help you:

IN THE US:

- The It Gets Better Project: itgetsbetter.org
- Trans Lifeline: translifeline.org
- The Trevor Project: thetrevorproject.org

IN THE UK:

- All Sorts Youth Project: allsortsyouth.org.uk
- Dewis Cymru: www.dewis.wales/
- LGBT Youth Scotland: lgbtyouth.org.uk
- Mermaids: mermaidsuk.org.uk

If you are experiencing abuse, here are some crisis support groups who can help you:

IN THE US:

- Childhelp USA: childhelp.org or call/text 800-422-4453
- National Domestic Violence/Abuse Hotline: thehotline.org or call 800-799-7233

OUTSIDE THE US:

- Child Helpline International: childhelplineinternational.org/helplines/

MAYA MACGREGOR

The Many Half-Lived Lives of Sam Sylvester

When you're haunted by past lives, how can you live your own?

Discover Maya MacGregor's debut novel, *The Many Half-Lived Lives of Sam Sylvester*

Kirkus Reviews Best Book
Chicago Public Library's Best of the Best
Book Riot's Best YA Books of 2022 list
Chicago Review of Books Notable Debuts by Trans, Nonbinary, and Gender Non-conforming Authors
Andre Norton Nebula Award for Middle Grade and Young Adult Fiction Nominee

★ "A top-notch blend of contemporary fiction and mystery with a satisfying conclusion. . . . Blending and transcending genres, the book's beautiful storytelling and the rich voice of the prose at times evoke poetry. This captivating story centers a memorable, relatable protagonist surrounded by a lovable ensemble cast. The central mystery is gripping and fast-paced, but the book never fails to give all the characters motivations and backstories, making even the tertiary characters feel lived-in enough to be believable. . . . A thrilling debut featuring lovable and well-developed characters."

—*Kirkus Reviews*, starred review

★ "MacGregor's exhilarating debut. . . . Heavy themes of early death, trauma, and violence are inextricably woven into the history of both the town and various characters, exhibiting myriad paths toward healing and justice. Equal parts delicate and devastating, MacGregor's thought-provoking prose, evocative settings, and vividly characterized cast combine to provide a hopeful look at survival and closure."

—*Publishers Weekly*, starred review

★ "This vibrantly written debut novel masterfully blends a suspenseful and satisfying paranormal mystery with a sweet and tender love story.

Nearly all the main and secondary characters identify as LGBTQIA+ and are fully developed with their own quirks and arcs."

—*School Library Journal*, starred review

"While the central mystery surrounding Billy's death makes for a page-turner with truly chilling moments, MacGregor stays focused on the characters, filling the story with a deeply lovable cast of characters and nailing the realities faced by Sam. Readers will leave this poetic book feeling that Sam and the people surrounding them are completely real, along with the ghosts of Astoria."

—Booklist

"Featuring ghosts, haunted pasts, a touch of romance and a ton of fantastic diversity and disability representation—all headed by its lovable protagonist—*The Many Half-Lived Lives of Sam Sylvester* is a gripping mystery novel with a truly satisfying conclusion. Watch out, folks, Maya MacGregor's debut will keep you on your toes until all is revealed!"

—Nerd Daily

"Look no further for your next favorite read, because *The Many Half-Lived Lives of Sam Sylvester* has it all: a gripping murder mystery that will keep you turning pages, ghosts, romance, and a treasure trove of queer characters with depth and heart. Here's something rare—a suspenseful story that also feels like a hug."

—Sarah Glenn Marsh, author of the Reign of the Fallen series

1

The first time I see the house, it's as it swallows my father.

I count to three—Dad's strategy for doing things I'm not ready to do—and make myself look up.

The sound of something rattling in a hastily packed box behind me has stopped. I've carefully kept my eyes on my phone, scrolling Tumblr, but I can't avoid it anymore. I sit here watching motes of dust drift in the slanting afternoon light.

The front door is even ringed in red like a mouth. Not a bloodied mouth, nothing monstrous. Nor are the two dormer windows at the top in any way aggressive. They droop. The house looks like it *tried* but that it had found whatever it tried just too hard, and it quit.

I can kind of relate to that. New house. New city. New school. Again.

I hope I do better than the house did.

"Sam!" Dad sticks his head out the door to holler. "You've gotta come see this place!"

He's so excited about it. I've seen pictures, of course, but he insists they don't do it justice.

I push a lock of lavender-swirled hair out of my face and open the car door.

Outside the wind is chilly, and I'm amazed that I can smell the ocean. The salt tang to the air and the brisk winter wind wake me right up. I shouldn't be surprised to smell the sea; it surrounds Astoria on all sides. There's even a damn palm tree in the yard next door. Aren't we fancy? I like it. There's no one around, but it's Wednesday afternoon, so I guess people are still at work. Just as I think it, I see a person with a backpack covered in She-Ra and Steven Universe patches and Pride flags turn the corner onto our new street. I'm pretty sure I feel their eyes on me as they look over their shoulder, and I hurriedly turn away, even though I want to know if I saw right—I thought I saw the telltale pink-purple-blue of the bi flag. I don't want to get my hopes up. Maybe I didn't see what I thought I did; it was just a glance. I'm used to being the only queer in the room (the only one who was out, anyway), and in Portland, I was still too terrified to even register that wasn't true anymore.

Tapping my thumb against my iPhone's screen, I trot up the few steps to the house. I close my eyes on the top step. The floors over the threshold are dark hardwood, maybe walnut. Even from here, I get a whiff of newish paint, the smell fading but not gone. The foyer's mostly offset by pale light coming through the windows. The house is oriented north-south, and I wonder what it'll be like in the golden hour if the sun ever *really* comes out here.

I can see it behind my eyes, all warm orange turning the dust motes to sparks instead of sparkles.

"Sam!" Dad calls my name again. He's upstairs, from the sound of it.

I open my eyes and let the house swallow me too, stepping over the threshold.

The house echoes around my footsteps. It's a strange sound, like I'm descending into a cave. We have zero furniture. There's supposedly a truck from IKEA coming in the next day or so, but for now, my feet on the stairs feel heavy, so heavy their thumps should be heard by the ocean and its waves three streets away.

I put one hand on the banister as I climb the stairs, and my trepidation grows. Like the sea wind or a wave at the change of the tide, it washes over me and retreats, slipping back into the deep.

At the top of the stairs is Dad, leaning on the railing. He's a smidge taller than I am, around six feet. I'm still not used to seeing him without his locs surrounding his warm brown face, always in contrast to my pale white skin and naturally dirty blond hair that is more half-hearted wave than Dad's gorgeous tight coils. He cut the locs off for his new job. I said I didn't want him to cut them. He said they were heavy and giving him migraines with extra pressure under his hard hat (plus his hairline's receding, and he's self-conscious about it), and then he chased me around the apartment after I buzzed his head. The downstairs neighbors pounded on their ceiling to tell us how much they appreciated *that*.

He laughed at the time, but I think Dad had more mixed feelings than he let on, and the silliness was him trying to hide it. He's worn locs since I was little, and while I know it was his choice and his reasons, I think he felt the weight of more than hair once it was done.

"Did you see the palm tree?" I ask. It feels important that he knows it's there. Palm trees are vacations and sun-drenched shores, and this move is neither of those things, but the tree seems hopeful anyway.

"I did, I did." Dad grins at me. "Not quite a tropical paradise, but I thought you'd like it. Come see your room."

I follow, trailing my hand along the banister. It looks like it's been freshly sanded and re-varnished, the same dark wood as the floor. My fingertips stick slightly on the smooth surface. I think if I bent over, I could see my face in the glossy reflection.

He's giving me the biggest room. He insisted that he's too lazy to climb stairs to get to bed, and his smaller room has an en-suite, which just means he gets his own bathroom. And when I walk into my new room, a little shock goes through me.

The room is huge. The windowsill directly ahead of me spans both dormers, almost a window seat, and is a solid two feet deep. The upper bit rises straight along the outermost edges of the windows and then curves inward to meet in a little point like the peak on top of an ice-cream cone.

Walking to one of the walls, it's almost too bright to look at. It's white. White-white, not eggshell or cream. It looks and feels hastily done. There's even a seam visible. Dad would be mortified if his crew did this. I rap my knuckles on it, and a hollow sound greets me.

When I touch the paint, I take a step backward, the way I saw a kid do once at the IGA supermarket when he called a woman *Mom* and when she turned around, it was a stranger. A thrill buzzes up the length of my spine, an echo of the premonition I hadn't even articulated in thought enough to consider being right. Someone *did* cover something up here.

It's not the sound of the hollow echo that startles me, but the feel of it. Like instead of wood, my knuckles touched an electric current—or the ghost of one. I fight the urge to pick at the seam, to dig into the wall to be able to touch whatever is waiting behind it.

"What do you think?" Dad gestures around with a flourish as I spin around to look at him. He had his back to me and must've missed my movement. "You're going to be Emperor Sam up here."

I rap my knuckles on the wall again, harder this time, trying to ignore the way it sends little shock waves zipping up and down my fingers. Yep, definitely hollow. I want in there. I can't figure out what's waiting if I can't touch it, and this crappily done wall is in the way. Dad watches as I circle him, knocking on each wall. Sometimes I knock a few times, listening to the variations in sound. I find a rhythm. Hollow at hip level, fading into shallower sounds in both directions, then back out to hollow again. Dad doesn't say anything. He's used to me by now.

"You can be yourself here, kid," Dad says.

I think he means what I'm doing right now—knocking on walls like the weirdo I am. I wonder if what he says is true. For one glorious moment, my universe expands like his words sparked a Big Bang. I could be me. Really me. For the first time. Maybe figure out who the hell that even is.

The moment contracts as quickly as it expanded. I pull my hand back, and I tap my fingernails hurriedly against my palm, stimming.

"There're shelves behind the walls, I think," I tell Dad.

He gives a little start at my words, then looks around. He's used to me not responding to emotional things, too. Walking over, he knocks lightly on one panel, and sure enough, it gives that same hollow echo a little too deep for it to just be regular drywall and beams. Like I said.

"Huh," he says.

He doesn't question, but he does look at the wall a bit closer. He gives an offended sniff at the shoddy crafting of that wonky seam and mutters, "Previous owner's attempt at DIY, maybe." After a moment, he beams at me. "It'll be a good project for us to open them up. If you want."

He looks so eager that even if I didn't want to, I'd agree. Besides, now that he's seen that seam, I wouldn't be surprised to wake up with him fixing it in the middle of the night. It's going to drive him nuts.

I return his smile. "Damn right."

"Don't say damn."

"Darn tootin'."

"That's worse. Say damn."

His phone goes off downstairs, playing "The Imperial March" from *Star Wars*.

"Uh-oh. BRB." He lopes out the door and thumps down the stairs calling at me, "Sam! No neighbors to yell at us now!"

"So you say!" I call back.

I haven't seen him this happy in I don't know how long.

I trail my hand around on the wall, feeling the uneven paint and that thrill just out of reach. My fingertips buzz against the paint like I'm touching one of those lightning balls you find at novelty shops. I can almost see where the drywall bows a bit between the shelves beneath it. There's something there, something for me to find. And this room is *mine*.

New town, new house, even a seemingly new dad.

I hope to hell it goes better than last time.